LOVE ON THE
Dancefloor

BY
LIAM LIVINGS

Beaten Track
www.beatentrackpublishing.com

Love on the Dancefloor

First published 2019 by Beaten Track Publishing
Copyright © 2019 Liam Livings

ISBN: 978 1 78645 342 6

Cover: Roe Horvat

Beaten Track Publishing,
Burscough, Lancashire.
www.beatentrackpublishing.com

DEDICATION & THANKS

Thanks to Deb for making my writing so much better by giving this a well-needed edit. Sometimes I have a tendency to write slightly tangled wordage which, even when I've self-edited still needs to be untangled. Deb, you and your editing rock.

Thanks to Roe Horvat for giving my story another splendid cover which captures the fun, love and setting of the story.

Thanks to Tim who helped me research into the orbital party scene of the early nineties, and who also, after I'd been through dozens of other options, came up with the title of the book. Thanks also go to Tim for being so supportive with my writing, especially when I bring it on our holidays and leave him reading while I write 'just another scene' in the sun.

Thanks to Younger Liam who read books like *Disco Bloodbath* by James St James, *Rachel's Holiday* by Marian Keyes and *Sharking* by Sophie Stewart, inspiring Present Liam to try and capture the chaos, fun, wild abandon and excess of those stories in a gay romance. Reader, I wrote it!

Thanks to you, reader, for stepping into Liam Livings' world, which I hope gives you an emotional, escapist and enjoyable gay romance.

Love and light,
Liam Livings xx

LOVE ON THE
Dancefloor

PART 1

CHAPTER 1

September 1996

I WALKED TO THE check-in desk at Ibiza airport, my small wheeled suitcase trailing behind me. My sunglasses rested on my head and I still wore flip-flops, shorts and a T-shirt. I hadn't had time to change, you see; once I'd made up my mind to leave, that was the only thing I had wanted to do.

Now, as I crept to the front of the queue, I felt my passport in my pocket. I stroked the shiny red leather case, and a tingling coursed its way through my fingers, up my arms and into my stomach. I noticed my feet were moving from side to side, in time with someone's mobile phone ring.

Hang on a minute, someone's mobile phone ring, why am I dancing to that? Shit, I'm coming up on those pills I double-dropped.

Double-dropped in a futile attempt to stave off the inevitable come-down at the end of the after-after-afterparty, before realising I really *had* had enough and finally making my way here, to the airport, to get away from the everything, to escape it all, in one fell swoop.

Only, the whole one-fell-swoop escaping business wasn't going to be as easy as I'd thought because now—having completely forgotten what I'd done just a few hours ago, and in case you don't know, that's what ecstasy will do for you—I was coming up on those pills.

Shit.

I inhaled deeply, trying to control my breathing, but instead my whole body willed me to dance, only now the mobile phone had stopped ringing, replaced by the beeping of an electric vehicle towing a long snake of luggage trolleys. The orange light rotated, giving the impression it pulsed on and off, on and off, on and off, with the beeping.

That bloody beeping. I needed to keep a lid on it all or I wouldn't be allowed on the plane. My stomach clenched and I regretted instantly the coffee I'd grabbed as I'd arrived at the airport. The bitter after-taste filled my mouth as the black liquid threatened to make a return appearance. I swallowed, closed my eyes and concentrated on staying in control. Or at least *appearing* to stay in control.

As I opened my eyes, I noticed the smiley woman at the check-in desk signal for me to walk forward.

I stood, just about managed to minimise the dancing motions of my arms and legs in time with the distant beeping of a…fire alarm, was it? I wasn't sure, couldn't say without asking. And I didn't want to talk to someone unnecessarily for fear of calling them a *geezer*, or saying it was a *nice one*, or how it was all *safe, man*.

"Yes, sir, if you'd like to come forward, I can get you checked in today," the woman at the desk said.

Me? Oh, yes, she was talking to me.

I used all the concentration I could muster to pull my suitcase forward, and I slid across the floor, not lifting my feet, as I had an inkling it would prove too much and I'd find myself moon-boot-walking around the airport. Even in my currently partly mind-altered state, I knew that would definitely *not* constitute keeping a lid on it.

"Hello," I said, quickly closing my mouth so I could resume chewing, chewing and chewing at nothing at all, except my cheeks. *Shit, I'm meant to be keeping a lid on it.*

"Are you all right, sir?" She stared at my mouth.

I laughed. "Nervous flyer. Happens every time." I rested my trembling hands on the desk, pleased at my body for doing something I'd asked of it.

"We'll make sure we take good care of you, sir. Do you have your travel documents, please?"

Travel documents. Yes, that's a good thing to have, isn't it? Now, what does she really mean by travel documents? Such a simple, yet strangely, for me at that point, confusing phrase. I checked my shorts pockets: only my wallet. I checked the front compartment of my suitcase: only some keys; to where, I wasn't sure. And a length of cable with two small black things at one end and a shiny silver thing at the other. *Bit complicated to work that one out now, I'll save it for later.* I pushed it back into the pocket and, armed with a smile and some hope, turned to the woman.

"Passport, please, sir." She smiled broader than before and, I sensed, with a touch of irritation.

I looked on the floor, then realised I'd already got my passport out in anticipation of this moment to smooth the process, and now look at what a state I had got myself in. *What an idiot!* A dark, red, shiny thing poked out from under my right foot. *Bloody sliding along the floor, this is what you get for sliding along the floor.* I lifted my foot, making sure it wasn't high enough to enter the moon-boot-walking stage, and handed it to the woman with an apologetic smile.

After a few clicks on her computer, she gave me a boarding pass and directed me towards the gates.

"Which gate was it?" I couldn't quite read the letters as they swam in and out of focus. I'd tried to listen to what she'd told me about how I should board the plane, but at this point, concentrating on anything more than standing still and not chewing my face off was beyond me.

"Twenty-four-C. Far end." She paused, took a deep breath, adjusted her perfectly coiffed hair, and added, "I've written it on your boarding pass."

I stared at the piece of card in my hand, trying to focus on the writing while not chewing too much. *Chewing gum, or maybe bubble gum is better, yes, some bubble gum for the flight. Just a few sticks of Juicy Fruit and I'll soon be back home. Now, what am I doing?* I squinted at the paper. *Bubble gum. Chewing gum. Two sticks.*

A voice entered my subconscious, the voice of an angel, starting quietly, then growing louder and louder. And then it was accompanied by a gentle hand on my elbow pushing me to one side. *What have I done wrong? What has brought me to this place to this time? Bubble gum.*

No. I remembered what I'd done wrong, I'd necked two speckled Mitsubishis an hour before getting on a plane.

"Twenty-four-C," came the angel's voice, this time much louder, filling my head.

I looked up from the piece of card, the mystical boarding pass the angel being person woman had told me about.

The woman behind the desk pointed, and someone standing beside me gently pulled me by the elbow.

Who is this person? I don't know her. I want the desk lady, she's kind.

"Follow me, sir, we'll get you some water and a nice comfortable seat near your gate, so you can stay there until the plane's called." The woman tutted loudly. "You all right to walk, or you want me to get a wheelchair?"

A wheelchair? What is wrong with me? I feel amazing. I feel like I could fly. I could have flown, actually, had she let go of my arm. I was floating above the shiny floor, still sliding my feet across it, not lifting them too high, for fear of the moon-boot situation.

Through columns of people parading towards me with enormous eyes and wide-open mouths, their clothes blaring at me at volume ten, and their voices shouting to me in red, green and blue, forcing my senses to eat, drink and be merry at them in screaming colour.

And then I was in a comfortable seat, holding a bottle of water, no idea where it had come from. A glass screen separated me from the outside, where the big planes moved. The big planes, one of which I was going to board and it would fly me back to London, float me away from all the stuff that had brought me to Ibiza in the first place and had become too much to bear in the end.

You're probably wondering what made me neck two ecstasy pills, disco biscuits, 'E's, Mitsis whatever, before flying. And you'd be right to wonder, because as I sat back and looked at what I'd done, I couldn't quite believe I did it.

Was it something to do with a man, you want to know?

What do you think?

When *isn't* something slightly bonkers you've done to do, in some small way, with a man? Who hasn't made a total twat of themselves in the name of love? I've spent most of my life doing it in various ways. And I thought when I met Him, I couldn't love anyone more than I loved Him.

'Love u More' was our song. *Is* our song? Do you stop saying you're together as soon as possible, or do you leave it? I mean, strictly speaking, I hadn't dumped him; I'd just fucked off, a short note left by his bed. *So long, I've had enough, I can't be that person in that situation anymore.*

Anyway, 'Love U More' by Sunscreem was—there I've decided, He's in the past—our song. We used to sing it to each other on the dance floors, believing every single word about making the sea turn turtle, making the sky turn purple, doing all these magical, impossible things but not being able to love you more. Not being able to love each other more.

Only, now I'm not sure if there was any love at all. Not real, non-chemically enhanced love—the proper stuff—not the smiling all night, touching each other, dancing so much you think your feet are going to fall off and your heart's going to burst out of your chest, love.

Don't get me wrong, it's not that I didn't enjoy the chemically enhanced love. Fuck me gently, we had some of our best times together in that state. The clubbing, the DJing, the partying, the everything kind of went together with the disco biscuits. They were, after all, meant for disco, for dancing, and oh boy, did we dance with them!

So how does a man who worked in a video hire shop end up headlining a club in Ibiza for the summer?

And, more importantly, why would he then fly away from it all completely banjaxed on pills?

They are very sensible questions, and if you'll bear with me, I will tell you the answer to both.

But the thing that made me saddest, as I tried to keep a lid on my pilled-up feeling on the flight, more than leaving what was the pinnacle of my career, the friends, the fans, the lifestyle…all that? The saddest thing comes right back to 'Love U More'. How I felt my whole relationship was over, the person whom I'd thought would be with me forever was no longer going to be there.

And that was what scared the shit out of me when I landed at Heathrow airport a few hours later, having chewed through four packs of gum and drunk three bottles of water.

CHAPTER 2

Summer 1993

I REPLACED THE RETURNED videos on the shelves in their proper places, having run the newest releases through the rewinder machine, for those people who found it too much effort to press rewind once they reached the end of the film. Lazy bastards.

It was Friday afternoon, and I could practically taste it— almost feel it if I reached out to grab it. Another few hours and the weekend would officially land.

The man I recognised but could never remember his name, despite looking up his account details on the computer every time he hired videos from us, turned up with three films and a smile on his face. He worked in the second-hand record shop a few streets over from the video hire shop. I knew because he'd told me, along with asking if I wanted the latest DJ extended mixes of the new dance trance hits. And he knew because I'd told him I enjoyed that sort of thing.

"Busy weekend?" I smiled at him, taking his card and tapping in his details. *That's it, his name's Paul, as in Oakenfield.* Only this guy wasn't Paul Oakenfield; he was Paul Stockton, as in… well, I didn't know what, but anyway.

Paul said, "Quiet weekend, as it goes. All me plans fell through. Was gonna catch up with some mates, check out what parties are on. See where the weekend takes me." He paused. "But now, not so much." He laughed.

"Flaky friends?" The question would have been an over-step for other customers, but we were well on nodding terms now.

He'd come in most weeks for the last nine months or so, and we always had this sort of banter, chatting about our weekends, what films we liked, what films we hated, laughing about the hype around the new films, agreeing on how most big blockbusters didn't live up to it and how we usually avoided them.

"Mandy's car blew up. She was our wheels, but without her, there's no way we can get there."

"Orbital party?"

"Meant to be, yeah. The usual driving round the M25, meeting at a payphone for the next instructions. All part of the fun, innit?"

That smile. I melted slightly inside my stomach. That cheeky, grinny smile with those twinkly blue eyes. These little chats were sometimes the highlight of my week at work. *Tell him you're DJing round the back of King's Cross station and he can come. Tell him you'll put his name on the door. Tell him.* "Err...maybe see you around?"

"Yeah."

We said this to each other every time we met, whether here, at my shop, or when I went to his to buy the latest twelve-inch dance tracks I'd heard on the radio and knew I'd need in my record case for my sets.

Whenever I went to his shop, he'd walk over, shake my hand, then hold his hands behind his back, hooking them in his jeans pockets, a smile on his face, his eyes darting from me, to the window, then back to me, and then back to the window.

See, we'd still not had *the conversation*, the whole, *are you, aren't you* thing. We got on. We liked the same music. But it always felt like the wrong place to have that conversation, at our works.

Like last Monday, for example...

"I was there," he said to me, as he always did when I told him where I'd ended up over the weekend. "D'ya go to the afterparty at Slickedy Jim's in Hoxton?"

"No. Went home. Too much of a good thing." I caught his eye, sharing a look that in an instant said all we needed to know about the clubbing, the after-clubbing, the comedown, the everything.

"Over-indulged in over-indulgence, did ya?"

I shrugged as he handed me a pile of must-have records for the month, sorting through them—those I'd heard of and needed, and those I'd need to listen to before committing to buying them.

He pointed to one of the records. "This one, you gotta hear. It's gonna blow your mind." He lowered his voice to a whisper. "Thought I was coming up when I put it on the first time. It builds and builds in waves till the middle, and then you think you're gonna fly right out the room."

"Well, I'd say, let's listen to that one first." Any excuse to hang around while he told me about the latest tracks and then watch him gently lower the record onto the turntable, his face showing his pleasure at the slight crackle before the music started. We'd had the digital versus vinyl conversation at length. Oh yes, no fear...

"Have a bit of everything last night, did ya?" He opened his eyes wide and gave an exaggerated sniff.

I smiled, bobbing my head slightly. "Something like that."

...but we'd never had the conversation where I told him I wanted to feel his white hands, with dark hairs on the back, grabbing me hard. No, we kept to music, records, club-speak. Probably because I assumed he wasn't into boys...men. Couldn't be. Obviously not.

Now, in my shop, he was taking the video cases filled with the right videos I'd collected from the filing system behind the counter, and he was waving at me, and he was telling me to have a good one, and he was walking to the door, and he was the other side of the door, and then he was gone.

I stared at the clock, watching the hour hand, willing it to go faster so I could leave, get home and sort out my set for the night, my first solo set at this new venue. It was the biggest venue I'd played. An old warehouse behind King's Cross, a maze of rooms segmented off the aircraft-hangar-sized building, playing different types of music in each. I'd managed to get a thirty-minute set in the trance room—you know? The one full of people holding glow sticks in both hands, making *big fish, little fish, cardboard box* moves. That one.

***

At home, I wolfed down my dinner, apologised to Mum for not being able to stay and chat, ran upstairs into the shower, threw on some clothes—baggy silver combat trousers, white sleeveless T-shirt—and styled my hair into a dozen or so individual large spikes. But as I stood at the door with my record suitcase in my hand, she barred my exit.

"Where's the fire, love?" Her foot tapped the ground.

Do I tell her about Paul and still not getting the guts to ask him outright if he's a gayer? Or do I make my excuses, say I've got to rush to get set up, sort my set order and go over things with the venue first?

"How you getting there with all that lot?"

"Tube. It's right next to the station. Easy life."

"Yeah, and you get mugged round the back of King's Cross. Full of druggies and prostitutes, that is. It was on the news the other week. And them needles, you got to be careful. There's people running up to complete strangers in night clubs, injecting them with blood and leaving a little note written on a sticker saying 'welcome to the happy world of HIV'. Terrible, it is. Saw it on the news."

"Yeah, you said. A few times. A few places."

"You taking care of yourself?"

I sighed. "I need to go, Mum. Can I go, please?" I slumped against the wall, the energy I'd had moments before leaving my body.

She unhooked her coat from the hanger and collected her keys from the tail of the green parrot that hung on the wall by the door. "I'm driving you."

As we made our way from our green corner of Brockley through the traffic of South East London, she told me how she wasn't happy with me travelling alone late at night.

"Not for no DJ job, not for nothing. You're getting a cab home. Don't care what your father says, I'm giving you the money. And if I find out you spent it on drink or a kebab, or drink and a couple of kebabs, I will personally kill you with my own two hands. Understand?"

She meant it. She'd given me murder a few times when I'd disobeyed what she'd asked me to do. Always in my best interest, but at the time, the sore head from her gold-ring-fingered slap didn't feel quite so much in my best interest.

"This fella. The one at work," I began, just sort of grabbing it like a stingy nettle of awkwardness.

"Works in the record shop?" She was chewing gum and staring straight ahead at the road.

"That's the one. We get on. We do, we really get on. We have a laugh. He comes to my shop, we talk. I go to his shop, we talk. It's great. We go to the same places. Same music, see. Never bumped into him yet, though. Small odds, I suppose. Anyway, I don't know."

"Don't know what, love?" She pointed to the sign for King's Cross. "Is this us?"

"Round the back."

We were at the entrance of the warehouse, a large, grey, squat building made of black bricks and a corrugated iron roof.

She stopped the car and turned to face me. "I said, 'Don't know what?'"

"If he's, you know, into lads." Since the hypodermics in night clubs, and all the guys who'd disappeared during the eighties, being gay wasn't really as cool as it once had seemed. Saying you were gay to a lot of people meant AIDS. HIV. Death. That's what being gay meant. And so a lot of us had sort of retreated back into our shells, taken the rainbow unicorn down a few notches. Down a lot of notches, actually. Not that I was really camp or flying around on my own unicorn. But little things about songs I liked from the seventies—Donna Summer, disco classics, that sort of thing—I kept that to myself. Unless you actually asked someone if they were, it was this shame thing, this sort of problem, like AIDS and HIV, people didn't want to shout about anymore. Especially when you were at work.

Mum rapped her red nails on the steering wheel. "Love, you just gotta ask him if he wants to go for a drink. Simple as."

"What if he thinks I'm just being friendly?"

"No one ever asked no one else for a drink cos they wanted to be their friend. Not deep down, they didn't. They might be pretending to be their friend, but really, they want to get inside their knickers. Simple as." She pointed to the bouncer who was waving outside the entrance. "I think you're wanted, love. Better get off." She tapped her cheek.

I kissed it. *Simple as.* Thing was, even if this Paul was gay, he'd never be interested in me anyway.

"What time you back?" she asked.

"Club closes at four, I think. My set's earlier than that. But I dunno."

She pressed some notes into my hand and said firmly, "Cab."

I walked to the entrance of the building, half kicking myself for not being so straightforward with Paul and half shitting myself about tonight's set, the crowd in the trance room, whether they'd enjoy what I played, whether they'd dance to what I played, whether I would be asked back again.

But as soon as I got behind the record decks, put my headphones on and started the first song—'For An Angel' by Paul Van Dyke—accompanied by a dance floor of people with hands raised above heads, some whooping and screaming as the strobe lights flashed in time with the 120 beats per minute, I knew I'd done the right thing, saying yes when I'd been offered this spot.

Of course, the half a speckled Mitsubishi I'd taken three-quarters of an hour before my set was also undeniably taking the edge off my nerves. I'd already told the previous DJ I loved him, as well as the coat-check woman and the man who'd shown me where to put my records. They weren't fussed; it was par for the course in this place.

***

I stayed after my set, realising I was way too *on it* to just get a cab home straight away. I'd done it a few times before and ended up dancing in the kitchen to the beep of the oven when the time was up on some chips I'd fancied but unsurprisingly hadn't wanted when I actually saw them cooked. Mum had arrived in the kitchen, arms folded and leaning against the door, asking me what time I called this, and what did I think this was, a frigging night club, before walking close up to my face, staring me in the eyes and saying, "Don't think I don't know. I wasn't born yesterday. I was a child of the seventies, remember? Drinking too, were you?"

One of the early rules I'd heard from one of the clubbing old campaigners I'd met at an orbital party a few years ago was to stick to water and never mix alcohol and pills. That was where the wheels started to fall off and why everyone was constantly sucking on a bottle of water as they threw shapes, danced, hugged and kissed everyone on the dance floor.

"Nope." I'd said half proudly, half ashamedly to Mum.

"Make sure you don't lose yourself. Plenty of people thought they'd discovered God or a higher state of being when actually a little bit of their brain had got left in a warehouse near the M25. Just make sure you keep a bit of yourself tethered, stuck to the ground. The real you, the Monday to Friday you. All right?"

I'd nodded.

She'd left me to it, a cold tray of chips and a still beeping oven as I made *big fish, little fish, cardboard box* shapes with my hands, eventually falling into a fitful sleep on the sofa.

Now, tonight—as the darkness left and the bright house lights filled the floor, revealing plastic pint glasses and bottles, bits of old glow stick and topless sweaty men with their arms round bra-on topless sweaty women, smeared make-up, wilted spikey hair and everyone looking for a familiar face who they could brave the journey home with or head to an afterparty—I wondered what the fuck to do to kill a few hours and get myself a bit straighter before going home.

"Tom, you coming round mine after?" Slinky Simon—the DJ who'd played after me—asked.

I held my jacket in front of my chest, my heart rate having almost returned to a normal rate. Tempting as it sounded, Sunday morning would soon bleed into Sunday afternoon and inevitably Sunday evening when, with my body empty of anything more nutritious than a Marlboro Light or some Juicy Fruit chewing gum, and with my energy and serotonin levels thoroughly exhausted without any chemical aid to mask this, I would have to make my way across London from the location of the afterparty, back to Mum and Dad's terraced Victorian house in Brockley, South East London. Mum would ask me if I was working tomorrow, and I'd nod, and she'd tut and I'd go to bed with a comedown the size of Lewisham, Greenwich and Bromley combined, threatening to crush my soul and existence.

I shook my head at Slinky Simon. "Soz. I've got work. Need my beauty sleep."

"When you working, Tom mate?"

"Monday."

He made a waving, dismissive motion with his hands. "That's a whole day away. Don't be worrying about that just yet. Come with me. Follow me and you'll love it. Trust me."

As far as DJing advice, getting me into that club or anything in that vein, I did trust Slinky Simon implicitly. But as far as me following him and being able to function in any way approaching a human being on Monday morning, I trusted him as far as I could have thrown him. And he was about twice my size, with very large, very high platform trainers.

I shrugged. "I'm empty. Nothing left. Can't go on." This, I knew, was a dangerous strategy, as admitting I was out of drugs could result in two outcomes:

1) end of conversation as the other person was out, too, or...

2) a cry of that not being a problem and he had plenty more, and it would be all good.

Slinky Simon grabbed my hand, pulled it towards his groin and squeezed it, where I felt a small lumpy mass with lots of smaller bumps on it. He wasn't coming on to me, not that he didn't know I was that way. He just wasn't into all that. He liked women and their bodies and the support, and the way they made sense to him too much to, you know, *go gay*. No, he was making me squeeze the bag of pills he was hiding in his underpants.

I held onto the wall, the wobbles and jelly legs from before returning. I needed to keep myself tethered to something, and if I followed Slinky Simon to his, I'd come well and truly untethered.

"Maybe next time." I waved, and before he could say anything else, I was gone, out into the cool, pale sun of Sunday morning. The bit of Sunday morning that no one except nightclubbers and central London refuse-collecting services ever sees. The bit of Sunday morning that's before even those mad people who get up at seven o'clock even at the weekend.

This was my favourite part of the day, after a night out shouting, chatting, dancing, loving it all, as you jumped onto a night bus—or a day bus sometimes if it was late enough—and floated on the remnants of the high from before, all the way back to a womb-like bed, with one last cigarette and a hot, sweet milky mug of tea.

I arrived home, followed my usual post-clubbing ritual: pint of water, tea, cigarette out the front of the house as everyone else was starting to rise for the day, then showered, closed the *complete blackout specially requested from Mum* curtains, climbed into bed, and slept.

***

Later that day, when I'd had enough sleep I could string a sentence together but no longer felt floaty and disassociated from the world as it was being presented before me, I walked into the kitchen where Mum was making one of her legendary roasts. I sat on the chair and let out a long, dramatic sigh.

"No sympathy from me. I'm telling you. None." She paused. "If you want a cuppa, you can make me one too."

I put the kettle on and assembled the mugs and bits for our tea.

"Auntie Luella rang. Said she'd sent you a letter and hadn't heard back from you. I asked if she wanted to talk to Dad, on the off-chance she'd have anything to chat to her brother about, but she said no, she wanted to check if you was all right. I said you was, but you was busy."

"Thanks." I'd been meaning to reply to that letter for weeks. I usually wrote to her every few months, making up for not visiting her in the last few years. I enjoyed reading her long, newsy letters and knew she loved hearing about whatever I was up to.

"Write back, will you, love? She asked if you were coming out to see her this year, like you used to. I said I didn't know, with your job and that."

"I will. I'll ask for time off and I'll fly to New York and see her. It'll be great. Just like it used to be."

"A letter would do," Mum said.

"The problem is, cos I'm so busy doing lots of interesting things, I don't have much time to write to Luella and tell her about them. Pretty ironic, don't you think?"

"A short letter. Couple of pages'll do. Anyway, I said I'd ask. So that was me, asking." Mum smiled. "So, last night, did you cab it home?"

Did I get a cab home? Hmmm, good question. I didn't one hundred percent remember what had happened to my suitcase of records, but I had confidence in myself that I'd not got too banjaxed last night to have left it in the club, on a night bus, in Trafalgar Square at the bus stop...

"Hang on." I ran upstairs, and relief flooded through my body when I saw my record-filled suitcase behind the door. I rifled through my combat trousers pockets, all eight of them, and found no money. I must have got a cab. As I arrived back in the kitchen, I said, "Yes."

"Well, why've you got a face like a bloody slapped arse? Go well, did it? This set of yours?"

"It did, as it goes. Yeah. Very well, actually. Hands in the air, shouting, people asking for more. Good set. Slinky Simon's asked me back. So…" I shrugged.

Mum pointed to the now boiling kettle. "Tea."

I made the tea.

Mum said, "Slinky Simon, eh? Well, what's up, then?"

I busied myself with the tea-making part of the day, concentrating hard while I thought about what to say about the Paul situation. I handed her a mug and took mine to sit back at the table. "He weren't there last night. Said he might be. But he weren't. Said we'd maybe bump into each other. We never do, see."

"I see." She tapped the ash off her cigarette into the flamenco-dancer ashtray, put the fag back in her mouth and resumed peeling the carrots, with her back to me.

"I was gonna go to his shop next week, casual like. Say I was stocking up on some new tunes, and tell him how it went last night. Casual like. And see if he wanted to come see me next time I'm back there. Slinky Simon said I could put him on the guest list. No bother. But I don't want him to think I'm too much, too datey, too going out, too boyfriendy. He might have a girlfriend and a little baby for all I know." Another protracted sigh escaped my lungs and filled the air of the kitchen, mixing among the steam and cooking smells and Mum's wafting smoke.

Mum sat next to me and offered me one of her cigarettes.

"Smoking inside?" This was a rarity, me being allowed to smoke indoors. Something was definitely on the horizon here; I could feel it in my waters.

She nodded, lit it, along with another for herself. "There's no good all this 'see you at my night, when I'm doing my set' bollocks. That doesn't say you want to get to know him. That says you know him a bit and if you bump into him, that's good, but otherwise you're not arsed."

"But I am arsed, Mum. I really am arsed." And rest assured, I'd had quite a few in-depth thoughts about how much I was arsed about Paul, whether he was straight or not. But that wasn't for sharing with Mum now.

"Fuck's sake, Tom love, it's no wonder you can't get yourself a boyfriend. You're not trying hard enough. I know you don't like just going to the gay clubs, you want to have a wider circle. You don't want to ghettoise yourself. But bugger me backwards, love, you're a lot more likely to meet a boy who likes boys at one of them places than one of these. And if not, then you'll just have to bloody well ask him to go for a drink. You and this Paul. A drink. If he's all vague and can't come and runs off like a cat when it thinks it's going to the vet, you'll have your answer—he's into girls, women, females…you know what I mean. And wham-wham-bam, thank you Paul, onto the next one. I can't stand all this fannying about you're doing, moping over him. How long you been talking to him, talking to me about talking to him? How long's it been, couple of months?"

To my shame, I worked it out on my fingers and very quietly said, "Eleven months."

"How many times have you seen him at your work?"

More counting on fingers. "At least twenty times."

"And you go to his record shop too?" She was shaking her head now and tutting very loudly between sucking on the cigarette as if her life depended on it.

I nodded. "But it's surfacey. Just nothing talk. Clubs, music, films we like, who we know from the clubs—a lot of the same people, actually. Nothing much."

"What sort of nothing much? Give me a for instance."

So, as the pans bubbled, and the meat roasted, and the potatoes did whatever it is potatoes do when you have them in a roast dinner, I told her about the last time when I'd gone to Paul's record shop, pretending not to know which songs I needed for my big set at the enormous warehouse nightclub behind King's Cross station, and how Paul had spent almost an hour with me, going through the DJ extended mixes of all the best trance songs, cos he knew that's what I liked playing, that was my thing as far as a DJ went.

***

"How'd you feel about bouncy house, or is it just trance you want?" Paul said, his hands hovering above a twelve-inch single version of 'Return To Innocence' by Enigma which had just been released.

"Think I'd better stick with what I'm building as my sound. If that's all right."

"No problem, but you might want to check this out, just for yourself. Here—" he handed me the record "—I'll throw it in with the rest. Call it mates' rates discount or some shit." He smiled. "I'm assuming you've already got the classics—the tracks where it all started?"

I knew my trance but not as well as Paul did. I thought I had a good variety in my record collection for the shows; I'd gradually worked my way from little pub back rooms to bigger venues, to some warehouses at orbital parties, to the proper London venue I'd told Paul I was playing that weekend.

"Jam & Spoon, 'The Age of Love'?"

"Hum it." I said, still staring at his beautiful blue eyes.

"Piss off, hum it. I've got it." With a few deft finger movements between the wooden trays of records, he pulled one out and put it on the record player, nodding his head in time with the music, closing his eyes as it built to a crescendo.

Allowing the silence while the song was at its best, I eventually said, "I'll take it. Any other essentials?"

Over the course of the next hour, he played me what he considered the essential trance songs right from the start, up to now, 1993, before adding one more essential track.

"'Love U More' by Sunscreem. It. Is. A. Tuuuunnnneee! Heard it?"

I had, but seeing as I was enjoying the attention and didn't have my own copy yet, I asked him to play it. He put the record on, then did the *eyes shut, head nodding, hands dancing* thing he'd done to the other songs, this time a bit deeper. He was really getting lost in the music.

We waited right to the end of the four-minute song.

I don't know if you've ever listened to a song in a record shop, right to the end, when there's others in the shop, clutching their records and eager to have a listen. Well, it's a long time.

It felt like another hour, but it was worth it to see Paul's face at the end. He lifted the record off the turntable, wiped it gently with a cloth, and replaced it in its sleeve. "Having it?"

I took it and added it to the pile of other records I'd agreed to buy, based on Paul's advice and music-playing temptation.

As he handed my change and the bag, heavy with records, he smiled and said, "'Love U More'. It doesn't get better than that, I reckon."

I told him, again, about where I was playing that Saturday night, and said he could come along; it'd be good for him to hear the songs I'd bought cos of him.

He looked away, with a smile, and said, "Yeah, sounds wicked. Cool. Yeah. Enjoy!"

I left, clutching the bag to my chest and replaying the bit of the conversation by the till.

***

Now, as I came to the end of telling Mum, I shook my head. "Still can't understand why he didn't come."

She snapped her fingers, stood to check the pans on the hob, then returned, lighting one more cigarette and offering me another one. "That, my dear, sweet innocent and naïve boy, is where you're going fantastically wrong. That's not surfacey, that's small talk. That's what most of us do most of our lives. Who wants to talk about politics or religion when you can chew the fat with someone about some film or other you liked, or hated, or thought was pretty painfully shit? That, right there, is the basis of a relationship. It's something more than passing moments over the tills at work. That *is* a relationship. Almost."

"Then why's he not come to the places I say I'm going to be at?"

"He doesn't know if you're into boys too. And love, although this may not be physically possible, he sounds to me like he's more shy than you are. Bless him, giving you the song about love, saying it was his favourite one, and letting you have it for free. Bless him. Bless you. Bless the bloody pair of you."

"It was, it's been everywhere, It's essential for me to have in my record collection."

"All right, love, you tell yourself that." She shook her head. "Like I said, that, my love, is almost, nearly, within a gnat's snatch of being the beginnings of a relationship."

"If he's into boys."

"True enough. So, sweetie, love, my darling, beautiful son, please can you promise me one thing?"

"Yes." I took a drag on the cigarette, flicking the ash at my end of the table into the basket on the back of the china donkey she'd brought back from her last Spanish holiday with Dad.

"Ask him the fuck for a drink."

"Understood." I shook my head, knowing it would be pointless. If he even wanted to go for a drink, Paul wouldn't want to go out with me. Useless. When someone tells you something often enough, you start to believe it. Useless. When it's all you hear about yourself for almost a year, it's how you start to think everyone sees you. Useless.

CHAPTER 3

Monday, as predicted, rolled round in all its horrific, dragging-on-for-the-whole-week glory. But fortunately, as I'd avoided going back to Slinky Simon's, I was able to do more than just stand by the rewinder machine because I was too banjaxed to do anything else.

No, this Monday, I took old films out of rental, priced them up in the for-sale section and checked in a load of new films. Some of them looked good, others looked terrible, and I knew which ones would walk out every week as if they had legs of their own. They didn't stand much chance against *Jurassic Park*, *Mrs. Doubtfire* and *Sleepless in Seattle*, which were on at the cinema.

I willed with my whole, slightly crumpled but not as bad as it could have been, body for Paul to arrive, with his broad smile and his twinkling blue eyes, so I could ask where he was on Saturday night when I had been making my largish-club DJing debut, and we could joke about how there was always next time, and he'd say he couldn't come because something had happened and he'd meant to leave a message at the door but he'd forgotten that too, and I wouldn't mind because he'd be standing, smiling, in front of me and I would have forgiven him anything.

Sadly, none of that little rom com actually happened. Not a sign of Paul for the whole day. I debated with myself about calling into his shop during my lunch break, but the bus journey across three high streets would have taken the whole hour, and I couldn't bear the thought of the smell of summer sweaty bus people on a minor comedown. Instead, I sat in the staffroom, hiding from the bright sunlight and read a copy of the *Daily Mirror,* which had a two-page article about the acid house scene and how it had changed, and how the world as we knew it was going to come to an end because young people were dancing to repetitive fast music and taking ecstasy like generations before them had done with different drugs and music in the sixties, seventies and eighties, but for some reason now signalled the end of the world.

Minor rant coming up, so brace yourself.

People don't glass each other in nightclubs on ecstasy. People don't fight about getting a drink at the bar if they're on a decent Mitsubishi turbo. No, that's the reserve of pissed-up people in pubs and clubs having drunk their body weight in alcohol. But because you can't tax and regulate ecstasy, this is why the papers see it as the end of the world as they know it.

When I returned to work, I pottered about, tidying up stray videos that had been put in the wrong sections and serving a few customers. The thought of flicking through the Yellow Pages to find the phone number for Paul's record shop escaped my mind right until the end of the day, when I checked the time and knew, by six o'clock, he'd be closing just like I was.

***

Life and time rolled on. I didn't call Paul and he didn't come to my shop. I didn't bump into him at any of the club nights I'd played, having been asked to return to the King's Cross warehouse for the next three weeks, gradually getting a bigger and bigger crowd until on the third week I was given the slightly larger room, usually reserved for the soaring melodies of house music, but they wanted to give me a try.

On a high from how well it had gone, and of course the two halves of a Mitsi I'd necked before and during my set, I threw caution to the winds when Slinky Simon asked if I wanted to come back to his to carry on partying, to celebrate the night, and agreed.

That was when, after we'd all piled into Slinky Simon's house—a fake-bay-windowed two-storey new-build semi in a close in some part of North London I neither knew nor cared where but somewhere north of Hampstead Heath with a lot of Turkish shops along the main road…

…once Slinky Simon had put a track on the record player, closed the curtains, made a round of teas and coffees for everyone, showed us where the toilet and sofa were and asked who wanted a little something to keep us going…

…that was when I noticed a familiar face, mug of tea in one hand, cigarette in the other, trying to concentrate on not chewing his face off as his eyes, widened, and he bobbed his head around in time to the music.

Paul bloody Stockton.

It was now or never. Remembering Mum's sage advice, I took my mug of tea, as much confidence as I could muster and a pack of cigarettes and plonked myself next to Paul on the wide arm of the low, slouchy leather chair in which he sat. "Fancy seeing you here!" I put my cigarette in my mouth and held out my hand for him to shake.

He turned to face me, spilling a bit of tea on his white combat trousers and very tight grey T-shirt covered in glowing pieces of fake computer circuit board. "Shit! It's you, I didn't… Do you know Slinky Simon?"

"Who doesn't?"

He squished himself over in the chair, leaving a space to his side, and gestured for me to join him properly in the seat. "I saw you, you know."

"Here? I was in the kitchen helping Slinky Simon with drinks, then I needed some water. Gotta rehydrate after dancing and sweating all night."

"Yep. No, I saw you in the club. Doing your set. You were wicked. Wi. Ked." He gave a broad grin, showing all his teeth. I could see he was concentrating with his whole mind to not chew, chew, chew.

"Want a Juicy Fruit?"

He put his hand to his face. "Soz. Didn't realise. Thought I wasn't too bad."

I handed him a stick of gum. "Occupational hazard."

He put it in his mouth and chewed with a look of perfect satisfaction. "Cheers. Yeah, you were wicked. Best I've seen in ages in that room. I was proper flying. When that song in the middle of the set got to the best bit, I thought the whole club was gonna, I dunno, fly. Everyone with their hands in the air, in time with the music. It was like some religious shit or something, weren't it?" He looked away. "I dunno."

"Don't stop, don't be embarrassed, I was enjoying that. Don't get people come up to me in the DJ booth telling me how much they love it. I'm not quite at Slinky Simon's stage just yet." I laughed to myself.

Paul grabbed my hand and massaged it with both of his, starting at my palm, moving outwards along my fingers, then up my arm and down towards my hand again.

The squeezing pulsed through my body, from my fingertips up my arms into my chest, and out the other arm—the one that wasn't getting any attention. I closed my eyes and took a deep breath. *Fuck me. I'm fucked, and I love it!*

We sat, snuggled up to each other as he massaged my hand, then the other, then I offered to do his, copying how he'd done it to me, staring at him as he sat, eyes closed, chewing slowly in time with the music, taking a sip of water every now and then.

I was the first to break the comfortable silence we'd fallen into. As I felt the courage building inside, I grabbed it with both freshly massaged hands and said it before I bottled it. Again.

"Wanna go for a drink sometime?"

There. That wasn't the end of the world. That was actually quite easy, short, simple. If he's not interested, no harm done. I'll make my excuses, nip to the kitchen for a drink and slip out before anyone notices.

"Yeah. That'd be wicked." He smiled.

Wi. Ked. I swear I heard a chorus of *hallelujah* above the music and a round of trumpets accompanying my thoughts.

"Really? A 'drink' drink, me and you, no one else? That sort of drink?"

"Yep, just us two."

"But I didn't... You didn't... We haven't... Have we?"

"No. I hoped the 'Love U More' record would make you ask me. About as subtle as a steamroller in a pub car park. Not that I love you...but I like you. Fancied some fun with you."

"Why didn't you ask me?" I was still trying to piece together all that this meant in my mind. It was, as they say, all new ground for me.

He shook his head. "Shy, in't I?" He looked away. "'Sides, at work. 'S not the sort a thing you come out with over the choice for a video weekend, is it?"

"Or while there's a queue for the record player."

"Exactly!"

Still trying to arrange all the new pieces of information in an orderly line, fighting with my floaty mind that just wanted me to stand and dance to the music, never mind sitting still, I said, "Can I kiss you?"

"Thought you'd never ask. C'mere." He leaned forward, spilling the last few drops of tea onto his trousers, his lips met mine and we kissed, squashed together in that slouchy leather chair in Slinky Simon's living room, kissing, exploring with our tongues, licking each other's lips, moving back to kiss each other's necks, returning for more kissing, but always, still, continuing with the kissing, losing track of how long we'd been kissing, breathing with our noses so we didn't have to come up for air, until, after a while, we pulled back from the kiss.

"That was worth the wait," he said.

"Yep."

The room filled with applause as everyone stood clapping in harmony, above the noise of the music, the room a fog of cigarette smoke and half light as a few streams of sunlight from the reality of the day outside streamed through the gaps in the curtains.

Slinky Simon said, "All right, you two? About fucking time! We'd started taking bets, how long before you came up for air."

"Who won?" I asked, squeezing Paul's hand, cuddling up closer to him, wishing I could meld with him like molten metal reforming in a mould, to become one person, a mixture of the two of us.

"Me, of course!"

**

Our first date—the second time we'd seen each other outside of our shops—we went for a curry in Brick Lane. We arrived at the decision after both of us had been noncommittal, saying we weren't bothered and didn't mind if it was a pizza or pasta or in Chinatown or just a pub, until Paul had said, with a pause and a quiet kissing noise made down the phone while I stood in the hall at home, "Fuck it. Let's get a curry down Brick Lane. Can't go wrong with a ruby, can you?"

"You weren't born in the East End, were you?" I asked.

"Don't think you can stretch Chelmsford to the East End, no."

"No." And so it was agreed. A *ruby murray* in the best Indian restaurant in Brick Lane, a road where the smell of turmeric and curry and smoke wafted along with the breeze as you moved from one curry house to the next, with barely any space between them, each with an Asian man standing outside, waving the menu and beckoning you in.

We walked past the parade of tempting Asian restaurateurs and arrived at the place Paul had booked.

"Sorry," he said once we were seated and the waiter had brought us poppadums and chutney.

"What for?"

"Being so crap. Taking so long. Not turning up to any of the nights you told me you were gonna be at. Everything, really. I thought I'd play it by ear. Take it easy."

I shook my head and gently rubbed his hand on the table. "Don't be so stupid. We're both as bad as each other. All that banter and small talk, and the whole time both of us wanted the same thing."

"Suppose so."

"I know so." I paused, breaking a poppadum with a satisfying crack and dipping it into the sweet sauce. "'Course, now you've got to come to see me playing. DJing. To the biggest room in the club. On stage at the front. The whole nine yards. Or it looks a bit funny." I wanted to see how he reacted to my statement that jumped ahead a lot of steps.

"That's what I thought. That's what I wanted to ask you. I've heard you chatting about it, but now you're going somewhere with it, I want to see it, hear it, dance to it for real. Your own stage, your own room. You know? It'll be a laugh."

Christ alive! This is getting pretty serious, pretty quickly. Is this normal? Am I making it go too fast? Or is he putting his foot on the accelerator and I'm not sure what to do? Do I want to go this fast? Or am I just wanting to pause on principle? It's not like we just met each other; we're practically friends, in a sense, so this is like date six or seven, isn't it?

"Yeah. I do," I said, thinking I'd just go with it at the moment. It had taken so much to get us to this point, I didn't want to bugger it all up by running scared.

"Sorry." Paul said again, and this time, he rubbed my hand under the table, squeezing my knee.

"What for?"

"Too much. Too strong. My friend told me. It's just... I've been wanting to be here with you now since I first saw you in the shop, and I've got so much to say I don't know what to start with. I want to make up for all the lost time when we should have been doing stuff together but we kept missing each other." He paused, taking a breath, then filling his mouth with a bit of poppadum.

"Why did you never just turn up to the nights I told you I was at?"

Before he could answer, the waiter brought our mains—a silver dish of sizzling bright-red chicken tikka masala and a black metal plate of sliced prawns in a yellow sauce, accompanied by enough rice to feed all the customers in all the restaurants on our side of Brick Lane. The waiter asked if we wanted anything else. I was tempted to say 'just to get to the bottom of this little matter, and then maybe to see what Paul looks like naked', but I simply smiled and shook my head.

The waiter gone, Paul continued, "I didn't know you were. So if I turned up, told you I was there, just cos I knew you, it felt a bit...I dunno...too much. Too...serious. You know?"

"Yeah, I do."

"But I always enjoyed our little chats. I used to look out for you every time the bell rang over the door. Sad, innit?"

"Not as sad as the time I spent an afternoon arranging on the counter all the films you'd mentioned were your classics and making sure I rented them myself—for free, of course, staff discount—so when you came back I could talk about them with you."

"That's well sweet. Wicked sweet, that is." He smiled as he forked some food into his mouth. "No point us renting them again, then?"

"I didn't say that. I'm sure we can make some arrangement. Do you live with your parents?"

He nodded. "Can't afford anything else. Not on what the record shop pays me. You do too, don't you?"

"Yep." I shrugged. "Mum's pretty cool, though."

"What d'ya mean?"

"Everything, the clubbing—and I mean, *everything* about the clubbing. She's the most liberal, not-arsed mum I could ever wish for. Sometimes I wish she'd be a bit more arsed, tell me off for something, like other kids' parents. She cares about me. Wants me to take care of myself. It's just she's worried about different things than most parents. When I was at school, I used to listen in amazement to the stuff others got grounded and bollocked for.

And me, it was carte blanche do whatever, as long as it didn't hurt anyone else. Came home from school when I was fifteen or sixteen and Mum had a condom, a spliff and an E on the kitchen table. She sat me down, told me to make sure to wear the first, there's a lot of it about at the moment."

We shared a look that, with nothing, said everything.

I continued, "And she said if I was gonna smoke spliffs to stick to weed and avoid skunk cos she'd heard lots of bad shit about skunk and people totally losing it and going paranoid with too much. Finally, she said if I was gonna get into the disco biscuits—and to be honest, by then I was already pretty well into them, that's the advantage or disadvantage of having older friends—I must drink plenty of water, avoid booze, and if I felt like curling up into a ball, that's not good E and should be avoided. Don't buy 'em in the clubs, she said too. Best off getting someone to trust and buy from them."

"Your old dear said this to you?"

"Yep. Every word."

"Wicked. How comes you're not, like totally fucked up and always on it?"

"It's like swearing," I said as the waiter collected our dishes and offered us a dessert menu.

Paul shook his head, so I did the same, and the waiter disappeared.

Paul said, quietly, behind his hand, "I had an Indian pudding once. It was shit. Same when I went to Chinatown, some lie chi and fried banana crap. Never again. We could go to Soho and get something from one of the cafés on Old Compton Street. If you like. Otherwise, I'm not bothered. Unless you've gotta get back. Whatever you want. But just no pudding here for me, all right?"

"Noted. Understood, Paul doesn't do pudding at Indian or Chinese restaurants." I was looking forward to getting to know hundreds of little quirks and foibles like this about Paul.

We sat in silence, paid the bill—split fifty-fifty, no *who did/ didn't have rice, I'll pay, no, you pay* rubbish; it was refreshingly simple. I allowed myself the briefest moment to hope the rest of Paul and Tom would be as simple too.

Walking back to the Tube station, he said, "We could go back to mine. If you like. The olds aren't in. They're never in. On holiday, working, something."

"Chiswick, isn't it?"

"They say Turnham Green, but yeah, Chiswick. Well remembered."

The thought of the hour's Tube journey out there wasn't too appealing, and although I knew we both wanted to go further than the opportunity the restaurant had allowed us, I didn't want to rush this. I wanted to take it slowly. I'd waited eleven months to get this far and didn't want to spunk my relationship load too soon.

I looked at my watch. "I've got work tomorrow, and I was up early. So I think it's best if I just, you know, get back to the delights of Brockley." If I slept with him on this first date, I'd never see him again. I wanted more than a one-night thing. If Paul wanted to see me again—which I really wasn't sure why he would—then I'd make us wait to sleep together.

"Me going out with a hard man from South East London. Who'd have thunk it?"

There was a bit of *awkward hug, brief kiss on neck and longer hug* moment, both of us conscious of where we were, then he said, "I want to hear more about this mother of yours. This swearing thing you started about."

"Yeah. That'd be nice. Next time."

"Next time." He leaned forward, hugged me again and gave me a slightly lingering kiss on the cheek before pulling back and winking a big brash, winky-wink at me and treating me to his broad, cheeky grin.

We went through the ticket barriers and waited on opposite sides of the platform, him heading west, me heading east. As his train arrived, he made the phone motion with his right hand, then jumped on and disappeared in a dirty carriage of strangers, taking him back to West London to an empty house, with no parents.

What a stupid idiot I am. Why have I passed up a guaranteed shag for a hot cocoa and a debrief with Mum?

***

Our next date was the cinema in Leicester Square to see *Basic Instinct*, a film everyone had been talking about and saying was unmissable, especially for the Sharon Stone legs-crossing scene. It wasn't a particularly 'us' sort of film, and understandably neither of us were remotely interested in seeing Sharon Stone's lady parts, but we both agreed we had a lot of dating time to make up, so it felt right to go there rather than shout above the throbbing beat of music at some underground nightclub behind Waterloo station, or some other shit date.

We sat in silence at first as the film started, not knowing what to say about a man being killed by a woman with an ice pick in the throes of passion, but once we started holding hands, Paul leaned closer and murmured, "I dunno how they're gonna top that." I giggled slightly and was met with a loud *ssshhhhh* from behind us.

At the scene where Michael Douglas shoots two tourists on a massive *I'm on cocaine and I think I'm the king of the world* high, I couldn't keep it inside any longer, since we'd both been passing minor critical comments to each other to this point. I laughed, loudly.

Paul put his hand on my mouth, shushing me. "We need to either shut up of ship out. Which is it to be?"

I stopped laughing, and turned resolutely back to the screen, holding Paul's hand for the tense moments of what we'd managed to successfully reduce to an over-the-top farce with ice picks and hard-boiled detectives.

When Michael Douglas read the final pages of Sharon Stone's book, I whispered to Paul, "I don't give a monkey's what happened to any of these vile characters. How d'you fancy a drink or something?"

Not needing much persuasion, he immediately stood, and we left, to a chorus of "Get out the way!" and "What's wrong?" as we giggled, climbing across seats and into the aisle.

In the cool air of evening, amid the crowds of tourists having photos taken, taking photos, buying tickets from theatre booths and generally milling about and wondering at London, we sat on a bench in the small grassed area in the middle of Leicester Square.

Paul offered me a cigarette, lit it, then lit one for himself and said, "Hype, eh? Same as always. Something's meant to be everywhere, everyone says you've gotta see it, and you see it and it's one big fat disappointment." He inhaled deeply on his cigarette. "What a load of shit, eh?"

I nodded. "Where now?"

"Any-fucking-where. I read some flyers someone left in the shop this week—there's a big housey, trancey night someplace down out the back of Paddington station. Looked good."

I crinkled my nose. "Could do, but will we be able to talk?"

"If we go to a quiet room. There's three or four rooms of different music and some bar bits between the dance rooms, which don't have music playing. You'll still hear it, but it's not loud, like in the other rooms."

"Or we could go Soho so I could snog your face off. Cos that's what I've been wanting to do all week. Every night we've spoken on the phone, I've wanted to jump in a cab and come round yours just to see you, to kiss your face." I stared into his eyes. I was obviously getting better at being more forthright about what I wanted. He'd not made me feel as small as I thought I was. Yet. Mind you, I reminded myself, it had taken the ex a few months to work up to full-on piss-taking, bullying and verbal abuse. And it had taken me almost a year to leave him. *That proves how useless I really am!* Shaking that thought from my mind, I concentrated on Paul, now standing in front of me, and my increasing desire to have sex with him.

Up to that point, we'd managed a quick fumble a while after we started seeing each other; he'd come to one of my nights at a small club in Brixton. The Fridge, cos it's, like, so cool. *Too Cool for Skool*, the flyers said. It was a bouncy, housey crowd, who all liked to get completely bouncy and chemically enhanced as soon as they arrived, if not before. Slinky Simon joked they handed disco biscuits out with tickets, but they didn't.

Anyway, we'd met there, and after my set, when he'd come up to the DJ booth and told me how much of a wicked time he'd had dancing and dancing until he thought his heart would burst out of his chest, he pulled me towards him, leaned across the booth and snogged my face off for what seemed like an age, until the next DJ asked if we were all right and did we need a room and could he start his set now?

We'd danced together, gradually taking our clothes off until, both topless with sweat pouring down our chests and a sheen of glitter across Paul's, we'd ended up in the gents', in a cubicle, necking Paul's last pill with a bottle I'd been refilling with tap water throughout the night, and he'd kissed me.

We'd got a bit more involved, even though someone had been banging on the door for us to get a move on, and he'd reached into my underpants, and I'd reached into his, squeezing him, trying to expand and respond to our kissing, which we'd been doing for so long we both had stubble rash. The great, really sexy stubble rash you get when you're so into a guy you don't want to stop kissing him, not for anything, and the next morning you're proud of the stubble rash cos it shows how much into the other guy you were. That sort of stubble rash.

Anyway, we wanted to whip each other out in the cubicle and give each other a go, but unfortunately, at that late stage of the evening, both of us were very much the worse for wear and although not quite completely banjaxed, we were certainly flying pretty high, we hadn't suitably responded enough to get anything much going. So we'd pushed ourselves back in our underpants, laughed, shrugged and left the cubicle to dance until the club closed.

Now, I said, "Let's get pissed. Like, really pissed. What you working tomorrow?" Alcohol always helped me feel more confident.

"Sunday, closed. You?"

"Late. Midday till close." I paused, a glint in my eyes at a plan hatched. "Ready?"

***

We were on the third round of pints in a Soho bar, laughing at everything and anything, banging our hands on the table as we told jokes, stories, and generally being fucking hilarious together.

It was wonderful. I chuckled to myself.

"What?" Paul chinked his pint glass with mine.

"Nothing. Silly."

"Come on. You've seen my ecstasy-shrivelled cock, I think we're beyond silly, don't you?"

"It's just… You know how you think things should be, how you think it's going to turn out, and somehow you stop and it's nothing like that?"

"That…is life."

"Like, if someone had told me I'd finish school and carry on in the video rental place I'd worked when I was at college, I'd have laughed. But you know what? I don't mind it, now I'm doing it."

"And you've got your DJing. Don't forget that."

"It's nothing." I waved it away.

"It's not nothing. It's wicked. Wish I'd done something like it."

"You could. Why not? You know the tracks. You're like an encyclopaedia of music. Every time I come in, you know who's new, who's old, what's classic, what's going up, what the clubs were playing—everything. That's *wicked*."

He smiled at me using *his word* for the first time. "I don't push myself, I suppose."

"Why not?"

"I knew you were gonna ask that. I dunno. I don't wanna say it's Mum and Dad. I don't wanna be one of those poor little rich kids who blames his parents for everything that's wrong with his life. Poor me, and my *private school, monthly allowance funded* life. I must be crying to the cashpoint every time I get the money."

This, was all news to me. I'd known his parents were well off, but none of the rest. It must have been the alcohol loosening things up for him, and now I knew he really was out of my league. I sat in silence, sipping the last of my pint, willing him to continue. This was what I'd wanted for our date, not some stupid Hollywood blockbuster film with ice picks and a no-knickers heroin.

"Anyway, we're not talking about me, we're talking about you—how it's not what you think it will be or something. You're much more interesting than me."

"I'm so not."

"You are, you know. With your liberal parents and your DJing and your plan. I don't have a plan. I don't need a plan. That's the thing about parents like mine—you don't need a plan." He shook his head. "I said I'm not whingeing about them. And here I am, whingeing about them."

We sat in silence for a few moments. I pointed to our empty glasses, already feeling pretty pissed, but not sure where the evening was going to take us.

"More is good. Three pints is great, four's gonna be brilliant, and five's gonna be—"

"Wicked?"

"Bloody right, wicked."

I returned with another round and told him about how I'd thought our dates should be all like in the films—dinner and then drinks, and then a film, and then a kiss at the doorstep, and then, and then... But now I was here, with him in the pub, just being, with no film playing in my head I felt we should be living up to, I was having the most fun we'd had together so far.

"Me too," he said, with that wink and that smile.

And when he said that, with the wink and the smile, I knew I was in so much trouble with this man, that I'd follow him, do anything that sounded fun with him, that I was jumping onto the Ferris wheel of our relationship while he sat in the booth, reaching out for me to take his hand. And we'd soar into the sky, high above everyone else milling around at the fairground, because I knew instinctively Paul would be my very own fairground of fun.

CHAPTER 4

I STARTED HAVING PAUL in the DJ booth with me. It was now DJ Tom plus one.

It was after one of these *DJ Tom plus one* nights a few weeks later that we jumped into a cab back to Paul's in Chiswick, both babbling about how well it had gone.

"I could feel the waves from the dancers when I picked the songs. It was like a bolt of energy from the clubbers." Paul held my hand, massaging it gently in the back of the cab.

"I was absorbing the energy from the dance floor, from the booth, I could feel it, and that translated into the mix of what I played next."

"Wicked," he said with his smile-grin.

"Did you see how it went down when Slinky Simon dropped a beat?"

He shook his head. "No fucking mercy for a dropped beat. Well bad." He leant forward and kissed me. "You know we got the house to ourselves tonight?"

I nodded. He'd mentioned it a few times—earlier that day, during the set, and as we'd left the club when I'd complained of feeling a bit tired and he'd said there was no place for being tired, not yet.

We'd been kissing and cuddling like horny teenagers whenever we were together in the club but hadn't had the opportunity to go any further. Yet. Paul said he wanted it to be perfect. Magic. Wicked.

We'd arrived. He paid the cab driver, thanked him and led me through the wide wood-and-stained-glass door of the sprawling three-storey Victorian detached house, just off Turnham Green itself, in the rich heartlands of Chiswick, nowhere near the rough Acton bits.

He danced me into the kitchen, sat me at the breakfast bar and made us tea. He swooped past, kissed me, lingering for just long enough, then disappeared into the living room where he remained for a while. He shouted for me to stay there with the tea and feel free to smoke if I wanted.

"You sure?" The kitchen all looked so immaculate, so 'Ideal Homes Exhibition', with its shiny black work surfaces, shiny metal oven, microwave, fridge, freezer, hob. The bin had opened when Paul waved his hand in front of it, magically, just like that. It was like some sort of a Dalek stood in the corner, waiting to consume the family's rubbish.

Wicked.

I kept expecting a TV presenter to pop up from the corner explaining how much it had cost and how long it had taken to install. I lit a cigarette, inhaled deeply and took a sip of tea. The combination of smoking and tea mixed to form one of our shared favourite sensations. We'd had a long, in-depth discussion about the joy of smoking and drinking tea in a nicely floaty, pilled-up state. Not the mad for it, wanting to dance and wave your hands above your head state; oh no. We'd passed that. This was the gentle glide from that to the beginning of normality. This, we both agreed, was the time when tea and cigarettes and cuddles and kisses and caresses and more all came into their own.

I found my head nodding in time with something. *Something.* What was it? Music, a gentle chill-out track we'd floated down together on a few times.

Paul appeared at the door, his hands either side of his body. "I am ready for you now. If you'd like to follow me."

I followed him into the living room, where the curtains were closed, letting in little light, but the room was filled with the flickering of a dozen or so candles, scattered around the table, mantelpiece, window ledges. The room was filled with a burning, sweet smell; a joss stick smouldered in the middle of the mantelpiece.

Paul knelt on a duvet he'd thrown on the floor, patted the space in front of him.

I joined him, and as we knelt, he pulled me close, kissed me slowly, gently, our mouths open as he explored with his tongue, no air between us as we both sucked slightly while kissing, as the tension built in my underwear. We fell sideways onto the soft duvet he'd scattered with pillows and cushions, and we lay on our sides, kissing each other, gently, then a bit more bitey, then stopping for more tea and cigarettes, gently flicking the ash in cleverly placed circular metal ashtrays round the edges of the duvet.

"I've wanted this since I first met you," Paul said.

And once he's seduced me I bet I won't hear from him again.

"Right back then?" I asked. "When I came into your shop asking for some ideas for singles?"

"Right back then." He smiled, kissed me, pulled back and removed my T-shirt.

I kissed him and removed his T-shirt. "And it took you all this time to finally get me into bed." I laughed quietly.

"Shy. I didn't want to ask in case you said no."

"So you waited for me to ask you. I see. Very clever."

He shrugged, put his lips on mine and unzipped my trousers, awkwardly edging them over my hips.

I leant closer, both of us lying on our sides; after a few awkward moments, his jeans were off too.

He raised his hands to mine and we pressed palms together, edging closer so our bodies touched skin to skin, straining underpants to straining underpants. We lay like that for a while, kissing each other's faces, necks, chests, pushing ourselves forward, brushing underpants. The sensation of his body against mine pulsed through me. The feelings, the tingling rippled up and down just like the hand massage in the club he'd given me, but now along my whole body.

He pushed me onto my back, then worked his way down with his tongue, starting at my face, over my chest, my nipples, my navel. Looking up at me, he edged my underpants off and threw them into the corner of the room before, sharing a glint in his eye, he took me, all of me, inch by inch, into his mouth. All I could do was lie, with one arm above my head, the other on his head, stroking him so he'd know I was enjoying him making love to me with his mouth.

I think he'd have carried on selflessly until it was over for me, but I wanted to show him how I felt for him, how much I wanted us to melt together like we were wax from two candles. As I reached a near crescendo, I gently lifted his head. I didn't want it to end just yet. I pulled him back to my level and kissed him, tasting myself and him mixed together. Manoeuvring him onto his back, I crouched across his body, leaning down to kiss him.

"Better get them off," I said, eyeing his straining underpants.

"Go on, then," he said, with a smile.

I grabbed the offending underpants at either hip, while he lifted himself off the ground, then I whipped them off, throwing them over my head with a triumphant flourish and a smile.

He leant forward to kiss me, but I pushed him backwards and, easing his legs apart so I could make myself comfortable between them, in one gasping move, I took him in my mouth.

We lay like that for a few chill-out songs, with him trying to pull me back to his level so he could kiss me, so he could reciprocate, but I wanted to take him as far as he'd taken me, just using my mouth, my tongue, my lips.

His legs tensed, and I knew he would soon be at the point of no return, so I allowed him to put me where he wanted me, and he kissed me, long and hard, as I lay on top of him, our bodies pushed together, skin against skin, hard and wet against hard and wet.

"Is that what I taste like?" he asked, with a cheeky smile.

"Pretty much."

"Bit salty."

We both burst out laughing, shaking as it spread through our bodies, holding each other tightly, not wanting to be separated for even one moment.

Afterwards, when the laughter had subsided, we lay facing each other, his head on my chest, curled like two apostrophes, interlocking, as close as we could be. We stayed like that, drifting in and out of dreams, the music and flickering candles lulling us to sleep like a lullaby.

After a while, I woke, still feeling a bit floaty but aware of Paul's body entwined with mine, and I whispered something about wanting our bodies to be twisted but never our minds, quoting an Alison Moyet song we both liked, saying *I love you* without quite saying the words.

He looked up from my chest, taking me in his hand. "Waking up, I see."

"You too." I reached to reciprocate to him.

"Let's keep our bodies twisted just like this, eh? But not our minds," Paul said as he pulled me, pulled me, pulled me.

We adjusted our position so we were sitting up, facing each other and enjoying the view as we gathered speed, mirroring each other's motions.

Paul moved, positioning himself above me so we were both facing the same direction with his legs either side of mine as he crouched over me. He lay back, on top of my chest, turning his face so I could kiss him as I pulled him with my hand, while I strained, pressing gently into him underneath. He moved on top of me, in time with my hand and my hips as I pushed against him.

He turned to face me, nodding slowly, lifting his legs slightly and pushing himself down, onto my hardness.

"Where's the..." I managed, my throat strained, hardly able to keep a lid on things. I had never felt so turned on as I did in that moment.

He reached to the ashtray, fumbled and knocked it over, cigarette butts and ash spilling on the floor. I started to sit up to tidy the mess.

"Don't move. Fuck it. Fuck me." Paul handed me two silver packets.

I tore the foil wrapper with my teeth, then tried to reach forward to put it on myself, but with Paul still lying on me, it soon became apparent that was not happening.

"What's up?"

"Not from this angle," I said, trying to keep the tone serious but having to suppress a slight laugh at the ridiculousness of the situation.

"Try harder, I'm just... It's almost..."

I sat up, bringing him with me, so we were sitting, him in front of me, on the duvet.

"I was enjoying that. What'd you have to go and do that for?"

"It's not happening. If you want it, then I'm gonna have to." I shuffled backwards so I had space to do what I needed to. "I'm leaning back now." I did so, pulling Paul with me, and after a bit of adjustment, we were back in the same position he had been enjoying so much.

He turned to kiss me, nodding, with a smile.

I nodded back, and after slicking both of us, I pushed myself to meet Paul, pushed farther as he gasped. I checked if he was all right. He nodded and lowered himself to meet me, and then, with a gasp from both of us, we were one. I kissed his neck, checked he was okay, and we began moving together, me pushing from below, him moving his hips from above, so we emphasised each other's movements. All the while I was pulling on him around the front, as he strained, hard as one of the candles around us.

We continued like this, moving together, rocking together, our hips grinding together, his back slipping with sweat over my chest, building our pace. A few times, Paul tensed *those* muscles and I thought my head was going to explode. I uttered a brief, "Fuck me."

To which he replied, "Wrong way round," followed by a little laugh, and some panting.

He held my arm as I continued pulling him, the candle on our birthday cake of sex, until his legs tensed, and with another few flicks of my hand, he finished, a white streamer flying high into the air, landing on his chest, just missing our eyes. I stopped thrusting into him, not wanting to make him uncomfortable. It took all my will to resist as I was close, so close, but I wanted him to get his breath first.

He turned to the side. "Why've you stopped?"

"What do you want now?"

He took a breath. "Really?"

"Really."

"A ciggie and a cuppa. But…if you want…you can…until… if you…"

"That's not how I want to make love to you. This isn't some random fuck. In case you didn't notice, there's a bit of a scene you've set here—moonlight, candles… No rose petals, I notice." I withdrew myself from him.

He climbed off me then lay, curled over my body, his head resting on my stomach, his breathing slowly returning to normal. "You sure?" He lifted his head, looking at me as I stood pointing to the ceiling.

"Amazing. I thought I was having an out-of-body experience when you tightened. Amazing."

He lifted his head to kiss me, and we lay like that, kissing, as I knew would be the case. With a few quick flicks of my hand, I finished myself off, sprinkling us both in my come. I kept expecting him to stand and want to shower, as had happened with most of the others I'd slept with, when all I had wanted to do was cuddle, kiss and lie in our own juices, bathed in the warm glow of our sex.

Paul didn't mention a shower. Instead, he pulled the duvet over us, kissed me once again, and that was the last I remembered until a few hours later when Sunday morning came streaming into our cocoon, with the low grumble of a bus pulling away from the bus stop not far from the house.

I looked down to my chest, staring into Paul's eyes and asked, "What time are your parents back?"

"Tomorrow, Tuesday, Wednesday. Who knows? He's doing some business deal in the Middle East and she's away with some girlfriends—all big hair, big jewellery and Mercedes convertibles. Mum thinks she's living in a Jackie Collins novel. And in fairness, she is. She won't be back till mid week, I think she said."

"No rush, then?"

He shook his head. "No rush whatsoever. Wicked, eh? Just us two, nice and casual."

When we eventually left the nest he'd created, we bathed together—bubbles and candles and more chill-out music—then we drank gallons of tea and ate half a loaf of bread, thick wedges toasted and smeared with butter and jam, while watching terrible Sunday morning TV, laughing at the presenters, flicking over to a black-and-white film. Sometime in the afternoon, when I was sore from going twice again with him, we finally ventured into the outside world.

He showed me the delights of Turnham Green, the end of the green to avoid, the end by the Chi Chi shops selling exclusive women's clothing and kitchen accoutrements more expensive than an elderly but battered small hatchback. "What do you want to eat before you go?"

"Must I go? Can't I stay here for ever and ever and ever?"

He smiled. "Probably best you go. I think Mum and Dad would have something to say about that. Not to mention your work."

"Oh." Maybe that had been a slushy step too far. I glanced at my watch: well past *going home and getting ready for the week ahead* time. "I'll be off. Is that the nearest Tube?" I pointed to the glowing red and blue sign at the edge of the green.

"Want to ring home first, let the olds know where you are?"

"They'll be fine. I'm a big boy now. I can look after myself, you know."

"Give 'em a ring before you leave. And then we can get chips. Fancy chips for dinner. Big bag of salty, vinegary chips, eaten out the paper on the breakfast bar back at mine. How's that sound? Mum would hit the roof if she knew, but she's not here so…chips on the breakfast bar it is, I reckon."

"If it's OK." I hung my head, pausing to look back at the Tube station in the distance. "Didn't mean to get all wuvvy-duvvy clingy-wingy, but after earlier, I don't know how I'm gonna be able to be without seeing you, touching you for a whole entire week. Sorry. Too much. Phone home. Yes."

He grabbed my hand, pulled my head up to face his. "Don't apologise for how you feel. Never apologise for that. This is all pretty new to me. Let's keep it casual, though, all right?"

"Yeah." *Casual? We've just had the best time and he's talking casual?* I'd started picking out curtains for our bedroom. But I didn't tell him that.

"One step at a time." He smiled and pointed to the chip shop in the distance. "Then definitely chips on the work surface together. Wicked."

Wicked.

I called home from Paul's phone in the large hallway that made our living room look like a caravan, the light from Sunday evening streaming through the red-and-blue stained-glass windowpane, leaving a pattern on the red-tiled floor. Mum was pleased I'd rung but hadn't been worried. She knew I would be with Paul. She asked if we'd done the deed; I cursed myself for being far, far too open with Mum about my love life. "Can't say now. Tell you later."

"Get back when you get back. Dinner or no dinner, I'm easy. Me and your dad are vegging out on TV, and I'm eyeing up a pile of ironing that should get done, but really, when I think about it, I could really just do one, stick the rest on hangers. Once you and your dad've worn it, it would be nearly as good. So you're not missing much."

After the chips and newspaper meal, it took twenty minutes for me to finally leave the house; We stood in the hallway and he pushed me back against the wall, kissing me, saying just one more kiss, one more goodbye, and then I could go. Eventually, my face red with stubble rash, my groin sore and a slight, lingering smell of sex on my clothes, I left the house, walked to the Tube station and made my way back home with one word ringing in my ears: casual.

CHAPTER 5

A FEW WEEKS LATER, Paul helped me pick the tracks for the set for the evening. As I mixed, listening in on my headphones to make sure the tracks flowed from one to the next, I explained what I was doing, and he asked me questions. I said he could have a go at the transition for the next song if he liked; having decided the order with me earlier, he might as well mix it himself. He slowed one track down slightly and sped another up to match their beats per minute, fading one out, fading in the next: 'Love Stimulation' by Humate. It was the track of the summer and had the whole club shouting and screaming at its introductory bars, while Paul nodded in time, smiling and winking at me.

Afterwards, we went back to mine. Although I couldn't quite recreate the cocoon of duvet and candles Paul had at his place, in the early hours, as the sun rose, we sat in the kitchen smoking and drinking tea—oh, such perfection, it was—talking about what we'd like to do in our dreams, bearing no resemblance to the nasty realities of work, houses, money, life.

Paul said, talking quickly, pointing with his non-smoking hand, "You could go to Ibiza and do a season. Get a place in one of the super clubs out there. Blissed-out Balearic Islands, they call it. Wicked, it'd be."

"Yeah, like that's gonna happen." I shrugged, flicking ash into the ashtray on the kitchen table. *As if I'm good enough.*

"This is dreams, remember? This is *imagine if.* Let your imagination fly, float above the rooftops and take you wherever it goes. Go on."

"Well, I don't want to be working in the video shop for ever. Didn't think I'd stick it after leaving college, but you know. Practical and all. We could get somewhere together. How about that? We must be able to afford something together."

"Yeah, us two. No parents telling us what to do, no worrying about them walking in on us. It's a bit of a passion killer, isn't it, sometimes?"

"You've not met my parents yet." I paused, glanced at the clock. "Which reminds me, we've got Mum's Sunday roast in seven hours. You ready for sleep yet, or too banjaxed?"

"I could sleep. And yeah. Snuggle. And... Let's carry on with this for a bit, though. Let's finish our ciggies then go to bed."

I lit us both another cigarette and asked what he wanted to do in his life, apart from the music shop; what was his plan.

"I don't have a plan. That's my plan. Don't like to feel tied down. Stuck to things. That's why the olds are so frustrated with me, see."

"What about the DJing? Would you make a go of it? In this fantasy, dream world?"

"Oh yeah, 'course I would. Yeah. 'Course." He didn't sound convinced.

"You're good, you know. Really good. Natural. If you were shit, I'd have put you as a plus-one and they'd have asked me to take you off next time. That didn't happen. Take that and remember it."

"I want to do something on my own, without help, that my parents can be proud of. That's what I want."

"And what would that be?"

Paul shrugged. "Guess that's the problem. If I knew that, I'd have been doing it by now. Fuck, that's a bit deep for five o'clock in the morning, isn't it? I dunno, have fun. Can that be it? Have fun, and work out how to make money doing it. That's a bit airy-fairy, isn't it? I don't feel any different from when I was a teenager.

Don't see why I should grow up, really. Why anyone should. Just live for fun."

"There's that Confucius thing—when you find a job you love that's the day you stop working. Not airy-fairy. We just gotta work out what it is. Together."

"Right." He nodded, but somehow it sounded a bit like a question.

"But for now, it's bed unless we want a tongue-lashing from Mum for not eating her roast. She's looking forward to meeting you, after all she's heard."

"That's what I'm afraid of. That's why I was hoping we could stay here, in this little bubble away from the real world. I've got a couple more if you wanted." He pulled two white pills from his pocket; they lay on his palm.

I shook my head. "That's another couple of hours before we can sleep. I'm just the right side now, ready for a bit of shuteye."

"But this is so fun. I don't want this to stop. If this is fun, doing this—" he looked at his palm "—is more fun. Logical, innit?"

This was a frequent conversation between us: Paul's desire to go with the flow and keep things going, floating at the clubbing or afterparty stage, and my acknowledgement of enough being enough and it being time for bed and all that it entailed. Both jostled for prime position and an agreed decision; sometimes he won, sometimes I won. Sometimes there was no contest and we agreed what to do.

"I'm going to bed." I stood. "I'm not sure I'll be able to sleep without a bit of a release. If you want to give me a hand... Well, that would be good. If not, I'm sure I can manage on my own." I grabbed my crotch, bent down to kiss his forehead and walked upstairs. As I left, I saw he was adjusting himself in his baggy grey clubbing trousers.

Once in my room, I stepped out of my clothes and into my single bed, lying on my back, remembering the events of the night, of all the previous nights with Paul, of the conversation we'd had in the kitchen, of his face, of his kiss, and I felt myself respond. My eyes shut, I grabbed myself.

The door closed. I opened my eyes and Paul stood, completely naked in the middle of my small bedroom, his hand on himself, trying to minimise the shrunken-drugs-cock look we often laughed about at times like this.

I lifted the duvet, exposing myself to him, and quick as a flash he jumped in beside me. I moved up against the wall, he next to me, under the duvet. It took a while, and we both agreed we'd never sleep without the release, but with Mum and Dad next door and our bodies feeling like an empty husk from dancing and smoking all night, gymnastics weren't called for, so instead settled for pulling on one another, while kissing and occasionally checking under the duvet, until first he finished, all over my hand and the duvet, and then I finished and said, "Right, roll over, sleep."

He rolled onto his left side, facing the wall.

I did the same, pushing myself close behind him, no gap between our two bodies, my right hand reaching round him, stroking his navel, and my left hand tucked behind me. I kissed his neck. "Night."

"Night," came his reply as he stroked my hand, then kissed it.

***

Later, Mum's shout upstairs woke us. "On the table in fifteen."

"Must we?" Paul asked, quietly, slowly kissing my hand again, his eyes still closed. "I might just nip home. Your mum won't mind, will she?"

"She'll mind. Yes. We must go. Both of us very much indeed, must."

"Really? I don't think I can eat anything. I'll slip out. Go home. We can do meeting the parents another time. I think I must have eaten something dodgy. I feel a bit fragile."

"And the two doves, pack of ciggies and dancing your tits off all night has nothing to do with it, eh? Whereas I'm feeling like I've been doing yoga, drinking water and breathing buckets of fresh air, aren't I?" I pulled myself away from his back, pausing briefly for a little kiss on his shoulder. "Shower, you'll feel better."

I grabbed a towel from the back of my door and jumped in the shower, standing under the water getting my head wet, noticing the nerves in my body returning to normal levels of sensitivity. I returned to my room to find Paul still in bed. I pulled the duvet off, threw him a clean towel and told him the shower was still running, then leant down to his level and whispered, "And you wanted to do those last two pills. Imagine if we had."

"I'm dying." He turned to face me, opening his eyes one at a time.

I kissed him and lifted him upright, so he was sitting on the edge of the bed.

He slowly walked to the bathroom, wrapped in a towel.

Eventually, he returned, wet, a smile on his face and a twinkle in his eyes.

I handed him some clothes he'd left at mine and Mum had washed and put back in my room.

I waited on the bed as he dressed, and once he'd put gel in his hair, forming it into thick spikes, as he had last night, he looked normal, like my Paul once again.

"Ready?"

"As I'll ever be." He stood, took my hand and we walked downstairs together.

Mum looked us both up and down as we arrived in the kitchen. "So, the clubbing wanderers return. Good night, was it?"

"Had 'em eating out of our hands, didn't we?" I turned to Paul.

Paul nodded while taking a seat and folding his arms.

"Didn't we?" I tapped his arm.

"Yeah. Out of our hands."

"Where's Dad?" I asked Mum as she sat.

"Working. He's fixing some streetlights in Lewisham. Why it couldn't wait till tomorrow, I don't know, but you can't argue with triple time, can you? Don't sit on ceremony, dig in. Anything we don't eat now, it's for dinner during the week. So it's in both your interests to eat up. I've saved a plate for your dad, so no holding back." She looked at me as I chewed my cheek slightly. "I *told* you this was the plan. I *said* would you be all right to eat after all night on the disco biscuits, and you *told* me you would. 'Yes, Mum, it'll be fine,' you said. So here we are, eating." Her eyes narrowed. "Eating."

I swallowed the ball that had appeared in my throat, then dug in, putting a small amount on my plate and encouraging Paul to do the same. Slowly, forkful by forkful, our bodies remembered the concept of food and that our stomachs hadn't seen any since lunchtime yesterday.

We told Mum how it had gone last night, the set we'd done together, the waves and shouts of the crowd, the reading the mood of the room, the songs we'd played. She hadn't heard of any of them, but when Paul hummed the chorus, she nodded in recognition. There was a pause and then Mum asked, "What about this Slinky Simon? What's he reckon to you two?"

Paul, with a mouthful of food, said, "Wicked," then looked at me, then Mum, swallowed and said, "Sorry. Mouth full."

Mum shrugged. "Don't worry. We're not posh here, are we, love? You should see his dad eating. Food all over the floor, chewing, talking, laughing. But that's who he is, and I love him for it. It's what's in here, I reckon." She tapped her heart. "Not if you know which knives and forks to use or how you hold them."

I shrugged. "We don't normally have these." I held up my napkin.

"He's right, you know. They're just kitchen roll, but I thought I'd best have them since you're from Turnham Green. In Brockley, we're a bit different." She smiled.

Paul said, keeping his food on his fork this time, "Mum wouldn't know a roast potato or a Yorkshire pudding if it landed in her lap. She discusses the menu with the maid and that's as far as she goes into the kitchen."

"Well, I do declare!" Mum's eyes widened. "Sorry, you'll just have to make do with us, take us as you find us, I'm afraid."

"At least you're here to find each other." He swallowed another mouthful.

Silence descended across the table. I reached underneath and squeezed his knee.

"Poor me, poor little boarding-school, trust-fund boy. I know it's stupid. Ignore me. This is family, not some French au pair who got fired one day after my parents' arguments went from frequent to regular. Mother told me the au pair was bad, and then a much older woman started looking after me. Then boarding school. Prison with blazers."

Mum raised her eyebrow at me, obviously not knowing what to say. She went with, "I could show her if she liked, a few bits. How to get the roasties crisp, some basics, you know? For your mum."

Paul shook his head. "Getting to be in the same room..." He wiped his hands on his trousers. "Sorry. I'm a bit... Ignore me." He wiped a tear from his eye. "Tired, that's all." He sniffed.

Mum rubbed his arm across the table. "It's all right, love. Eat up and we'll say no more about it."

Paul explained what his parents did after Mum asked. His dad was in the property-rental business, owning much of certain streets in West London; his mum was a woman who didn't have to work and enjoyed that.

"So, Paul...what's your surname, I don't think Tom's told me."

"Stockton."

"So, Paul Stockton, I need to ask what your intentions are for my son."

Paul shot me a look of pure, undiluted terror, eyes wide open, lips pursed.

I said, "She's joking."

"I bloody well am not. I want to know what you intend to do with my son. Is this serious, or are you just, you know, messing about? Don't mind if you are. Trust me, in the seventies, I was very good at messing about. I could have taught an Open University course in it, blokes before your dad, and then eventually between me and your dad. But if it's not that, if it's more, then I'd like to know."

"Mum, behave would you?" To Paul, I said, "Take no notice. She's joking."

"I told you, I am not bloody well joking. I've not met any of his other men before. Not that I minded, if it was just messing about. But I'm assuming, since you're here with me, meeting the mother-in-law, you're aiming for something a bit more than just messing about. Or am I wrong? Who knows how you kids do things these days, I can't keep up with it all. It's hard enough knowing about the new music, the new clothes, the new parties, not to mention the new drugs, never mind what you do for relationships now."

Paul looked at me, one eyebrow raised.

"She knows. We had the drugs talk years ago. She knows."

Mum adjusted her bra under her top. "And *she's* sat here in the room with you, so *she* would prefer it if *she* wasn't referred to as *she* if that's all right with you both." Mum helped herself to another serving of roasties.

"I said she was laid-back, didn't I?" I offered.

"Yeah, but I didn't think you meant this laid-back." Paul sipped his water. "This is, I don't know, this is…"

Mum laughed. "Fucking horizontal!" She assembled herself, then said, "Look, there's no point pretending it's not happening. You're young, you live in London, you're into clubbing. I know all you lot don't stay up all night on water and fresh air. Cos neither did I when I was your age. Only it was different stuff.

Same, really, I suppose. Broadly the same. Anyway, I think it's best to be open about it, not make it something forbidden, cos soon as something's forbidden, it's all kids ever want to do. It's like swearing."

Paul said, "Yeah. Tom was starting to explain it was like swearing, but we never got round to finishing that, did we?"

I shook my head.

Mum continued, "Swearing, if you ban children from swearing, it's all they'll want to do when you're not there. If you're grown up about it, explain it's part of language and is used appropriately, it's not this magical forbidden thing. Same with alcohol and drugs and sex. No point me pretending you're not gonna do them all. Fuck me, I did. I got right involved when I was your age. But any more of that's not for now. I knew he was gonna be into the music and the clubbing. Ever since we bought him his first record player when he was eleven, he's been dancing in his room."

"Wish my parents had the same idea. It's not talked about. They must know, the number of times I've come home totally banjaxed as they've got up the next morning. Once, I was dancing on my own in the living room, facing the hi-fi system and doing *big fish, little fish, cardboard box* to some track I'd bought from work and had been playing nonstop. Mum walked in and asked if I could keep the noise down as they were going to make breakfast and did I want any."

"That's what she said, your mum, faced with you doing that?"

"My eyes were like bin lids, I tell you. I was chewing the Juicy Fruit like my life depended on it. In fact, I think I'd dropped another one just before she got up. I was flying. I was having my own little party. A one-man party. Didn't want the night to end."

I briefly reflected on how sad that was, but didn't mention it.

Mum put her knife and fork down. "See, that's a conversation. Here, that's a mum-and-son talk. If it's not forbidden and off-limits, then there's no risk with it getting out of control, becoming a big thing. Between five and ten percent of people take drugs every weekend and carry on with a normal life in the week. Getting on it at the weekend with a few pills and some pot is very different from injecting heroin or smoking crack. Against what the papers and the news says, all drugs aren't the same. People die of alcohol and smoking all the time, but we carry on selling that. And do you know why?" She paused, as Paul shrugged, then went on, "Because the government tells us it's all right."

"And they can tax it," Paul added.

We'd finished eating now, so Mum offered pudding—trifle or nothing. "Them's the choices. Take it or leave it."

Sitting back in his chair, stroking his full stomach, Paul said, "Trifle please." He looked at me. "Wicked."

Wicked, indeed.

We finished eating, both much more than we'd anticipated being able to eat. "Told you once we started it'd slip right down."

"You can clean this lot up," Mum said. "I'm going down Lewisham to meet your dad, see how he's getting on. He said he'll be back at the depot so I'm taking him a flask of tea."

I stood and started collecting plates together. "Shall we come too?"

"Na, don't be daft—sure you've had enough of parents. I'll be out for a while, so if you want to go back to bed and really let yourselves go, be our guest. Empty house, see. 'Spect last night we cramped your style a bit, didn't we, sleeping next door to your room?" She kissed my forehead, then Paul's, and left the room.

Paul leant forward. "She having a laugh?"

"She wouldn't joke about that."

"Wicked." Paul rubbed his hands together. "Best get this lot cleared and then nip back upstairs."

"Oh yeah, bloody right too."

We'd cleared everything within twenty minutes of Mum leaving the house, ran upstairs to my room, and once the door was closed were naked again in thirty seconds flat.

Paul looked me up and down, then pulled me towards him, skin touching skin. "What have I done to deserve you? To deserve all this fun?"

"What have I done to deserve you?"

And we stayed in my room until the front door banged with Mum and Dad returning and Mum shouting upstairs if we'd finished yet and was Paul staying for his dinner. I shook my head.

"Unbelievable. Wicked, but unbelievable," Paul said, nuzzling into me.

"You staying or what?"

"I'd best go home."

***

I did meet his parents. After much to-ing and fro-ing of dates and noncommittal noises from his end, we finally arrived at a midweek nibbles-and-drinks meeting.

"You sure you want to meet them?" Paul had said after I'd insisted he arrange it.

It felt like the logical next step of us being together. "You've met Mum, so I'll meet yours."

"Can't we stick to just us two? See how things go?"

I was starting to think he was embarrassed about me, which reconfirmed all my beliefs about myself, so I'd stopped mentioning it for a while and gone quiet, until Paul had announced he'd arranged it, adding, "It's nothing. I've had a few offers of other things to do that night, so we can see what else is happening."

It had felt like a reasonable compromise.

Now, the four of us stood in the conservatory, the sun streaming into our eyes, the immaculately manicured garden drifting off outside to a large outdoor pool and pool house, us holding champagne while a bemused-looking French au pair circulated with trays of tiny smoked salmon, mushroom and ham nibbly things.

Paul's father, never 'Dad', Roger shook my hand awkwardly. "Sorry it's taken so long to get round to this. It's been absolutely manic with work. I've been flying off left, right and centre. Some weeks I've been in three time zones before breakfast."

I eyed him up nervously, taking a sip of champagne to give myself more time to consider my response, knowing I would, no matter how good I was, never live up to their expectations of a suitable partner for their son, specifically because I was male, and because of a whole host of small reasons I could do nothing to change about myself or my family.

"What is it you do?" I asked Roger.

He began to explain about asset management and liquidation and leveraging all sorts of things, and he'd been chatting away reasonably well until his wife, Marilyn—a vision in an aquamarine cocktail dress and shiny aquamarine six-inch heels—sailed over to us with a wave of her green-nailed hands, bracelets jangling.

"Do please ignore him. He's so tiresome once he gets going on his little projects. Now, Tom, isn't it?" She didn't wait for me to indicate that was my name and ploughed on, regardless, with, "This is all new to us. Quite the novelty."

"What is that?" I frowned.

"Getting to meet one of his friends. He usually keeps them to himself, only casually mentioning names at dinner sometimes. But with you, it was quite different. The same name kept popping up at dinners over the months. The same name. I thought to myself, this can't be the same person he's still talking about. Most uncharacteristic behaviour."

Paul shook his head and mouthed *ignore her* to me.

Maybe things aren't as casual as Paul says…

Fingering a dangly diamond earring, she went on, "I said to Roger, I said there was something that's shifted with Paul. *Something* different I can't quite put my finger on." She looked me up and down, licked her lips, then took a sip of champagne. "So, here you are."

Feeling as if I should shuffle off to the toilet and remain there until we left, and sensing there was an expectation for me to speak, I said, "It's lovely to meet you at last. I've heard so much about you both."

"All of it lies, I'm sure," she shot back instantly, like a cannonball over the deck of a ship. She laughed. "Sorry, a little private joke." She stared at Paul.

Paul visibly shrank from her gaze.

I remembered Paul's response when I'd first asked if I'd meet his parents, like he'd met mine, if we were all in, if we were taking it seriously, this whole relationship thing, and Paul had said simply, "I tend to keep her away from friends. It's usually best. She's wicked, but not in the way you'd want her to be. If she were an animal, she'd eat her own young."

Of course, at the time, I hadn't believed that for an instant, so had insisted on meeting her. Now, in the conservatory, with cannonballs firing over my head, running out of conversation and a feeling of awkwardness slowly unfurling itself like a long, black snake emerging from a basket, I wished I'd taken Paul's advice and left this until absolutely necessary, whenever that would have been in the far, far distant future.

"The biggest disappointment of it all," she continued, "was not having any grandchildren." She shook her head slowly, moving closer to Paul to wipe a crumb from his mouth and hold his cheek for slightly too long for his comfort. Turning to him, she said, "No chance of you going out with the girl you were friends with from school?"

Paul said, tiredly, his whole body showing me he'd said this dozens of times before, "I was eleven. She was eleven. I am gay. I will be gay forever. No girlfriends. That's how it works, Mother. I'm seeing Tom."

Seeing? That's at least one click down from dating, isn't it? Definitely more casual than 'going out with', I'm sure. I knew it wouldn't be long until Paul saw the error of his ways and realised he was a good eight or nine and I was, being generous, probably a six or seven.

"Yes, but darling, I do always live in hope—hope you'll do something worthwhile, worth reporting to us, worthy of bringing home." She glanced in my direction. "I don't mean to be rude, dear Tom, but you must understand the disappointment a mother feels when one finds out one will be *denied* grandchildren." Clasping her heart, she said, "Punctured, I felt."

I knew it best not to respond to that, so instead said, "Mum wasn't fussed. She said it means she doesn't ever have to be Granny, or Nanny. She can stay forever a bit young, like I will. Peter Pan syndrome, she called it. Sounded fun whatever it was." I smiled at Paul's mother, wishing I could reduce her to a pool of melted goo and smoke like the Wicked Witch of the West in *The Wizard of Oz*. I quickly told myself off for having such an uncharitable thought.

Frowning at me, she said, "What *do* your parents do? I believe Paul has told us, but somehow I've a mind like a sieve, and it has simply slipped through."

"Dad works for the council, doing roads and repairs. Mum looks after him and the house. Does a bit of ironing for neighbours too."

"The council?" Her tone was of undisguised disgust. "And which council is this?"

"Lewisham." And now, not only did I feel inadequate but I felt it on behalf of my parents too. *Christ on a bike, why did I agree to this?*

She sipped her drink and collected one tiny smoked salmon nibble from the passing, terrified serving girl as she slunk past, shoulders hunched, shrinking from Marilyn's touch. "I thought you lived in London."

"I do. Brockley is London. Lewisham is the same borough we live in." I thought she was joking, then remembered Paul's advice that she rarely joked. "London Borough of Lewisham. South East London."

"How extraordinary. Did you know this, Roger? Lewisham—a whole new part of London we've yet to explore. We must make a trip there to see what this so-called Lewisham is all about."

"Well, I wouldn't make a special trip for it. I wouldn't go through the West End to visit Lewisham. It's not that...well, it's..." I stopped talking, not knowing where I wanted to go with that sentence. It had somehow left me marooned in the middle of a conversation I neither wanted to continue nor knew quite how to get out of. Where was my conversational life raft when I needed it?

Roger dived into the silence with an enthusiastic, "We must go. Check it out. Perhaps we could drop in on your parents. Wouldn't that be lovely?"

Marilyn shook her head very slightly. "Let's not get ahead of ourselves, Roger. I'm sure Tom's parents have better things to do than entertain us at the drop of a hat."

"I didn't mean just drop in on them. It would be arranged. A time, a place. An occasion."

Under her breath, Marilyn said, "What occasion would there be to go there?"

Paul shot her a look of daggers. "We can soon go."

Marilyn checked her watch. "It is dragging on rather, isn't it? This. Are we done? It's such a blessed relief." She put her drink down and strode from the conservatory, her heels making a clacking noise on the tiled floor. "Paul, do tell us when you've decided what you're doing with your life."

"Later. It's still a work in progress. Playing it by ear. I don't want to get stuck with something I'd hate in five years' time." He turned to me. "Sorry. She's no manners. I did say we needn't have bothered." He leant forward and whispered, "Let's go out and get on it, forget all this terrible shit."

"On a Wednesday night? I don't think so." I nodded towards Roger, who was chewing a mouthful of canapé and sipping champagne while thoughtfully staring out at the garden.

"Bye, Father, we're off." Paul put down his drink, took me by the hand and walked me out of the front door, into the middle of the green outside their house, where he knelt and shouted "FUCK!" at the top of his voice. "I'm so sorry. For them. For it. For everything. All that terrible shit. I should have persuaded you otherwise, but you wouldn't believe me, would you?"

"I couldn't believe anyone's parents could be as you'd described without them being part robot or wicked Disney villain."

"Wicked's the right word. You won't see them again." He strode towards the Tube station.

"Where you going?"

"Anywhere except here. I don't care. I just can't be near them at the moment. I'm so sorry. I should have known. My fault. We won't do it again. I'll shield you from them."

"Not your fault. Stop apologising for other people. I'm sorry for forcing you into doing it. I thought it would be nice. How stupid was I?"

"Don't you apologise either, not for being you, for being *optimistic, looking on the bright side* you. That's one of the reasons I like you." He smiled.

"Is it?"

"You betcha. Fancy going The Bush?"

"Shepherd's Bush?"

"Bit grittier and more urban than here. Check out the bars, see what shops are still open."

I shrugged. "Could do. But grittier? It ain't got nothing on Lewisham. Lewisham takes your Shepherd's Bush, raises it, like, three clicks and is still in another league of its own."

"Like you." He held out his hand, beckoning for me to follow him, to jump on the Ferris wheel of our relationship and join him in the next adventure as we soared above the buildings of London together.

"And you." I held his hand and we made our way to Shepherd's Bush together.

I was still guarded about using the L-word with him, having been burned before, after I'd thrown it into the relationship mix never to see the guy again. I'd never felt this way about someone, about how we could do anything and nothing together and it still just flowed, went, rolled, and was...well, it was wicked.

Did we argue? 'Course we argued. Who doesn't argue? If you don't argue with the person you're going out with, it's cos you don't care enough to bother arguing. We argued about whose house we stayed over at after playing; we argued about which songs to include in the sets; we argued about whose turn it was to make the next round of drinks, or roll the cigarettes when we were particularly poor and unable to afford normal cigarettes. We argued when we'd see each other in the week for a snatched couple of hours, both exhausted from work but wanting to do more, jump each other's bones, climb inside each other's bodies, melt together like the candle wax on the first time, but we couldn't. And we argued about who was the horniest, who wanted the other person the most. Oh yeah, we argued. But never about anything that mattered.

We didn't mention the evening in the conservatory ever again. It was like a murder we'd both committed.

He continued seeing his parents when they were in together, while they continued paying him his small allowance, leaving him notes about whether he'd thought about going to university, or working with his father in property, or whether he'd consider a job his mother had found through one of her lunching circles, helping organise a charity ball. I said it didn't sound so stupid; it would give him useful skills on party organising, especially if he wanted to go to Ibiza with me.

One evening, after discussing him helping his mother out and putting on an event for her, Paul frowned. "Like that's ever gonna happen."

"You never know," I said. "If it makes her happy, do it. Make it an amazing, wicked, perfectly Paul charity ball. You could have a theme—you'd enjoy picking the music, I bet."

"For forty-somethings?" Paul shook his head. "Imagine them throwing some shapes and getting on it on the dance floor! I could dissolve some pink doves in the punch, see what happened then."

"Yeah, or you could organise it like a proper party, picking the music from the record store. You like all music, don't you? Not just dance music."

"Yeah, I like the back catalogue, the history of it, the touch of the records, the crackle of the vinyl under the needle, the album art. There's some wicked stuff from the seventies—big, brash, gatefold albums. I could theme it seventies. Or is that a bit naff? Is twenty years ago too soon for retro?"

"Not if you do it right. Not if you do it well, like I'm sure you would." I paused, allowing myself a small internal smile for my powers of persuasion. "Tell her you'll do it. Of all the job suggestions they've given you, it's the best. Give them a bone, eh? We can do it together if you want. I'll be your wingman, like you are to me with our clubbing nights."

"Maybe. I'll think about it."

CHAPTER 6

B EFORE LONG, WE were sharing half the DJ set each, seamlessly blending our styles together, moulding the music to fit each other, to fit the mood of the club of sweaty, dance-hungry dancers bouncing, jumping, waving, throwing shapes with glow sticks in their hands and blowing green glow-in-the-dark whistles around their necks.

We sailed into the club, into our club, where we had our hour-long set on the posters and flyers, exactly as Slinky Simon had told us we would. We greeted the bouncers, the coat-check man and the barman who always winked at us. Slinky Simon asked if were we all set, did we need anything? They were expecting a full house that night as it was the Friday at the end of the month— "After pay day, so everyone's wanting to spunk their money up the wall, to have a bit of an escape from the Monday to Friday, the nine to five, to have a bit of magic, and we're...*you're* here to give them that magic, aren't you, boys?"

Although it was quite a tall order, we'd been going there for months, most Friday or Saturday nights, and it felt like coming home in a way. The people in the club, the people who worked there and the dancers who came up to us week after week, requesting the same songs we'd added to our collection, shouting and jumping up and down when we played their requests...it was like a spiritual family meeting. More like a family meeting than it had been in Paul's conservatory.

They say friends are the family you choose for yourself, in which case Paul and I had created brothers, sisters, uncles and aunts joined by the love of music, the love of letting the week go, disappearing into our movements on the dance floor, eyes closed, hands in the air, waving in time with the music. In that moment, we were all joined by that particular genius that filled the club when the music, the mood, and the drugs all combined perfectly.

So how could we be nervous playing again, when we were among family? We couldn't. We didn't stay nervous; any worries and thoughts about anything bad disappeared as soon as we stepped into the DJ booth with our records to the cheer of the crowd.

Halfway through our set, Slinky Simon joined us in the booth, a big smile on his face as he nodded in time with the music and his hands snaked around his head. "This is what it's all about, boys. Told you, didn't I?"

I nodded, an ear taken out of the headphones so I could hear what he'd said.

"This—" he gestured with his arms to the jumping crowd, waving glow sticks, dancing, flashing lights "—this is a beautiful glimmer of tranquillity in what can feel like a hate-filled world. Where's the hate here? Nowhere. Enjoy your time in this life." He kissed my cheek, then Paul's, and then disappeared into the dancing crowd.

I didn't think we'd be able to top that, but it was that night when it happened.

In our dirty, cluttered kitchen, an overflowing ashtray on the table between us, a mug of tea each, having our own two-man chill-out party as we had so often before, both of us at that perfect moment, post being a bit too high to breathe without feeling sick and before the reality of life, the comedown approached on the horizon. That perfect floaty, feeling connected with the world and everything in it, feeling that all would be well, now and forever...

That moment.

We were discussing what we'd do if we could go to Ibiza and take up Slinky Simon's offer of a tryout spot at one of the clubs out there.

"We'd need the summer off work." I continued with the list of requirements.

Paul counted them on his fingers. "Yeah, go on."

"And the flights."

"Yeah, and what else?"

"Somewhere to stay." I took a drag on the cigarette, closing my eyes and welcoming the slight rush I felt as I inhaled deeply.

"What else?"

"Someone who can put on a party, someone who knows how to put on a show for the clubbers. Inflatable statues, foam blowers, whistles and glow sticks, the lot."

"Yeah."

"I mean you. You know how to put on a party. You've been to enough in your time, haven't you?"

"It's nothing."

"Tell your mum you'll do the next charity ball thing she's asked you to do."

"Don't wanna."

"Do it. Or…I'll withhold sexual favours until you do."

He grabbed my hands, placing them on his lap. "Like to see you try."

"Do it," I said.

"All right, but only cos I love you. Cos you make me be a better person just by being with me. Is that cheesy? Is that too much? I don't care, you really do."

"So that's a yes, then?"

"That's a yes," he replied, nodding, staring into my eyes.

"Paul."

"Tom." He was still staring at me.

"I love you."

And then he knelt in front of me, put his hands on my knees and kissed me. "So, so much."

***

"I've been thinking," I said to Paul the day after we'd both dropped the L-word.

"Right?"

"Maybe we should get a place. Together?" I was a bit uncertain as I couldn't quite believe we were still together, but given we were in his bedroom, having just spent an afternoon doing not much but each other, we did seem to be still together.

He sat up and his eyes widened. "Isn't this OK?"

"It's OK, yeah, but don't you think being in our early twenties and still living at home is cramping our style a bit?"

"Maybe." He sighed. "Or we could just leave things how they are. If it ain't broke and all that. Play it by ear."

"Maybe." It certainly wasn't broken, but I was getting a bit sick and tired of having to plan our sex lives around our parents being out of the house.

"Way I see it, we should give it a few months and then see." He kissed me, and I felt him stiffen as he pushed against me.

"Paul!" Marilyn shouted, then, without knocking, burst into his bedroom, face aghast in horror at us obviously about to have sex. Staring at the floor, she said, "I assumed you were alone. I want to talk to you about something."

"Give us a minute, will you, Mother?"

She stood, tapping her foot on the floor.

"I'll be out. Door please." He stared at her.

With a huff and an aggressive closing of the door, she was gone.

I kissed him, but he didn't respond. "Killed it, hasn't she?"

He shrugged. "Let's have a look what we can afford. Just a look. Maybe we could get some help from my olds if I tell them I'm going to find myself, work out what I'm going to do with my life."

"Yeah, let's have a look," I replied with a smirk as I pulled on clothes.

***

We found a large, four-storey crumbling Victorian redbrick mansion in an unfashionable street in an unfashionable corner of South East London, beyond Lewisham, thrusting its way towards the M25 orbital motorway, and beyond the Catford gyratory system which was, basically, a big roundabout. And when I say we found a mansion, what we could afford was one double room in which we put our entire lives: bed, wardrobe, desk, records, clothes, TV. No VCR. We bought a top-notch hi-fi system to go with Paul's record deck and our growing record collection instead.

Mum helped us move in. Paul's parents said they would have helped, but they couldn't spare the time away from the essentials, and did he want any more money to help him settle in?

Mum held a box in front of her stomach and the door with her hip, a cigarette in her mouth. "It's gonna be snug with you two in here, but fair enough, it is time you flew the nest. Is there a lounge, or is the landlord squeezing another room's rent out of it?"

I said, taking the box from her and putting it on the bed, "There was a lounge, but now it's two bedrooms. Landlord put in a wall and split it. He said that's how come our rent can be so cheap."

"Sounds all heart, does this landlord." Mum picked a cookery book from the top of the box. "This should make sure you eat more than kebabs and beans on toast."

"Thanks."

"I've also packed some of our spare kitchen stuff so you have some bits—cheese grater, plates, a saucepan, that sort of thing. Save you having to get it all. Sorry I couldn't give you nothing else." She looked at Paul.

Paul said, "It's very kind of you. Between our parents, we're here. Even if I didn't expect to be quite yet..."

Mum clapped her hands. "I've left the kitchen-stuff box in the kitchen. Let's stake our claim on a cupboard and I'll show you how to whip up a mean macaroni cheese that'll have you the envy of the rest of the house."

She took a drag of the cigarette, scanned the room full of boxes on and next to the second-hand unmatching furniture we'd begged, stolen and borrowed from various corners of our lives, having decided to keep the contribution from Paul's parents for things we couldn't buy second-hand and for rent, deposit, bills, food and so forth.

"Couple a days and you'll be right as rain. Proper settled in, the pair of you. Your own place together. I remember when me and your dad first got our own place. Well, I say our own place, it was a bit like this—a room in a big house. And when I say house, I mean a hippy commune, and there was a bit more commune living than we'd first thought, but we soon got used to that, and then moved out to our own flat, when we could afford it. Still, you've got all that in front of you now. Good times." She stared wistfully at the packing boxes and jumbled furniture. "Right, come on. Food!"

We followed her to the kitchen where, using the second-hand cookery book she'd bought us, she showed us how to cook, instructing us to chop, mix and bake, while she perched on the corner of the kitchen table, holding the cookery book in one hand and a cigarette in the other.

A while later, we sat together at the table eating our creation in silence.

Mum was the first to speak. "Have you actually met any of the others who are living here? It's locks on all the doors, isn't it? So it's more like a boarding house than a student house share, or a commune." She got a faraway look in her eyes, staring out the window, then returned to the macaroni cheese.

Paul said, "We asked, didn't we? Landlord said it was some couples, sharing like us, lots of single men who he didn't know what they did all day, and a few women on their own, and one couple with a baby, but they're a few floors from us, so hopefully, no noise."

She did the washing-up, despite our protests, stayed for a few hours helping us unpack, wished us goodbye, hugging both of us and kissing our cheeks, and then with a wave and a "Get used to doing the washing-up yourselves, cos I'm not doing it again," she was gone.

"Fuck," I said to the quiet kitchen as the noise of people in their rooms all round us gradually became audible.

"Just us two now, babe," Paul said, with a smile and a wink.

"Have we just made the biggest mistake of our lives? Walking out from free rent, food and washing, to this." I looked around the room, the grease-stained corners, tiled floor with mysterious marks across it and the yellow-stained work surface we'd had to bleach before using it.

"We'll be fine. Us two. I know we will." He looked around the room, then opened a box and started unpacking. "Besides, if we want to go to Ibiza, this is good practice for living together. Imagine flying there and finding out we couldn't stand each other and couldn't live together." He stood at the window, staring at the street below.

I walked up behind him, put my arms round his waist and kissed his neck. "Imagine that."

He turned to kiss me. "Shall I get a Chinese? Save us cooking."

"Celebrate getting our own place."

He nodded. "The next chapter of us. We can eat what we like here with no one nagging us. I think I'm gonna enjoy this."

"No need to sound so surprised," I said.

"I'll be back in a bit. Usual for you?"

I nodded and he was gone.

***

One night, at the club round the back of King's Cross station, the manager said, "Have you thought about the Ibiza idea? Slinky Simon says you're interested. He'll set it all up. I'll put in a good word for you too. I know a guy who runs a club out there."

"We thought about it, but it's not practical. We can't just leave everything and fly there for the summer. We've got stuff here," I said, looking at Paul, who nodded.

"Yeah, but that's *all just stuff*. Things to stop you going. If you really wanted to go, you'd make it happen and just go. You're ready for it. I know you are. Feedback we've got from the punters here—ticket sales are high on the nights you're here. I know that's not just you, we've got some other DJs too, but you're certainly not hindering things."

"We can't afford it. We can't just fly there for a try out. We need to see how things work out here. Besides, there's this whole orbital party scene Slinky Simon reckons we should check out."

"Why?"

"Because," Paul said, "we need to earn our stripes, do our time, do more than just your club before fucking off abroad and expecting to get into one of the big clubs in Ibiza, that's why."

The manager shrugged, gestured for us to go in and we got on with our set for the night.

Believe me, we really would get right involved in the orbital party scene. Fields of five to ten thousand people not far from the M25, the exact location kept secret to prevent interruptions from the old bill. You drove to a motorway service station, waited with hundreds of others, listening to a pirate radio station for the exact location. Then you all moved off in convoy and got right on it, in a field in one of the home counties just off the M25. But I'll come back to that. Trust me, it was wicked.

***

Both to keep in with his parents, and because I'd persuaded him of the value of putting on what was essentially a big party, Paul eventually agreed to organise the next charity event his mother was on the committee for. He'd said he didn't want to get involved, to have to be responsible for it, because he knew what he was like. "I'll just bail when I can't be bothered," he said.

"You won't. You'll do it cos it's important for your mum. Put your hand up and follow through with the offer of help. It'll mean so much to her."

"Sounds a bit serious to me." Paul frowned.

"More serious than us living together?" I smirked.

"It sounds like a lot of commitment to me."

"See previous question."

Paul nodded.

Now, Marilyn was sitting at the table with her head in her hands. "It's all finished. I am finished. I simply do not know what to do."

We'd nipped back to his parents to pick up a few things from his old room. We discovered his mother in the dining room. I indicated this was his opportunity to impress her.

At first, Paul shook his head, shrugged and pointed to the door. I insisted, pointing strongly and gently edging backwards to the corner of the room to leave them to have their conversation in some privacy, even though I heard all of it.

I was so proud when, after a few moments, Paul swooped in, asked his mother what the matter was, putting his hand on her shoulder, as I'd instructed him.

She explained, at length, how this current event had been doomed from the start since it had been dumped on her when the previous Women's Guild chair had resigned in a fit of pique over an argument to do with butter, margarine and Victoria sponges. She didn't go into details, just left the words hanging there, a very serious look on her face.

"This is the ultimate case of having greatness thrust upon me. And it couldn't possibly have gone worse than it's gone so far. The venue's contracted, at huge expense. Extortionate, actually. We've sold some tickets, but there's still so many unsold it's not going to even cover costs. It's a charity ball, did you get that bit?" She returned to head in hands resting on table.

Quietly, so as not to scare her off, I suppose, Paul said, "What's the latest thing? It can't be insurmountable, surely?"

"Darling Louis is no more." She clutched her hands to the left side of her chest.

"Oh, I am sorry, Mother. What happened? Was it sudden, quick, painless, or expected?" He shook his head and raised his eyes at me above his mother's perfectly coiffed hair.

"He's not dead, darling. He's...I believe the term is done a runner. He's gone. Disappeared. Left me in the lurch, holding the baby. So to speak."

"And Louis is?"

"The party planner for the Women's Guild. Well the previous chair who'd been in charge, pre-Victoria-Sponge-Gate, had contracted Louis to lead on all the little details, pulling it all together. And now, he's gone and I'm in charge. It is, as they say, all on my head." She shook her head, and my immediate thought was *heavy is the head that wears the crown*, but I said nothing.

Marilyn turned to her son. "Did you want something, darling? What brings you here? I'm rather busy, can't you see?" She gestured dramatically to the piles of paperwork on the table.

"Getting a few bits. Post, mainly. Look. I want to help."

"Me?"

"Yes, Mother, you."

"Why would you want to help put on a Women's Guild charity ball? You've never shown the slightest bit of interest before, and here you are, at my hour of need, and you're some sort of knight in shining armour. Or some such metaphor. I've told you I can't up your allowance, Father simply won't allow it. And I gave you the deposit for your little flat escapade, so you'll just have to manage where that's concerned, I'm afraid."

"I want some practice at organising events, parties."

Marilyn sighed. "Why on earth would you want that?"

"I don't want to work in the record shop for ever. I'm doing this DJing with Tom. Together with his music, and my party skills, we make a good team. I do the music too, of course. Anyway."

"Oh." Her eyes widened in surprise.

"So, can I help?" He pointed to the piles of paperwork on the table.

"I was just about to call the venue and cancel it. I simply do not know where to start with the rest of it. It's not so much the money, I have plenty. I can pay back the Guild for any losses. No, it's the shame. The shame of it all. Of it being a failure on my watch. Louis has up and left. All I've got is a few phone numbers and the contract from the venue." She pushed the papers away from her. "It's giving me one of my heads as I sit here."

"When is it?"

She checked her watch. "A fortnight Saturday." She moved to stand.

Paul gently pushed her from the chair and took his position in the driving seat. "Can I use this?" He held the cordless house phone.

Marilyn waved, nodded and walked to the cupboard to retrieve some cups. "Where is that woman? She's meant to be here, ready if I want coffee. Honestly, what's the point in having a maid if you have to do it all yourself?" And she was gone, charging towards the kitchen in search of the maid.

I edged forwards into the room, surveyed the folders and envelopes and papers in front of Paul. "Is it really that bad?"

"It's a right mess, but no one's going to die. It'll be fine. This near the date, they'll be past the refund point in the venue contract. So, may as well plough on and sell those tickets."

I kissed his forehead. "Listen to you, talking like an event planner already." I allowed myself a little clap, noticed Paul was dialling a number, and indicated I'd leave him to it, see him back home later.

As I reached the front door, I caught him saying, "Minimum contracted numbers, please? And what AV equipment has been organised?" I smiled to myself and closed the door quietly.

***

I'd never seen Paul so focused on anything as he was on making the charity ball a success. He was up before I left for work, slaving over our hot telephone, ticking things off his master list, then, at the end of the day, he'd tell me how he'd gone to the printers to print flyers and posted them by hand through the houses of his mother's Women's Guild members for them to share with others who they thought would be interested in attending.

Over dinner one night, he said, "We've sold out. I have a waiting list now. Did I tell you that? I forget what I've told you and what I haven't."

"I'd have remembered that."

"It needed a good theme. It was a bit all over the place before. Bless Louis, but he'd only really done the basics, very poor party planning, I feel. OK, so he'd booked the venue, arranged for a DJ and done a bit of promotion with the people who were always going to come anyway. But when I asked the hotel about the decorations, they were blank. Nothing. Slack Louis."

"What's the theme?"

"I thought about this for a long time. Thinking of the age group of people who're going, my parents' age basically, I thought something from the sixties would be fun. But then I thought... should I do the seventies instead?"

I started to say something, but Paul continued, really getting into his flow now. "If they're all roughly Mother and Father's age, they were our age, early twenties, twenty years ago, they were us in 1973. And who doesn't want to relive their early twenties? In the sixties, most of them would have been young teenagers. And those who are a bit older would still probably remember the seventies fondly. Also, I thought a sixties night was a bit, been done to death, you know?"

I hadn't really thought about it in any detail, but impressed by Paul's flow, I just nodded. "Has she asked how it's coming on?"

"Who?"

"The Queen of Sheba! Your mother, who'd you think?"

"When I've been working from their place, she's made a big show of making herself a drink—which she never does, as you know—and occasionally asking how ticket sales are going, and did I want a hand with the decorations for the theme?"

"Did you get a 'well done', or a 'thank you'?" I knew the answer but hoped I'd be wrong.

"Not yet. Early days. Father couldn't stop talking about how I'd found *my metier* when I stayed for dinner last week after working there that afternoon. He was beaming. And Father doesn't beam, at least, not about me."

"Great. All sounds like you've got it under control. Any problems?"

"Daily, hourly, by the minute some days. But you know what I found out? I'm a really practical person. Despite the best efforts of my parents to insulate me from the realities of life through throwing money at everything, I'm actually not too bad at, you know, solving problems."

"And modest too."

"Piss off. Oh, shit, do your parents want a ticket? They're about that age, aren't they? Weren't they hippies or something, a commune your mum said."

"Bless, you're very sweet, but Mum would think you'd got the seventies all wrong. I'm sure your version of that decade wouldn't be particularly close to her experience. How much are tickets again?"

"Seventy-five pounds."

"Per table?"

"Per person."

I shook my head. "I'm not gonna mention it to her. If she finds out your parents are there, she'll feel the need to come and won't accept free or cheap tickets, not if it's for charity. Best we steer well clear of the whole topic." I paused. "Awkward."

"A bit. Best we don't tell your parents then, eh?"

I nodded.

CHAPTER 7

O N THE NIGHT of the ball, Paul had to squeeze extra tables into the hotel's biggest room as his mother told him there were two groups of Women's Guild people who hadn't paid but couldn't *not* attend, so he would have to find space.

Paul said he'd wanted to tell her to get stuffed, but since it was all for charity and he could add a bit more onto the price for last-minute additions, he just thought of the children's charity, and the money, revisited his table plan and begged the venue manager to squeeze them in.

I stood at the door of the full-height hotel ballroom, hiding behind one of the psychedelic patterned curtains Paul had installed, watching the guests tuck into their prawn cocktails in stemmed dishes. The theme was Fabulous Seventies, and the words, two feet high in purple sparkles, were in an arch above the stage. The tables were covered in a variety of bright, brown, flowery and geometric patterned tablecloths Paul had picked up from charity shops when he'd discovered no out-of-the-box seventies-themed decorations were available at a budget he could afford.

On the stage, an ABBA tribute band, white jumpsuited up, long brown wigs on the men and a blonde and a brown wig on the women, played quietly—everyone's favourite songs. I remembered Paul's anguish about the band, whether to go with something more cool, more rock, like Yes, or Roxy Music, but with my simple question of, "When you think seventies, which band comes into your mind?" he'd said, "Abba," and I'd said, "I rest my case."

The guests had made an effort with their outfits: bright kaftans, flared trousers, kipper ties and shirts with collars you could go gliding in.

Paul appeared next to me. "You eating? There's a seat for you there." He pointed to a table near the front where his parents were both talking loudly to the others.

"Thanks, but I just wanted to see the results of all your hard work. After hearing you talk about nothing else for the last two weeks, it's amazing now it's all come together."

"Wicked."

"It's definitely that."

"Come on, stay and eat. Promise my parents won't be too bad. They're both pissed. They had two of the cocktails at the one-cocktail-each reception before the food even arrived. Bjorn from the ABBA tribute band told me earlier one of the women was getting a bit lairy. Of course it was Mother."

"Where did you get the pictures of the seventies cars?" There were large pictures of mainly beige, mostly vinyl-roofed cars from the era—Cortinas, Marinas, Princesses, Minis, Escorts—on the walls, peeking out from behind the curtains.

"All right, aren't they?"

"Babe, they're better than all right. You know it. Don't be so modest." I nodded towards the door. "I'm off. You don't need to be worrying about me. Enjoy your moment in the spotlight."

"Stay, for the main course, will you please? It's chicken Kiev. And I'll bring some Arctic roll home for you. I can put you on another table if you can't bear my parents." He looked at his clipboard, flicking over a few pages.

"Don't worry. I'll sit with them. What's the worst that can happen?"

As he led me to their table, he said, "You've not seen Mother with two bottles of Blue Nun in her."

As we arrived at the table, Paul introduced me to everyone as his other half, which I liked, as he said it out loud.

Marilyn asked her husband to move one seat over, then she patted the empty chair between the two of them.

Paul kissed me, whispered in my ear, "Good luck." And then, louder, once I'd taken my place in the chair between his parents, "Bet you never thought your old car magazines in the attic could look so glam, eh, Father?"

Roger looked at the walls. "I did wonder where I'd seen them before. I told your mother they'd come in useful at some point.

Marilyn rolled her eyes, taking another sip of wine. "Twenty years sitting in boxes in the attic, but at last their day has come. With a little help from a colour copier, it seems."

Paul said, to himself, but loud enough for everyone to hear, "Must send a thank-you card to the librarian in Chiswick." He wrote something on the paper on his clipboard, and then he was gone, leaving me between his parents, reaching for a large glass of wine to help the evening pass smoothly.

Later, once we'd eaten the chicken Kievs, full of buttery, garlicky goodness and covered in golden breadcrumbs, accompanied by many comments of how much they remembered these, and why didn't they have them nowadays, and would the band play 'Waterloo' again, Marilyn made her way to the stage at the front of the room. She silenced the band, tapped the microphone and began.

"Everything you see before you…" She suppressed a very small hiccup. "Excuse me. My digestive system's not used to chicken Kiev. Evidently."

I caught Paul's eye from the back of the room. He winked back at me, with one of his perfect, big, wide grins I was by now so used to, but cherished every time he shone it in my direction.

Marilyn continued, holding onto the microphone stand with one hand and the microphone with the other. "What was I saying? Oh yes, Paul, my son, has made all this happen. He rescued me somewhat from a bit of a situation, no thanks to a certain party planner who up and dropped me in it." She paused, pushing her hair behind her ears. "But that's not for now. Paul, can you come here, please? Where is he?" She shaded her eyes with her hand and made a bit of a show of searching the room.

Eventually, accompanied by a purple-kaftanned woman with bright blonde hair, Paul was brought to the stage and stood next to his mother.

"They say some people are great. Some people have greatness thrust on them. Well, I had no idea Paul could do this. Faced with having a mess thrust into my hands, and a complete flop of an event, I knew I couldn't do it and didn't think I had anything to lose by asking him to help. He's managed to break all records, and we're pleased to announce we can send the most money for any single event to the children's charity I know is dear to all our hearts."

There was a cheer and some applause from the audience.

She continued, turning to Paul. "And he did seem so eager, didn't you, darling?" She stroked his cheek and then snapped her fingers. Someone appeared from the edge of the stage with a wicker basket containing wine, chocolates and various glass jars of nice things, wrapped in a distinctive green bow that said 'Harrods' across it. "We, the woman of the West London branch of the Women's Guild, would like you to accept this as a thank-you for your help." She handed it to Paul.

He took it with a smile, then moved to the microphone. "It was sink or swim, and I think I've swum. It was wicked."

His mother took the microphone back. "That, I'm reliably informed, is a good thing." She began clapping and indicated for Paul to leave the stage. Some of the tables were moved to the edge of the room, making way for a dance floor with coloured flashing lights. The volume and tempo of the ABBA impersonator band distinctly increased.

I thanked my table companions and slipped out into the night, and then home, back to our little unfashionable corner of Catford, where I waited for a bouncing, talkative, Arctic-role-bearing Paul to greet me a few hours later.

***

In the small hours, he woke me with a kiss.

Paul said, "Wait till I tell Slinky Simon! Ibiza, here we come."

"One thing at a time, babe. Let's not run before we can walk."

"Honest, I'm calling him now. Tell him what I've done."

I checked my watch. "How about you do it tomorrow?"

He reached into his pocket and pulled out a small clear bag containing half a dozen white pills. "Come on, just a half each. Celebration." He took one from the bag and bit it in half, handing me one part.

There he was again, beckoning me onto the Ferris wheel, onto his own one-man fairground ride. And I knew it would be fun; it always was with Paul, but I just wasn't sure I wanted that now, at this moment, when we had lunch plans with my parents the next day. I told him as much.

He stuck out his bottom lip. "Don't you want a bit of a dance, a bit of a kiss and then some floaty sex?"

That, I couldn't deny wanting, but the impact it would have on the next day was something I tried to restate to him.

"Too late, I've necked my half." He shrugged. "She didn't have to, but Mother paid me for organising it. Not loads-a-money, but enough to pay for flights and some rent in Ibiza."

"That's your money. You earned it."

"It's for us. Our money." He kissed me.

And with an *if I must, I must* attitude, I followed suit. Reaching to the bedside table for a swig of water, I jumped onto the Ferris wheel car, and together, we floated to the sky.

I'll pause my story for a moment to say that anyone who says they can have just a half a pill is a liar. A total and complete liar. If there are more pills to be had, you will want to take them. Trust me. Once you're on it, once you're in the zone, the dancing together in the bedroom, smoking like your life depends on it, glugging water to cool your sweaty body down part? All you want is more, more, more of the same. If some is good, more is better, right?

Back to my story now.

As predicted, we finished the bag of pills, danced in our bedroom, then the kitchen, then on Catford green as the sun came up, smoking, drinking water, both our T-shirts off, sweat dripping down our bodies, bouncing about on the grass like a two-man outdoor party, as passers-by on their way to their sensible Sundays probably gave us looks of disgust we were oblivious to at the time. Because you are. I was. I was oblivious to everything except what was happening in our little floaty bubble, our very own fairground ride.

Mum was livid. I could feel the anger radiating off her, boring into me. We arrived at hers, both of us hanging onto the doorframe for support since the floor was doing that bumpy moving thing it sometimes did—after necking three pills each, yeah, that's when it does it, in case you didn't know.

Mum ushered Paul into the living room, where he sat talking cod-shit to Dad.

I followed her to the kitchen. She peered close to my face, looking at my eyes. "When did you get to sleep?"

"We're here, aren't we?" I shrugged. That couldn't be argued with, I felt.

"In body but not mind. You're both totally bollocksed. You gonna eat my lovely roast, are you? My roast I've spent all morning preparing for the two of you, so I could enjoy a nice chat with my son and his boyfriend, to hear about how things are going in your place, what you've been up to. What's the good news?"

"How'd you know?" I stared at my hand in front of my face, moving my fingers in time with the music that was playing in my mind.

"Random guess."

"But how, though?" I persevered.

"His party last night. How you are this morning. Call me Einstein, but I've put two and two together. Go well, did it? Last night? The seventies night."

"It was wicked."

"Bit too wicked by the looks of it. Go through to the lounge, talk to your dad. I don't wanna see you at the moment." She bundled me out of the kitchen.

I sat next to Paul on the sofa, and in a rare gap in the rubbish he'd been spouting since Dad had left the room, I said, "She's fucking livid. Told you."

"It'll be fine." He grabbed my hand and squeezed it tight. "I'll tell her it's my fault. Leading you astray. How's that sound?"

"Better. Fuck knows how we're gonna eat. My stomach's like a bowling ball."

We managed to pick at some of the food Mum had put on our plates.

Paul told her about the charity ball, and apologised for us. For him. For me. For now. For everything.

Mum said, "Yeah, all right love, don't apologise for everything. It kinda loses its impact. You'll be apologising for World War Two next. Try and eat a little something, would you both, please?"

Paul explained he wanted to do more event planning, party planning really, and we were going to talk to Slinky Simon about being in charge of the decorations, promotion, everything for one of the club nights.

Mum said, "And he'd let you do that, would he, this Simon bloke?"

"He's really keen. Wanted us to go Ibiza, but one step at a time, I suppose."

"Yes. Best walk before you try to run, eh?" She cut her potato, allowing herself a small smile, before chewing the food.

The conversation moved on to her and Dad's holiday in Spain and what he'd been doing at work, and soon she'd cleared the plates and returned to the table. "Don't suppose you both fancy a trifle, do you?"

We shook our heads.

"Didn't think so. How about a cuppa and a ciggie? How's that sound?"

"Oh yeah. Thanks, Mum." I caught her eye, mouthing *sorry* to her.

"That's the thing, never can stay angry with you long. Neither of you. Cos I'm a stupid soppy daft apeth and I love you both. And, in fairness, it's nothing I haven't done myself a few times before." She turned to start making the tea. "When did you actually get to sleep, or have you just gone through, surfing the waves, in for a penny in for a pound, sort a thing?"

Quietly, I said, "That. Pretty much."

"Thought so. You won't want a walk in Greenwich Park later, will you?"

Paul jumped in with, "Wicked. Better than trying to sleep and not. Good walk, fresh air, then we'll be ready for bed when we get home tonight." He yawned, trying to suppress it with his hand.

"We'll see, eh, love?" Mum replied, putting mugs of tea, a bowl of sugar and a Spanish donkey-and-basket ashtray on the table.

"Thanks for lunch," Paul said to Mum. "And sorry again. For us being. You know. All over the place."

***

We managed half the walk around half of Greenwich Park, Mum asking us about how the flat was going, if we needed anything, when we were next playing a set at the club.

We sat on a bench, the warmth of the sun and the tweeting of the birds and Mum's voice lulling us into a sudden, deep sleep.

We woke to a gentle shaking as Mum rocked us. "Let's get you two reprobates back. You've not done bad. Six o'clock. By the time you get back to yours, you can jump into bed and you shouldn't be too fucked for work tomorrow. Is it back to reality, back to the world of the living tomorrow for both of you?"

We nodded.

She led us to the train station, put us on the right platform, kissed Paul on the cheek, hugged me and said, "Watch it. You can have too much of a good thing. Trust me, I've seen people fall apart at the seams, get totally fucking lost from too much of a good thing, all right?" She tapped her cheek.

I kissed her hand.

"Written that letter to Auntie Luella yet, have you?" She waved as she left us, disappearing into the crowd of the station.

My lack of reply said all Mum needed to know. I'd started to write the letter and got a few paragraphs in and then left it, never to return. I could have told her where it was: in a draw in our bedroom. But I knew that was no good. Pointless.

As our train arrived, I said to Paul, "Never again. Sometimes I don't know if you're a bad influence on me or if I'm a bad influence on you."

Paul looked at the train. "Is this us?"

I nodded, and we boarded the train together, travelling back home in silence.

PART 2

CHAPTER 8

A MONTH OR SO later, we were in the back of Rob's white Ford Escort XR3i—lowered with blue lights under the wheel arches and the boot full of an enormous amplifier and speakers— on the way to the designated service station, all nodding in time with the music blasting from the speakers, our entire bodies pulsing with the bass. Rob's girlfriend Sinead was in the front, and Paul and I were joined in the back by someone else whose name I've forgotten. Alec, or Alex, I think he was called.

Who was Rob? Good question. He was a mate of Slinky Simon's—'safe as fuck, sound as a pound' Rob was how Slinky Simon had described him. We'd met him at an after-afterparty following a night at the King's Cross club, back at someone's house somewhere off the A3 in South West London. Rob had mentioned the orbital party scene and said we should give it a go. We'd agreed a night even though Slinky Simon couldn't come as he had some head office clubbing management stuff to do, but he'd told us to fill our boots and that Rob would look after us.

Now, we stopped the car at the service station, hanging round a payphone with thirty or so other cars full of people dressed in baggy clothes and dancing to the music from their car stereos.

I tapped Rob's shoulder. "What now?"

He turned. "We wait."

"Wicked," Paul shouted from the seat beside me, his head nodding, well bollocksed already and immersed in the music.

I coughed, swallowed, trying to assemble my thoughts, to marshal them from where they were currently floating above my head, somewhere between the car roof and the white fluffy clouds. "What for?" That was it, that was what I wanted to ask. I pointed to the crowd assembled round the payphone. "What's that about?"

Rob handed me a flyer.

I scanned it: today's date, then a junction number and afterwards it said *PP*.

"Still none the wiser. Sorry." I shrugged.

"Payphone. We wait. Then someone calls that payphone with the location of the party. Which field it's in, which warehouse we're gonna take over. Then—" he pointed to the other cars and people dancing outside them "—we all drive to the location and then…"

"Yeah, and then what?"

"We all get right on it."

Paul said, "Wicked."

Rob tapped the steering wheel. "It definitely will be. Once we get there."

After a while, someone ran to the payphone and answered it, scribbled some things on a bit of paper, then got into his black, lowered Ford Sierra with a spoiler as big as a whale tail. It was so large I swear it would have taken off had it been driven fast enough. The air filled with hundreds of engines starting, bursting into life, doors slamming as people ran to their vehicles. Music was turned up, and everyone followed the car in front, all of us in convoy behind the black Sierra with the spoiler. Some hands poked out the windows and started clapping.

Rob started the engine. "Guys, keep an eye on that Sierra. In case we're following some random car and they're not going where we want."

"Eh?" I asked.

"Just make sure I follow the big black Ford, all right?"

Paul and I nodded, and we kept our eyes glued to the magical black Sierra.

An indeterminate time later—it's hard to judge these things when you're coming up on a white dove, I've found—we arrived at a field full of cars. People had abandoned them wherever was convenient and were walking a few hundred yards to a rusted corrugated-metal warehouse the size of an aircraft hangar. It may have been a disused aircraft hangar, actually. At the door, a row of men in black T-shirts took a fiver off us, stamped our hands, then waved us on.

Once inside, the heat of thousands of bodies dancing, jumping, shouting, enjoying, hit me in the face. The far end had a raised stage with a DJ playing records. Each wall had moving lights on stands projecting red, blue, green and white light filling the space. There was a twelve-foot-tall inflatable snowman with a wide grin and huge red eyes next to one wall. The other wall had a similarly sized red Father Christmas which inflated, then deflated, then inflated again, creating a sort of hypnotising rhythm. One wall had a green triangle with red tips inflating, then deflating.

"What's that?" I pointed.

"Christmas tree," Paul said with a laugh.

"It's summer, innit?" I looked at my watch, not sure why as it had never told me the month and didn't on this occasion either.

Paul said, "Must have got the decs from some old Christmas party. Pretty wicked, though, isn't it?"

"It's certainly something."

Once I got used to the fact I was dancing in a warehouse in a field nowhere near anywhere else, I started enjoying myself, dancing with Paul and Rob, who kept disappearing to make friends with strangers, bringing them back to us, then walking off again.

I found myself sucking on my cheeks for no reason. Once before I'd bitten the inside of my mouth to pieces. I couldn't stop chewing due to the red-and-black cap I'd dropped as we'd arrived at the field.

Paul handed me some Juicy Fruit chewing gum. "All right?"

"Yeah." I chewed in time with my dancing and the music, and all was well with the world again.

"Wicked." Paul hugged me.

Rob joined in the hug, shortly followed by his girlfriend, Sinead.

"Where's him, beside me, in the back?"

"Alec," Rob said.

"That's him."

"Last I saw, he was stage diving off the speakers next to some Transit vans."

"Then where?"

"Dunno. He'll turn up. He can wait by the car and we'll see him. It'll be fine."

***

The first time I realised this whole orbital party scene wasn't quite like anything else I'd experienced was in the back of Rob's car, a few weeks later. We were following little signs at roundabouts that didn't say anything, just tiny red arrows, but the people who needed to know what they meant just knew.

"What's it mean?" I asked, pointing to the second red arrow we'd followed.

Rob, who really was sound as a pound and definitely safe as fuck, said, "It's where we're heading. It's where our whole week's been leading to. And it's gonna be..." He paused.

Paul said, "Wicked?"

"Fucking right, it is."

A few more roundabouts, turnings and red arrows later, we arrived at a field full of new-age travellers' vehicles—old school buses, caravans and double-decker buses with the seats ripped out and replaced with beds, some of the windows blanked out. The rust was mixed with coloured painted flowers, CND signs and general statements about love and peace.

"Is this it?" I looked around.

The field stretched as far as I could see, the near side filled with travellers' vehicles, beyond that cars parked in rough lines, marshalled to their resting place by men waving orange flags, and beyond that were two white marquee tents.

"You got tickets?" I asked.

"Follow me." Slinky Simon led us to the booming with music, strobing with lights, filled with sweaty people, dance tents, where we were met with a man taking money and stamping hands.

It cost a fiver each, and we were there for twelve hours. Twelve hours of solid dancing and partying and talking and laughing and soaring above the clouds.

And it was fucking brilliant.

I knew we weren't in Kansas anymore, Toto, when the normal rules of drug selling didn't seem to apply. Once inside the tent, there was a row of men shouting out what they had for sale, bumbags of money and pockets filled with plastic bags and drugs. "Come and get your ecstasy, acid, dope. Come and get it here. Pills a fiver, acid a tenner and dope fifteen for a tenth. Come on, you lucky people, come and get what you want."

The man next to him was shouting a slightly different version of basically the same patter, a queue of people in front of him asking for supplies, handing over money, then moving on to the next person.

They were selling drugs like they sell fruit and veg on a market. That thought hit me, suddenly, as they shouted about their wares, and people queued up with their hands ready to accept the purchases, like customers waiting for a couple of pounds of apples and pears.

I looked over my shoulder, expecting a bouncer or someone to stop the men selling. But no. No one came, and they didn't come for the whole night. Don't get me wrong, it was well organised—parking, hand stamps, even an area for first-aiders when the clubbers had gone too far and needed a lie down, or to be taken to hospital, mercifully rarely. But as for police or anything like that, not so much. People danced around huge bonfires, ran around swinging balls on ropes, or twirled batons. There was a man on a unicycle, and another on a pair of six-foot-high stilts. No one batted an eye at anything; they just kept right on dancing and chewing and chatting and getting lost in the music.

After eight hours of dancing, the sun came up, a large, golden orb appearing on the horizon, covering everything in an orange light, and a gentle warmth that contrasted with the cool of the night. As the morning properly greeted us, the crowd I was with, outside the tent, continued dancing, throwing shapes, moving, always moving with the music. A few of the new-age travellers emerged from their old buses, caravans, school minibuses.

A woman leant against the door of her bus, staring at us dancers. She didn't say anything, but that long stare, followed by a slight shake of her head said it all. She'd been there before; she'd been to Woodstock; she'd danced semi-naked around a bonfire in the moonlight. But she'd not taken quite as many drugs as we had to have stayed up for twelve hours of solid dancing.

As the music reached a crescendo and everyone lifted their hands above their heads, waving in time with the chorus—as much as trance music has a chorus—the woman was joined by a man—long beard, long hair, yawning—and he too shook his head at me, then started making a fire out the front of their bus.

That was the first time I wondered to myself if maybe we'd overdone it somewhat. The thing about nonstop fun, the thing about using the logic of *one being good, so four being fucking amazing* was it ended in a field, somewhere off the M25, with the sun rising and a few washed-up, drugs-addled new-age travellers disapproving of you. Yes, you.

I told Paul as much, pointing subtly—as subtly as you can after three doves and twelve hours of dancing—to the old hippies.

Paul shook his head, saying, "Don't worry about it. That's in-the-week speak. That's not for now. This is the weekend. We're weekenders. Let's enjoy it while it's still here." He looked at the sun, then reached out to grab it. "While we can still touch and feel it."

And at the time, it made perfect sense, as do most things when you're absolutely nutted off your face.

***

Another time we ended up—Slinky Simon nodding along to the beat of the music, very much out of his head—driving in the dark and rain, none of us knowing where we were going, except that we needed to follow the white Vauxhall Astra GTE in front. After a bare-knuckle journey in Slinky Simon's tiny red Peugeot 205 GTI, which cornered like it was on rails, we ended up in a field near Wisley Woods, with much the same boom-boom hypnotic music that ran through my body, flashing coloured lights, random inflatable things, a bus and an ice cream van in one corner of the field, groups of people dancing, chatting, lying on the ground all over the place. The only way I knew we were dancing outside, in my *head-bobbing, hand-waving, forgetting the real world completely* state, was the steam coming off the people around me. If we'd have been dancing inside, in a warehouse or some random building, there wouldn't have been any steam.

After dancing for a while nonstop, I ended up staring at a topless white man with long, dreadlocked hair, wearing a pair of light-blue combat trousers that seemed to be inching lower and lower, exposing more and more of his navel. I alternated my eyes between his navel, his white, slightly hairy chest and the green glow stick and whistle round his neck that swung as he moved his arms over his head in time with the music. Staring, always staring, transfixed by his body, the sweat glistening on his arms, his chest, a light dusting of glitter over his arms.

Someone stood behind me, kissed my neck, put his hands over my eyes, and said, "Rude to stare. Didn't your mum tell you that?" It was Paul, eyes wide, grin wide, arms wide for me to lean into and be enveloped.

"I wasn't staring. It's the music. It's hypnotised me."

"Yeah, and his nips too." Paul laughed.

My head still bobbing, my hands still above my head waving in time with the music, I said, "His what?"

Paul pinched my nipples and I understood.

Another night, not long afterwards, five of us crammed into Slinky Simon's Peugeot, and he flashed a car in front, suspension low with the weight of five people in a tiny hatchback, windows open and music and smoke pouring out.

"What you done that for? Paul asked.

"I know where we're going. Tell them we're off to have it, and he can follow us. No hassle."

"Right."

After a short while, the car he'd flashed pulled over to the hard shoulder. Slinky Simon followed, getting out to ask them what was wrong. I leant forward from the passenger's seat.

The driver of the other car said, "What you gone and done that for?"

Simon explained his slightly odd logic.

"We thought you was the fucking filth and we've all necked our pills."

"Oh. That's not what I meant. Do you know where you're going?"

"Hackney Marshes, follow me."

"Sorry," Simon said.

"Safe."

A face appeared, squashed against the back window of the other man's car, banging on the glass.

Simon walked back to his car. As he started the engine, he said, "Twenty-four-carat-gold twat, I am."

I said, "What's up with the bloke in the back?"

"Said his mate had better get a fucking shift on cos he'd double-dropped and was coming up fast. Didn't wanna be stuck in the back of that fucking Nova when he could be dancing his nut off in Hackney."

"Fair enough."

Simon pulled away, following the other car, and asked me to give him some chewing gum before he chewed his fucking face off. "You ready, we're on the flyer for this one, remember?"

I had remembered, but during the car journey and the intervening drama, I'd managed to forget this was our first set DJing at one of these parties. It was, understandably, much less formal and organised than playing in a nightclub, but our names were on the flyer so that meant it was real. I took the flyer from my pocket and read it again.

Up For It Promotions presents a private party.
From dusk till dawn
12 hours of music
two dance areas
food and ice cream
no alcohol
lasers
projectors

Legal venue
for ticket holders only
location guide—call 0831 124874

Fabio Fun Town
Mad Max
Slinky Simon
Tommy T & Paulie Paul

At the bottom of the flyer, but all the same, that was us: me and Paul.

After getting over the whole 'we're playing music in a field' concept, we followed Slinky Simon to the stage where he introduced us to the guy from Up For It Promotions who'd organised the whole thing, apparently legally. Slinky Simon did say the other guy's name, but the music, the noise and generally being a bit floaty about everything meant I missed it.

Very emboldened by this point as I was as munted as everyone else, I asked, "*Is* it legal?" I chewed the gum quickly.

The Up For It guy said, tapping his nose, "It's a private party. My birthday, as it goes."

"Happy birthday!" I gave him a hug, because it felt just the perfect thing to do.

He said to Slinky Simon, "Where'd you get him from? Is he gonna be all right to play? Looks a bit fucked to me."

Simon replied, "Isn't he sweet. You met Paul, other half of Tommy T and Paulie Paul?"

Paul shook his hand and said, "So is it your birthday?"

The man replied, with a wink, "Yeah, I have a big fuck-off birthday like this every fucking weekend in summer."

Paul and I stuck together as we always did at these parties, agreeing on an *if all else fails* meeting point by the ice cream van, listening to how the other DJs responded to the crowd, building their sets to a crescendo that seemed to mirror the waves everyone felt in their bodies. I borrowed a man's juggling balls on sticks, and after he'd taught me how to dance while spinning them in opposite directions without them colliding, I tried my best to give it a go, to Paul's and the man's amusement. In the end, I handed them back to the man, who offered them to Paul, who shook his head, and then the man hugged us like we were long lost friends, telling us to have a good night before disappearing, his swinging balls cutting a slice through the crowd.

Paul said, "Fancy getting some ice cream?"

I shook my head. I didn't feel hungry in the slightest, as usual at this point in a night out.

"Fancy going for a walk, see if he's selling any?"

That sounded like fun. Pretty much anything he'd have suggested at that point would have sounded like fun, so I nodded, and we strode off, hand in hand, towards the ice cream van, a little piece of the real, everyday world amid the magic, manic chaos of the big partying bubble we were in.

As we approached the ice cream van, which surprisingly had a queue of people dancing outside it, Paul said something so beautiful, so touching, so wonderful I couldn't help but kiss him and hug him tight.

A girl wearing white furry trousers and a black bra asked if we were all right.

"Yeah. Cheers," I replied.

"Wicked," Paul said.

Can I remember what he said now? No, as soon as he'd said it, it was as if its beauty was too much to be alive on this world, so it disappeared before either of us could grasp it.

I said, "Where did that come from?"

"What?"

"What you just said."

"What was that?"

"Gone." We joined the back of the queue for an ice cream, dancing with the others.

That morning, as we drove back to London and civilisation in Slinky Simon's car, the sun rose and the radio quietly wafted the early breakfast show into the back, along with the air from the open windows. The air of a new day. The first day after we'd played a crowd of ten thousand clubbers in a field in Hertfordshire. Paul's suggestion of a new track he'd managed to acquire through means he wasn't at liberty to disclose, a track by Paul Van Dyke, had gone down so well we ended up playing it three times in a row to the shouts of the crowd.

That night was always referred to as our 'For An Angel' night—the night that Paul Van Dyke launched Tommy T and Paulie Paul's career outside the M25.

As Slinky Simon stopped outside our house, he turned to face us and said, "Same again next weekend?"

Without pausing, I said, "If we must, we must."

Paul nodded, took my hand and we walked, slowly, slightly wobbling, up the path to our front door.

Later, in bed, as we were pressed skin to skin, our sweat mixing, our hands grabbing each other's hardness while we stared into each other's eyes, Paul repeated something he often told me: "Sometimes I don't know if you're a bad influence on me, or I'm a bad influence on you."

"If this is bad, I don't want good." I kissed him, closing my eyes, and we continued to make slow love until we fell asleep in each other's arms.

CHAPTER 9

O F COURSE, IT wasn't all drugs, dancing and amazing sex. Oh no. We still had that inconvenient thing called the real world to deal with. No matter how many hours we stayed up over the weekend, in the name of fun or work, we still both had that immovable reality to face each Monday morning.

I became very good at spending the whole Monday morning rewinding videos slowly; videos I'd saved during the week, for just such an eventuality. My cheeks were sometimes sore from accidentally biting them. My jaw ached from all the gum-chewing, the talking deep meaningful wonderfulness that actually turned out to be nothing but at the time felt like the answer to life, the universe and everything.

You may be expecting me to say I saw some terrible things in those parties—ambulances rushing people off to hospital collapsed and foaming at the mouth, people getting into fights. Sorry to disappoint you, but none of that happened.

Just like me and Paul, all the other weekenders resumed their real lives on Monday morning—working, studying, whatevering—with no problems. Except for having a head full of cotton wool and a big case of the midweek blahs on Wednesday.

For those who don't know, that's the delayed lack of serotonin in your body catching up on you. The energy, the euphoria, the connection you feel with all human beings, the wish to be open, to talk about things you couldn't contemplate talking about if you were straight, all comes from your own body's hormones, not the drug itself. The drug makes your body flood with serotonin, the happy hormone. Which is why, midweek, you always feel a bit sad, a bit low, cos your body's usual levels of the hormone are all gone, since you used a week's worth in one night.

Paul was less good at dragging his sorry carcass to the record shop each Monday morning when the alarm went off. He called in sick a few times, and I told him he'd lose the job if he wasn't careful.

"Who cares? I've got the allowance," was his reply.

To which I reminded him of his desire to be free from the parental strings attached and if it was good enough for me, it was good enough for him to get his arse to work on a Monday morning too. "Also, if we ever want any chance of affording a flight to Ibiza for this tryout Slinky Simon's offering, your job is needed."

He couldn't argue with that, so he didn't; he got out of bed, jumped into the shower and I walked him to the Tube station.

"Fancy dinner tonight?" he asked as we reached the barrier.

"What for?" I didn't want to splurge money unnecessarily.

"Date night. Us two. Pizza. My treat."

I nodded and spent the day looking forward to it. This was something he'd introduced which we kept up while we lived in Catford. Every Wednesday, we would go out, just us two: cinema, dinner, bowling... Once we went ice-skating but never again cos Paul kept falling over. We'd go to the theatre if we could get cheap, standing-up tickets at the last minute.

This was our time, when we forgot the everyday talk about taking the bins out, making dinner, work and vegging out in front of the TV. This was *us* time. We talked about plans for Ibiza, whether we could stick our jobs much longer, and argued over which music tracks were the best. I listened to him explaining why he'd moved from Chelmsford, where he was born, to West London—

"Mother couldn't bear living in Essex although it was easier for Dad's work. She said she'd always been a Londoner and couldn't believe how she'd allowed Father to persuade her to leave Chiswick after they'd married."

—and I explained how rarely I saw Dad—

"He's not much of a people person, really. Prefers things. Prefers working than leisure. Means he's given me a good work ethic. At least your parents are both there for you."

Paul debated this for a while, and we agreed his parents were physically there, but that brought its own challenges. We even talked about future, getting a bigger place, maybe a dog or cat, and whether we were interested in children. I said I'd got used to the fact that since I was gay, which I'd known from about thirteen, I wouldn't have kids.

"I like 'em," Paul said. "I think you'd make a good dad. I think together, we'd make good dads. Somehow."

I shrugged at that because I couldn't understand how on Earth that could be possible.

Paul replied, "You never know. If you want to, we'll do it." And it felt like anything was possible.

***

A while later, I had been telling Mum about Slinky Simon setting us up for a tryout slot at Manumission, the big club in Ibiza.

"What you still here for, then?" she asked.

"It's flights, hotels, hire car when we get there. It's all stuff we can't afford. Not to mention getting a month off work." We'd been saving but still didn't have enough money because every month there was always something else needed paying for with the savings: electricity, council tax, water, gas. Living alone was proving dearer than we'd expected.

"A month? Bloody long set."

"It's a series of clubs he's got tryout slots for. Different vibes. Different music. See which suits us best. Slinky Simon says it's very important to find the best fit of club for our sound."

"Does he now? Vibes, eh." She paused. "Love, I'd help you if I could, but as you know, I've only just enough to keep this house running, never mind money for flights and hotels and God knows what else for you and Paul. Sorry."

"It's all right. Besides, at the moment we're saving up for a little car so we can get to play places outside London. Don't need to always rely on lifts from Slinky Simon, Rob, and whoever else there is."

"How exciting. I'm so proud of you, love."

"It's nothing, we're just gonna get a beat-up Fiesta or something. Five hundred quid. Paul reckons we should get something bigger. That way, we can sleep in it if we need to, save on hotels."

"Very sensible, is your Paul. Speaking of which, where is he tonight? How comes he's not gracing us with his presence?"

"He's had to stay behind at the shop. The manager wanted to talk to him about something. He didn't say much when he called during the day. Sure it's nothing."

"Yeah, sure it will be."

"Mum, it was like fucking Woodstock or something. There was ten thousand people dancing like their life depended on it, balancing on stilts, unicycles, inflatable whatevers, laser shows, an ice cream van. It's totally mental. You'd fucking love it."

"Woodstock... That's quite something to live up to. Sounds lovely, but I'm not sure my knees would hold up to dancing all night, you know what I mean? Not at my age, love."

"You could chill out. Sit and talk to strangers. Share in the collective emotion of the music."

"Maybe, love, maybe. But for the moment, lay the table, will you? Your dad's due back soon and I don't want to miss *Coronation Street.*"

"I wrote the letter," I offered optimistically. Finished it, actually.

"What letter?"

"Auntie Luella." I was proud that I'd finally sat down to write the reply—three months after she'd written to me. l I told her what I was doing, my job, the DJing, the house in Catford with my friend, Paul... Auntie Luella wasn't stupid and she knew, but she was twenty years older than Dad and from another generation, so she didn't need me to spell it out to her. When I came out to everyone else, I'd kept it to a minimum with her. She had just nodded slowly the last summer I had visited her in Manhattan, mentioning the clubs and having fun with the boys but making sure I looked after myself.

***

When I'd re-read her letter, I was immediately transported back to her apartment in the Dakota building on the edge of Central Park, with its portered entrance, high ceilings and floor-to-ceiling windows overlooking the park, endless lunches and shopping trips across Manhattan, the bar at the top of the Empire State Building where she'd bought me a cocktail even though I had been underage.

A wave of her hand, and a "He's with me, darling," to the barman, it was all so simple and such enormous fun, as always.

The last time I'd visited her, the summer I turned twenty, which was three years ago, we had walked across Brooklyn Bridge as the sun set, and we stood on the river front, looking back to the crowded, high Manhattan skyline. She'd pointed out the names of all the big buildings: the World Trade Centre towers, the Empire State Building, some of the towers in Wall Street.

"Why have you left Manhattan? Remind me," I said.

"You've seen it, done it, know it. I wanted to show you some of the unseen New York—the bits the tourists don't usually go to." She paused, taking a map from her pocket. "I read an article in *Vogue* saying the only way to really live in a city like this, is to discover new things, every week, every day, every month. Or a part of you starts to die."

"Well, if *Vogue* says it, then we must obey."

"Quite." She strode off purposefully, back towards the bridge, and led me into an Italian pizza restaurant under the arches.

The inside was a haphazard mess of tables squashed over two floors. The wood-fired oven behind the counter filled the entire place with a strong smell of fresh pizza dough being cooked, mixed with cheese, tomatoes and garlic. The waiters and waitresses rushed from the on-display open kitchen to tables and then back again, scribbling orders on their pads.

As we sat, the waiter handed us menus, and explained alcohol was off as they'd lost their liquor licence.

"Iced tea, please," Luella said.

"Same." I shrugged, and once the waiter had left, said, "When in Rome."

"Eat lions? It's quirky. The article said you can eat in high-class restaurants downtown and you might as well go to a high-class McDonalds. This—" she gestured round the restaurant "—this is the real New York."

"Do you think you'll ever come home?"

"Back to London? Oh no. This is home now. Although, even after twenty years, I'm still a strange old British lady. The porters all know me."

"I think that's kind of cool. I'd like to be known by the porters of my building, especially if it has…how many flats does it have?"

"Couple of hundred. Must do."

The pizzas were enormous; loads of red tomato sauce and dripping with cheese, and they had a smoky, woody taste. We couldn't finish them, so we took the leftovers back to Luella's apartment.

We rowed on the lake in Central Park. Well, I rowed, and she pointed out the buildings along the edge, next to her Dakota Building.

As we ate cupcakes on a bench from a small independent bakery in the East Village, she said, "How are your parents? I must phone that brother of mine. He's terrible on the phone, it's like having a conversation with a stunned mullet. He's all 'yes, no, OK', and that's it. There's no flow to the conversation, you see, not like with us. Or even with your mum. How is your mum?"

Although almost completely opposite in so many ways, Auntie Luella and Mum got on well. I suppose it was the fact that class, background, income and education all pale into nothing in comparison to enjoying a good drink and a chat; plus they had me in common.

I told her they were both well, and Luella suggested they come over next year—all three of us, she was happy to pay. Her royalties from a Christmas song she'd written and sung, which had been number one in 1962—a one-hit wonder endlessly repeated every Christmas since—had effortlessly taken her from then till now, no further need to work.

I had talked to Mum and Dad about her offer to pay for their flights and understood the undeniable awkwardness such a generous gesture made them feel, but Luella would hear nothing of it. She didn't see any difference between paying for my flight—her nephew and surrogate son, in lieu of her having any children—and extending the generosity to her brother and sister-in-law.

After a few more attempts at asking me to convince Mum and Dad to come with me next time, I changed the subject and said, "What's this new club in SoHo you read about?"

"It's all the rage. It's wonderful. It sounds similar to Studio 54, but now." She leant forward. "And it's for your sort of people, of course."

"Do you want to go?"

"Oh no, don't be absurd. A woman in her sixties? I do have some dignity left. A little bit. Mind you, that would really get me known with the porters. No. You must go with my accountant. He is divine. Please promise me you'll meet him and you'll go to the club?"

I knew the chances of her letting this one go were slim to nothing, since she'd been mentioning it in letters earlier that year, and then almost nonstop since I'd arrived. She seemed hell-bent on setting me up with her accountant, Sam, who had just come out of a long-term relationship, and although he'd sworn off men and was throwing himself headlong into his accountancy work, Luella was convinced I was the man to end his swearing-off of men.

We had sat at opposite ends of Luella's dining room table, sipping our Manhattan cocktails she'd made, while she tried to get the party going, talking about things we had in common— "Sam is an accountant. You are good with money, aren't you, Tom?" and "Have you been to this club before? They have this sort of club in London don't they, Tom?"

Once we were on the street, next to the crowds taking pictures of where Lennon had been shot, Sam said, "You don't have to do this. I'm not gonna tell if you don't." He shrugged with an awkward smile.

"I'm flying home in a few days. I've not been to clubs here before."

"Do we have to go to the one she suggested? I talked to some friends and they said it was, like, totally full of tourists, and bridge and tunnels."

"Thanks. What's a bridge and tunnel? I mean, I know what they are, but what do you mean?"

As we walked to the subway station, he explained it meant the people who came to Manhattan at the weekend, all through bridges and tunnels, so they were out-of-towners, almost as bad as a place full of tourists.

As we sat on the subway train, a large American flag lit on its side, I said, "So where do you suggest? Oh, and you know I'm underage, don't you?"

"Where I'm thinking, you won't need ID. You won't need alcohol." He raised his eyebrows and smiled.

Tonight's suddenly looking up.

We swept into the club through a metal door in the side of a white brick building somewhere off Broadway below Houston, whatever that meant.

Sam said, "You check our coats in the coat check, I'll meet you by the bar. Water?"

A short while later, I met him at the bar, where he handed me a bottle of water and two white pills.

"Did you get them with the water?"

"I know the guy who serves up in this place. That's why we're here. And the music's fucking ace." He winked, and in one smooth movement necked two pills and took a swig of his water, winking again as he swallowed, his Adam's apple bobbing up and down.

"Double-dropping?" I shouted into his ear above the music.

"Always do." He pointed to the dance floor. "Coming?"

I followed him, taking his hand once I'd double-dropped too.

As expected, it hit me like a train. My lips tingled, my stomach curled itself into a ball, and I was hit by a sickness which made me rush to the toilet a few times, convinced I was going to throw up, but I didn't. I held on to the metal sink, staring at myself in the mirror. My eyes were enormous, my breathing fast, and my heart beat as if I had been running. I closed my eyes, took a deep breath.

A hand grabbed my arm.

It was Sam. "How you doing there?"

"I'm a bit fucked, to be honest. Actually, I'm very fucked. Just about keeping it together."

"All right, you can't look too fucked up or they'll throw you out. Sit in the john, close the door, and do some breathing to concentrate. Don't resist it, just let it…" He paused as he took a breath, then started chewing quickly. "Want some gum?"

I nodded.

"What was I saying?"

"Don't fight it…"

"Don't fight it, just go with it, feel the waves as you're coming up, then you'll be sweet."

I took the gum, then went to the nearest open cubicle and followed his instructions. This double-dropping was not for the faint-hearted.

Fuck me if we didn't end up lying on the coffee tables in the chill-out lounge, kissing each other as everyone else around us nonchalantly sipped their drinks, took more drugs and smoked cigarettes. I don't know why I started kissing him, and later Sam told me he didn't have a clue why he'd started kissing me either. But at the time, I needed something to hold on to, to ground me, to stop me floating away with the clouds, so once we'd taken our position on the tables, I leant forward and kissed him.

Afterwards, we laughed, danced and moved between the three different dance areas playing different music. I wanted to stay in the trance room, but Sam preferred the house room. We developed quite a routine where we'd follow each other onto the desired dance floor, then, after a while, one of us would shake our head, point, and we'd swap to the other room. It was brilliant. I know it doesn't sound so marvellous now I'm telling you, but at the time, it was perfectly brilliant, for no apparent reason.

We left the club as it closed, greeted by the morning sun and the sound of New York starting for another day. Sam high-fived me as we leant against a phone box. "Not bad for a crappy night, huh?"

"Not bad at all. We should do this again, next time I'm over. If you ever come to London, you should see me."

"Definitely. You all right getting back to Luella's?"

I pointed in the direction I thought was the nearest subway station. "Downtown!"

He hailed a cab, opened the door and said, "Get a cab. I'm not having you ending up lost in Queens 'cause you caught the wrong train."

"Queens." I laughed to myself.

"Just get in." He hugged me, kissing my cheek.

I got in the cab, told him the address, and we were gone.

***

"Sent the letter, did you?" Mum asked, obviously familiar with my trick of starting something and not finishing it.

"Stamped, posted, gone," I replied.

Nodding, Mum said—again, "Lay the table, will you, love?"

I did as asked, or started to. There was a knock at the front door. "Shall I get that?"

"Bloody cheek, who's that at this time? Bet it's those door-to-door pains in the wotsits." With a clatter, she threw down the serving spoon and ran to answer the door. A short while later, she shouted me to come through.

As I entered the hallway, I saw Paul standing, panting, red-faced and looking pretty sweaty. "What you doing here?"

"Finished early. Wanted to see you." He stared at me as Mum left to continue dishing up. "I missed you. Stupid, eh?"

It wasn't stupid. It was adorable. "Since this morning?"

He nodded, hugged me, pulled me tightly to him, and rested his chin on top of my head. One of the best things about him being taller than me was being able to rest my head on his chest and listen to his heart beating.

"'S all right, me crashing in, isn't it?" He kissed my forehead.

I took him by the hand and led him into the kitchen where Mum had finished laying the table. "He's asking if it's all right if he crashes in." I rolled my eyes.

Mum sighed. "I didn't receive your reservation. I mean, we're very particular about who we accept in this establishment. Let me see, are your intentions honourable with my son?"

Paul held up his hands in surrender. "I can't promise that, I'm afraid."

Gesturing to the chairs, Mum said, "Sit. Eat. I've not seen you in a while. Tom was telling me about this Ibiza club tryout stuff. How's it going?"

We talked about how we'd been saving and how the savings were less than what we thought we needed. All the while, he held my hand under the table. I rested the other one next to our glasses, we sat in silence and he rubbed his thigh against mine.

CHAPTER 10

WITH OUR BEATEN-UP Ford Escort estate, we travelled round the clubs outside London, mainly the Southeast, not too far, not too much petrol money taken away from our fee for the night. We slept in the back of the Escort, seats folded down, sleeping bags, pillows and the box of records on the front passenger seat. Word got round about the orbital party we'd done; flyers changed hands between Slinky Simon and other similar Slinky Simons from Bedfordshire, Hertfordshire, Essex and Surrey, and soon we were turning places down. Paul would ask what they were paying, if we could have a higher billing on the next load of flyers if we came back, and whether they had any other venues we could play in.

We were flying, really flying, our clubbing wings spreading a little bit more as each week passed.

Of course, it wasn't all WICKED. We were both suffering from what we and our weekender friends called 'in the week-ness'. This was a deliberate play on words, as we often found in the week we felt so weak and just about able to cope with the 'activities of daily living', as a clubbing friend who was also a carer described them.

"They're the things you do every day—dressing, feeding, grooming. Basics like that. When you get old, it's harder to do those, that's why people have carers," he'd explained, between chew-chew-chews of his Juicy Fruit in the early hours of the morning in a field somewhere.

I'd been telling him how tired me and Paul had been feeling during the week. "Eat, sleep, work, and that's it. Anything else is too much to think about, never mind do."

"In the week-ness. That's what that is, mate."

It was a sort of midweek blah stretching beyond Wednesday, when you usually got the midweek blahs. The in the week-ness started on Monday and lasted till Thursday. "Funny, though," he said, "by Friday it's gone and you're well up for doing it all over again, innit?"

"And what can you do about it? I don't think I can cope with it, week after week after week."

"Stop getting on it every weekend. Stop doing all this wickedness." He shrugged. "It's easy. But who's gonna do that, eh? I'm off for a dance, coming?" Off he went, arms waving in the air as he joined a group of people dancing round a bonfire.

When I mentioned it to Paul while we were both in the grip of in the week-ness the following Wednesday, he said, "It's fine. It's not for ever. Something'll turn up. Let's plot our escape from it all."

"Everything?" I asked, while using the will and concentration of my whole being to make beans on toast for us.

"Not you." He kissed me. "Not each other, obviously."

And I thought no more of it, until that morning in Walthamstow.

***

I woke up with Paul lying next to me, both of us semi-clothed under some blankets in a room. I looked around at the various other people, sleeping bodies scattered on the floor, sofa, some covered by blankets, some just lying still fully clothed. It was light, so I worked out it was the morning. Which morning? I wasn't a hundred percent sure; after the club on Saturday night, we'd gone to another club, then to an afterparty at a lock-in in a bar, and then ended up in the house where we were now.

I shook Paul awake. "What day is it?"

Paul rubbed his eyes, leant upwards to kiss me. "Dunno." He rolled over.

I put my underwear and trousers on under the blankets, picked my way over bodies and reached the kitchen where I found a radio. I switched it on quietly, careful not to wake anyone else, for at this point I was the only person moving in the house.

"Welcome to the breakfast show, it's Monday and it's five past nine. And what a show we've still got for you, another twenty-five minutes of the best breakfast show..."

He said Monday. He definitely just said Monday. I was due in work five minutes ago, and I was still...actually, where was I? I didn't even know where this house was.

I ran back to Paul, told him what I'd found out, asked where the hell we were and said we needed to get to work. "No time to pass home, to pass Go, to collect two hundred pounds, it's straight to work."

As I shook Paul to life, a woman appeared in a pink dressing gown, hair sticking up and a cigarette in one hand. "All right, love? Do you think you lot could get a shift on? This isn't a doss house."

"Is this your place?"

She held her hand for me to shake. "Charmed, I'm sure. Last night, you was my best friend. We were going clubbing next weekend, you were gonna have me round your place and everything."

"Sorry. It's just, I've...we've got to be at work—" I checked my watch "—fifteen minutes ago, and see, the problem is, we're still here. Actually, err, what's your name?"

"Nina."

I shook her hand. "Nina, where is this? It's not anywhere near Acton is it? Or Ealing maybe?"

"What's in Acton and Ealing?"

"My work and his work." I pointed to the Paul-shaped lump under the blanket on the floor.

Nina perched on the arm of the sofa, crossed her legs and lit another cigarette. "Fancy a cuppa? Hoping if I make enough noise, this lot'll fuck right off. I'll put a wash-load on in a minute and bang some plates in the sink. That ought'a do it." A plume of smoke puffed from her mouth as she closed her eyes in pleasure. "Fuck, I thought I weren't gonna come back to earth last night. And whoever's idea it was to drop the last pill at six this morning needs their 'ead seeing to."

"So where is this, please?"

"My sofa. My living room. Well, it's me and my flatmate's living room. She's still in her room with her boyfriend. Least, I think it's her boyfriend. Anyway."

"Where is this house, please?" I was trying to keep the anger and frustration out of my voice, but failing. I clenched my hands into fists by my sides.

"Walthamstow, love."

"Fucking shitting wicked."

In the taxi on the way to West London—where our jobs and the things that paid for the taxi, our food, rent and other wild luxuries like that were—I asked Paul how it had happened. How, after all these months of clubbing, always knowing when we had to return to the real world, this weekend, had we missed the turn off for Monday Morning Normality?

Paul shrugged, staring out of the window. "It's like I said before. Sometimes I don't know if you're a bad influence on me or I'm a bad influence on you."

"Answer the question."

"There was the set at the club, which was wicked."

It had been. I couldn't deny that.

"And we stayed till the end. Of course."

Of course.

"Then this club, somewhere south of the river, then it gets a bit hazy. I remember somewhere else, some more taxis. Actually, this weekend, I bet we've spent that much on taxis we could've bought another car." He laughed.

I didn't. "And then where? What happened that we ended up in fucking Walthamstow until Monday morning? Who the fuck is Nina? And who were the others on the floor around us?"

"Nina's a mate of Rob's, and she knows Slinky Simon."

"'Course, all roads lead back to Slinky Simon. And the randoms?"

"Randoms, I suppose. Didn't Nina know 'em?"

"She wanted everyone out so she could get on with her life, whatever that is."

"Yeah, wonder what she does. She did tell me. I think. I think she works in fashion, or music, or maybe it was the BBC."

"I think we're getting off the point. Aren't you worried about losing your job?"

He shook his head, staring out the window, then eventually said, "Not really. I'll get another one, I suppose."

"In a recession? Good luck with that one. Two million on the dole, and you want to join them as your own choice?"

"We'll manage."

"Will we? Will we really? Why's it always me who does the worrying about things. Why don't you worry about anything? How comes, in this relationship, I'm doing the worrying for two of us? It's like being pregnant with your worry as well as mine. Fuck's sake." I shook my head, willed the feeling of hopelessness, anticipation of a serious bollocking at work and the beginnings of a monumental comedown to subside. But they didn't. It was all too much and I started to cry.

Paul comforted me, told me it would be all right, something would turn up, and if all else failed we could always move back in with our parents.

I turned to face him, wiping my eyes with the sleeve of my dirty hoodie that I'd worn for thirty-six hours. "That's your answer, we move back home? That's going backwards. What happened to going forward, always moving forward with our lives? You want to be in your early twenties in a relationship, having to worry about when Mummy and Daddy are home so we can have sex without worrying? Well, I'm telling you now, I don't."

Quietly, Paul said, "I suppose this isn't a great time to tell you I got a written warning at work, is it?"

"No, it fucking well isn't." I paused, trying to gather my thoughts among the comedown that had moved beyond the horizon and was now sitting next to me, dragging me down into its black jaws of sadness. I cried again.

"Sorry. It'll be fine. Promise."

"I can't have this conversation now. Tonight, we'll talk about your job. If you still have one by then. Look at me, look at what you've made me do. You've turned me into your mother, or my mum. Actually, turning into my mum wouldn't be so bad. She'd cope with this, she'd deal with it. But your mother...how did I end up turning into her, telling you off? I'm stopping talking now. I think it's best, before I say something I'll regret."

Paul squeezed my arm. "I'll stop too. I think we're both a bit sore, you know, mentally, from the weekend."

***

I'd love to say the day improved from there onwards, but unfortunately it fucking well didn't. That morning in the taxi was just the starter to a three-course meal of a day of shit.

I arrived at work two hours late, was taken straight into my manager's office where he formally bollocked me, added a warning on my file and told me if I had two more I would be dismissed. "Same with everyone else. Just because we're friends, I can't cut you any slack."

Friends? I wouldn't have gone that far, but since it was my first, I'd hoped he'd be a bit more lenient. I tried to explain it hadn't happened before, and it wouldn't happen again, and it had just been one of those weekends.

He knew about my DJing and had been really supportive, but now he said, "Do what you want, but you've got to be here when you're due. Partying or no partying. That's the deal. You're here for the hours we pay you."

As I walked back to the shop floor, he shouted after me, "I don't mind you spending the whole day rewinding tapes. Don't think I've not noticed. At least that's doing something useful."

That evening, when I'd dragged my sorry sad carcass through the longest day on record—six hours of real time, but for my body it felt like six days—Paul and I tried to have the conversation about his job and his warning.

I said, "That's two of us. Matching, his and his. Aren't we the clever couple?"

Paul said, "No need to be glib, it doesn't suit you."

"Fuck off."

"Fuck off yourself." He picked up a letter I'd left by the door. "What's this?"

"Must've meant to open it when it arrived on Friday, but then…well, then the weekend landed, so…" I smiled. "Sorry."

"Sorry too." He smiled at me.

"Open it then, don't stand on ceremony."

He opened the letter, read it and said, "It's the landlord. Giving us a month to pay the rent owed, or we have to leave."

"How come the rent's not been paid? I thought that's what you used your allowance for?"

He took a deep breath. "I'm sorry."

"What have you done? And why didn't you tell me about it?"

"I used the allowance to pay for the promotion and flyers and things for the last few nights we've done. The warehouse party too. Make sure there was a decent crowd, so we'd get booked again."

"A month's rent on flyers? That's a lot of flyers."

"And the partying too. Where'd you think I got the money for the cabs, the drugs, the everything?"

"Where it usually comes from—your record shop wages."

"About that."

I could have killed him. It took all the strength in my body to hold myself back and listen to him explaining what had happened. What had been happening behind my back for weeks—months—it seemed.

He'd lost his job after getting a third and final written warning for being late and falling asleep at work. Yeah, really. And when he was meant to be going to work, he'd been meeting the DJs for lunch and sometimes more, and club promoters, getting us better billing on the flyers, having flyers printed, delivering them all over London and further.

Because it was so organised, and in the pursuit of the goal we'd set ourselves, I couldn't stay angry with him for long. What really hurt was the lying, the ongoing lying about him going to work at the record shop and instead having a whole different day planned out for himself. That, and spending the rent money, obviously.

"I'm sorry," he mumbled. "I thought I'd get another job so wouldn't have to worry you. But it wasn't that easy. That's why I was putting it all into the clubbing promo. I was sure it would pay off. It still might."

"Yeah, and in the meantime, we can't pay the rent." I took a deep breath.

"I hated lying to you. But it felt like I could justify it, you know? Only now I'm not so sure." He hung his head.

After working out how much rent we owed, and when I would be paid, it didn't take long to realise we were, technically speaking, fucked, and not in a good way. "What about your parents?" I offered quietly.

"Mother already thinks this little chapter in my life is a joke. She'll be expecting me to come running back home, tail between my legs, asking for money. And can you imagine her face when I ask her for money? All the good work I'd done by doing the party for her, undone in one quick mess."

"Of your own making," I slipped in.

Paul put his hands up. "I deserved that. Fair enough. My fuck-up—but while I was trying to do the right thing. Come on, admit that at least?"

"As far as fuck-ups are concerned, this is the nicest, most well-meaning fuck-up I've seen, or been a part of. So if that's any consolation, you can feel free to take it. Is that still a no to your parents?"

"It's still a no. With a side order of massive sorry and I am a naïve idiot and shouldn't have lied to you. But it's still a no, I'm afraid."

"No it is, then. If that's what we've got to work with, that's what we've gotta work with."

"Could we ask your mum and dad?"

"When was the last time you saw anything there that showed they had money? A car that's not slowly rotting in the front garden, covered in mould and hasn't moved for years. Or maybe the clothes Mum wears? Homemade or second-hand, the lot of 'em. Trust me, if they had money, they'd lend it to me. But that's immaterial."

"I didn't think… I don't really think about money, I suppose." Paul bit his bottom lip.

"That's because you have it. No one thinks about money if they have it. It's like, air, it's like light, it's just there. But it's not like that for everyone, babe."

"Sorry." He hung his head. "Patronising poor posh lad that I am."

"Easy, tiger. Don't go so hard on yourself. Our parents are very different. This isn't a surprise to either of us, and it's what makes us who we are. Normally, it's fine, but it's times like this, I wish there was a bit more money to spread around."

"How many days till we have to leave the flat?"

"Ten days. We're fucked."

***

I tried to beg work to give me an advance on my wages, but they said it would have taken as long as it was until pay day anyway, so not much point. A few days later, no money on the horizon, another letter from the landlord confirmed what he was going to do. On the day of the eviction, I arrived home to find Mum standing at the front door.

"All right?" I kissed her cheek and hugged her.

"I see the area's looking up." She pointed with her eyes to a man rifling through a bin under a lamppost.

"It's gonna be the next High Street Kensington. It's on the up. All we have to do is wait forty years."

"Easy life." Mum followed me inside and upstairs to our room.

Once settled on the sofa we'd decided to leave in the room, by the window, and with a cigarette and mug of tea in hand, Mum said, "Now, tell me this, are you all right? And what's with the boxes? You leaving?

"Long story. I'm fine."

"Really? Cos if I'm honest with you, you look a bit…well, a bit fucked. And not in a good way, do you know what I mean? Burning the candle at both ends, are we?"

"It's hard, isn't it?"

"What is, lover?"

"Life."

"Thought you knew that. Didn't we bring you up to know that? Isn't it evident from our house?"

"It is, but it's not the same as when it's down to you. When everything's down to you. Every letter through the door, every phone message, is up to you to deal with." I sighed.

Mum patted the sofa, indicating for me to sit.

I joined her. "Give us a drag on that, would you?"

"What's happened?"

I told her about the row with Paul, about his job and his lying to me. "I think this might be the end for us."

"Really?"

"Really. It was a big row, Mum."

"This is the beginning for you two." She tapped the ash from her cigarette into the silver spaceship ashtray we'd stolen from a nightclub.

"What do you mean?" I asked.

"Do you love him?"

128

"You know I do." It was all I ever said to her: how he made me feel, what he did, how he made me laugh every day, how we were so different yet somehow fitted together like two pieces of Lego.

"Well, then."

"What? Is it a play, or a book, or a show?"

"It would be easy to walk away, but if you really love him, it'll be harder to leave, won't it? Imagine not having him. Imagine him not being there when you come home from work. Imagine having to start dating someone else. Imagine having to tell this new man about yourself. Imagine sleeping with someone else." She paused.

I blinked away a tear.

"Sad, innit?"

I nodded.

"Exactly. And although he's lied, was he doing it in your best interests?"

"You know he was."

"Do you trust him? Do you think he's cheated on you, stuff like that?"

"No. Not for one minute. We hardly leave each other's side when we're out. Everyone takes the piss out of us, says we're, like, stuck together, all night, dancing together, coming up together, coming down together. The lot."

"That's sweet. Do you think I'd still be with your dad if I'd chucked him at the first stupid thing he did?"

I shrugged.

"I'm telling you now, if I had, you certainly wouldn't be here. If you know what I mean." She tapped the side of her nose. "Look, I'm not saying he's got open season to treat you like shit, start knocking you around, dipping his wick elsewhere, but this? It ain't that big of a deal, is it, really? What he's gone and done?"

I thought for a short while. "Not now I've thought about it."

"Well, then."

"Give us a drag on that, would you?"

She let me have a drag on her cigarette. I inhaled deeply and let her simple words of wisdom settle into my mind. Mum's common sense yet again won through.

She reached into her handbag. "That reminds me—nearly forgot why I'm here." She handed me a white, A4 envelope with a window addressed to me at Mum and Dad's place.

"What is it?" I felt for the thickness and stared at the address window. It was definitely for me.

"Thick, isn't it? Postage paid, so…"

"So…what?"

"Dunno. How about you stop fannying about and open the bloody thing? I've not got all night. Gotta get home and get your dad's tea on, as much as I'd love to sit here gassing and smoking with you. You never did tell me about the boxes—what's going on?"

I told her about the rent and the landlord and Paul's new career in club promotions as I opened the letter.

"Why didn't you tell me?"

"Didn't want to worry you. We needed money."

"I see." She sipped her tea. "Come on, what's it about? I'm on the edge of me seat here."

It said the solicitors had tried to contact me on a number of occasions unsuccessfully, but they enclosed a photocopy of the signed will relating to which I was a beneficiary. I stopped reading and looked up at Mum. "It's Auntie Luella."

"What's she gone and done now? You were going to write her a letter, weren't you?"

"She's gone and died."

"She hasn't, has she?" She shook her head, then hugged me, and after a polite amount of time pulled away and said, "When did you last see her? Hear from her? Get in touch?"

Guilt stabbed through me. I hadn't visited her for the last two or three years, since I'd turned twenty. Somehow, for some reason, going to America to visit a maiden aunt had seemed a bit unseemly, a bit odd, a little bit creepy somehow. Which was stupid. I'd gone every summer since I was old enough to fly unaccompanied. "We still wrote to each other." And I had replied to her last letter a while ago.

"Love, I'm not trying to make you feel guilty. It's not like you killed her, did you?" She paused, then stared at me, a dead serious expression on her face. "Did you?"

"No. How could I?"

"So what's it say? I've your Dad's tea to get on."

"You said." The solicitor's letter explained they'd highlighted the relevant part of the copy of the will, and that I'd need to contact their office to see the original and begin proceedings. Begin proceedings? What was the man on about? I scanned the highlighted sections, which said I'd been left the sum of fifty thousand pounds. There was something about the grant of probate and having to meet the solicitor in person.

I handed Mum the letter, asked her to read it, see if I'd understood it right.

"Fifty fucking grand! Bloody hell! What about her poor brother, what does it—oh, same for him too. That's all right. But you, at your age, that's a bit dangerous, isn't it? Who knows what you could do with it? Life changing, is that." She paused, put the letter on her lap. "Wonder what she died of. Does it say?"

"You're holding the letters and that."

"So I am. I'm a bit dazed. All at sixes and sevens. Fifty grand. I'll call your dad, tell him. No, I'll see what she died of first. Seems a bit undignified, doesn't it?" She scanned through the papers, shuffling them in her hands. "Nothing here about it. I suppose you'll have to see the solicitor, find out if they know anything. Will we have to come, as we're benefactors too?"

"Who knows?" Poor Auntie Luella, with her big hats, and her Manhattan apartment next to Central Park, in the building where John Lennon and Yoko Ono had lived and outside which Lennon had been shot, where tourists always crowded for their photos to be taken in what I'd always thought, even as a ten-year-old boy, to be pretty poor taste.

Mum said, "There's something else. Another envelope. Here." She handed it to me. "It's like Christmas, this, isn't it?"

> *To my darling Tom,*
>
> *If you're reading this, it means I am no more, I'm afraid. But don't fret for me; it's simply the same as before I was born, and I didn't mind that part one bit.*

Always straight and to the point as usual. It continued...

> *I have given you and your parents an equal share and you must spent it unwisely—such enormous fun—I want you to enjoy the money. You are to do whatsoever you wish with it, ignore what I would have approved or disapproved of, just promise me you'll enjoy it.*
>
> *As you know, you were my favourite nephew, and the son I never had myself. Damn suitors springing from everywhere when I was a young girl, and then where were they when I needed them? No point dwelling on that now.*
>
> *After I moved to New York when you were a little boy, I missed you so much, but it was the right thing to do. I even, I'm afraid to say, missed you more than my own brother! I think he knew this really. And I've been so fortunate in your parents allowing you to fly out to see me so regularly, even if this somewhat tailed off in later years. I say this, not to make you feel guilty or any such nonsense, but probably in later years I was, as a septuagenarian aunt with parts of me seizing up, or dropping off, or needing ointments and medication to keep in serviceable order, somewhat less fun to spend time with than my younger self.*

As I watched you grow up, each year you visited me, as you turned from a little boy to a teenager, to a surly teenager, into a young man, it all gave me such pleasure; more pleasure, I think, than if I'd been your real mother. I had all the holidays and the fun bits without having to worry about whether you got up for school and all such day-to-day issues.

So you see, my darling, wonderful young man, Tom, this is to say thank you, both to you for giving me that, and to your parents for letting me be such a part of it, your growing up.

Lots of love Luella XXXOOO

"What's she on about?" Mum asked.

The vision of the letter blurred before me. I wiped my cheek with the back of my hand. "I'll really miss her. I'm such a shit nephew, not seeing her for the last three years. What a shit thing to do, eh? And look how I'm thanked." I shook my head.

"What about all those years you did see her, every summer holiday, sometimes the whole six weeks you were out there. And, let me tell you, me and your dad, we weren't half grateful too. It wasn't like we didn't see enough of you. She was like your one-man finishing school in New York. You'd always come home with a new word or a new sort of food you wanted to have. It was great." She paused, scanning through the letter. "Bless her heart."

"I should've gone to see her this summer. Or the one before."

Mum rubbed my shoulders. "You was busy. You was working and DJing and everything. You couldn't have gone for six weeks, and it's a long flight for a week."

"Excuses, excuses. She knew, you know."

"What?"

"The clubbing, the DJing, everything. The *whole* scene."

"*Everything*, everything?"

"When I came back to hers that night after getting right on it with that Sam man, her accountant, I was bollocksed. And do you know what she did, when she greeted me in her dressing gown as I walks through the door, eyes like bin lids and still wanting to dance a bit more?"

"Dropped one herself? She was a game old bird, wasn't she?"

"She wasn't a cartoon character. No, she asked if I'd had a good time, did I want to chill out or did I still want to dance, and had I got on well with Sam, and how did I feel?"

"Just like that?

"Just. Like. That. She said she'd been trying to persuade Sam to let her have a try of the X herself, but he'd dissuaded her. With a heart as old as hers, he didn't want to have a dead woman on his conscience. But it didn't stop her badgering him every time he came round to do her accounts. She made me describe exactly what it felt like, why I did it, what the comedown was like. And once I'd described that, she just said she didn't think she could cope with that, and that nowadays a hangover almost did for her, so she didn't think she'd be able to deal with any chemical enhancements on top of her daily tablets."

"What are you gonna spend it on?" Mum asked.

"Not sure, but I've got a few ideas. I'll talk to Paul first. What about you and Dad?"

"Same as you, I suppose. It's gonna be fun working out how to spend it, though." She put the letter down on the table.

CHAPTER 11

Six months later—Ibiza

WE WERE LYING on our towels on the beach a few hundred yards from our apartment. Playa D'en Bossa had the longest beach on the island, something the locals never tired of reminding us.

The sun warmed my skin. The gentle lapping of the sea, yards away, had just lulled me back to sleep, but now I was reading, a thick paperback written especially for the beach. I found reading—the silence it demands, the silence it created in my mind while doing it—was exactly what my body needed after the days and nights stuffed with music, lights and movement.

Last night hadn't been any different. We'd played to five thousand at an underground club a few streets back from the beach, Swifeys. The club prided itself on being all about the music, none of the foam-party, water-filled dance floors, inflatables and lightshow gimmicks of the other clubs. No, Swifeys was all about the music, and so were we until we'd finally crashed in the early hours of the morning.

Paul was swimming in the sea, his head visible from where I was sitting. He turned to wave at me.

I pushed my white Ray-Ban Wayfarer sunglasses down my nose and waved back at him. I could get used to this. I *had* got used to this.

A few moments later, Paul was lying next to me, on his towel, dripping water everywhere. He leant across and kissed me.

"Good swim?" I asked.

"Wicked."

"What do you fancy doing today?"

"We've got a busy week." He talked through our four appearances over the next seven days, some during the day, others at night, in the three main clubs in Playa D'en Bossa, each catering for a slightly different dance-and-party-hungry crowd.

I squeezed his hand. "Best stay here, then."

"Best we did." He lay on his back, his hands behind his head. "Hard life, isn't it?"

"Bless Auntie Luella." I returned to my paperback.

"And Slinky Simon—don't forget him. This time, we can say it really was what Luella would have wanted. When someone dies, people justify anything by saying that, when in reality the dead person wouldn't have wanted it at all." He shrugged. "That was a bit deep for—" he searched for his watch "—what is the time?"

"Four. Where's your watch gone?"

"Must have gone missing last night. It'll turn up, I'm sure." He reached into the beach bag I'd packed. "Get us a water, would you?"

"I'm not made of money, thanks very much." I was a bit sensitive to the whole inheritance and money-being-no-object thing; despite Luella's insistence, I didn't want to spunk it up the wall in a few months.

"Lost my wallet."

"What else did you lose last night?"

"You called the police?"

"Wasn't much in it. Anything really. Besides, I wasn't pickpocketed. I just…" He was still in the bag pretending to search. "Sort of lost it. I think that's the best way to describe last night, don't you?"

To be fair to Paul, it had been one of those nights where everything seemed a bit slanted and was so far from the day time, when the usual rules applied, that you have to remind yourself what's happening at regular intervals, lest you become completely untethered and float away into the ether world of the clubbing and after-clubbing people. People who were weekenders but now weekended all week long. Like causalities of war, these pill-heads would wander from party to party, from club to club, falling asleep wherever they stopped, until the next party and batch of pills were acquired. Last night, we'd met some of these week-long weekenders, and although fun at first, I had eventually wanted to return to the real world.

Turning my mind back to Paul and his missing wallet, I said, "Do you reckon one of the randoms nicked them?"

"Nicked what?" His eyes were closed now, his arms above his head. His armpits were still as sexily irresistible as always.

"Watch and wallet. Come on, lover, pay attention. I do worry about you sometimes."

"Right. Yeah, they're well gone. No worries. Wicked night, wasn't it?"

"But do you reckon they nicked them?" I persevered.

"Who?" He turned so he lay on his front. "Gotta get an all-over tan."

"The randoms. Like I said."

"No way. They were as sound as a pound. Safe as fuck, they were."

"Fucked, they were definitely fucked. When had they last slept, do you think?"

"Didn't ask 'em. Do my back, would you? Put a bit of that factor five on, would you? And do one of those massages you're so good at."

He knew how to flatter me, and I let him. Because so often, after doing the massage, we would run inside together and tear each other's clothes off.

After finishing his back, I wiped the spare sun cream on my chest and asked him to do me, then, as I lay on my front while he massaged it into my back with his expertly soft hands, said, "Are your parents actually coming over?" They'd been threatening to visit us since we'd arrived five months ago, but I had yet to see the evidence of it being planned.

"Father said he could combine it with property searches—reckons the Ibiza housing market is set to do an upturn, or make the most of a downturn, anyway. And Mother said she would come so she knew what to tell her friends her son was up to next time they were children-boasting at a dinner party."

"She's all heart, isn't she?"

"That's heart. I think she's controlled by a big IBM computer in Winchester. She mentioned she wanted a mobile phone rather than always having to rely on her Mercedes car phone."

"What does she need a mobile phone for?"

"The Women's Guild's ex-chair has one. Anyway, I had to stop myself asking didn't she have a phone built into her hardware?"

I laughed. "Do you reckon we'll ever get them all to meet?"

"Meeting of the clans."

"That's the one." I'd often envisaged it: Marilyn and Roger regarding my parents like they were artefacts in a museum; Mum and Dad not having anything to say to them; me and Paul running between them, feeding them conversational morsels to keep the party from dying.

"Don't think I could be arsed with the hassle. Do you know what I mean?"

"What if they just turn up, invite themselves?"

"They'll check into some five-star hotel. We'll have dinner, get them drunk and leave them for a club. It'll be fine." He paused. "It'll be fine cos it'll never happen, I'm telling you."

I enjoyed the feeling of his hands rubbing the cream into my back. When he finished, I opened my book and, as the sun warmed me, I re-joined the fictional bubble of the characters I'd been hanging out with before Paul had returned from the sea.

***

Since we'd settled on the beautiful island of Ibiza—with some help from Slinky Simon's tryout club slot and Paul's party-planning skills and ability to take seemingly anyone out for dinner and end up their best friend at the end of the night—we'd become well known as the British DJ couple. The more we played, the more sets we did, the more clubs we filled, the more we were asked to appear at other clubs all over the island.

As Mum always said, 'things come of other things', and our time on Ibiza certainly was full of things. *DJ Tommy T and Paulie Paul* on the club flyers was starting to pull in crowds in numbers we could only have dreamed of before coming to Ibiza. Sometimes we headlined a club night and got top billing, right at the top of the flyer and the posters, our names side by side with all the other names below us.

It was, as Paul often said, wicked.

Tonight, we were playing Space, a legendary club in Ibiza, with four rooms of different sizes playing various types of music: house, trance, Euro trance, bouncy house and lots of different genres in between. Space had some open-air areas, where clubbers could dance under the stars until the sun came up again. They also had daytime parties for those clubbers who refused to go to sleep from the night before, or the more sensible people who wanted to dance all day and sleep all night. Tonight, Paul and I were in one of the smaller rooms, capacity only five thousand!

Our room had a ceiling of white lights like enormous jellyfish, with plastic tentacles trailing from their edges. The DJ booth was raised along the shortest wall, offering an uninterrupted view of the entire dance floor, allowing us to judge the mood of the music and the vibes of the clubbers when picking the next song.

We came on halfway through the night, after the crowd were well warmed up, hands waving in the air, and we managed to keep them floating at just about that level for our entire ninety-minute set. Paul and I had each dropped, just a half, so we stayed in control of what we were doing. It gave me just the right floaty feeling, sympathising with how the clubbers felt, allowing us to choose songs that flowed from one to the next.

Towards the end, we were playing one of our favourite songs: 'For An Angel' by Paul Van Dyke. We'd built the crowd to a crescendo, holding them at the high point of the song, the bit which would have been a chorus if trance music had choruses of any sort. The crowd shouted, jumped in the air and screamed, so we played it again, and again, finally moving off the podium after playing it three times.

The next DJ, Wayne, stood outside the booth—white vest and baggy trousers, shaved head and mouth frantically chewing—while we played our last track and greeted him with a kiss on the cheek and a 'safe' and a 'wicked' before he stood between the two turntables and took over the reins of the club.

We walked through the dancing crowd, and Paul pointed to them as they surrounded us.

Paul started dancing, but I wanted to sit, to chill out with a cigarette and a drink in the club's office, tucked away in the bowels of the building, where we could cuddle on a squashy leather sofa, talk about our set, then drive home in our new little Seat Ibiza, which Paul had persuaded me to buy—"We need something to get around. No point managing with some old banger. It's what Luella would have wanted."

He held my hands and pulled me back towards him, in the middle of the dance floor. He kissed me and pushed a pill into my mouth.

I shook my head. "Let's have a quiet one tonight?"

"Why? Come on, just the one. Let's dance, let's relax, we've been working. It'll do us good."

And so, with all the inevitability of the sun rising tomorrow, I swallowed the pill that was on my tongue with a swig of water Paul handed me, and we danced together until the lights came on and the staff cleared up the rubbish on the floor into black bin bags and the crumpled dancers tumbled out of the club's doors.

We went to an afterparty, invite courtesy of some guy Paul had bumped into at the bar buying water. I had been standing by the entrance, ready to go home, but Paul introduced me to this guy and his friends: an assortment of men and women in various states of messiness, dreadlocked hair, smudged make-up, sleeveless T-shirts, pierced eyebrows and crop tops.

Despite my protestations that he was totally banjaxed, Paul planned on driving to the guy's place. He walked in a straight line along the pavement. "Fine. I've not dropped for an hour or so. Besides, it's not far. What's-his-name says it's, like, five minutes away."

"Can't we walk?" I was high, but I wasn't fucking stupid.

"Are you sure you don't want to go in this?" Paul stood by the open car door.

"Are you still spannered?"

He shrugged, jangling the keys. "Not spannered, maybe a bit forked, a bit floaty. But no worse than anyone else we used to get lifts from back home."

I folded my hands and noticed I was chewing a bit too enthusiastically; the inside of my cheeks were becoming sore. "Doesn't mean we should do it again. I said why bring the car? I said let's get a taxi. But no, you wanted to bring the car. I knew this is what would happen."

"Wait there." Paul ran off to talk to his new friends, who were crowded round a pink car with dents on all four corners and each door.

I pulled some gum from my pocket and chewed that instead of my cheeks. *Fuck, I really am pretty spannered still. So much for an early night.*

Shortly afterwards, back at the man's flat—a zigzagged walk from the club, there never really was any need for driving at all—we carried on, dancing, drinking, talking and dropping. I still don't remember the name of the man whose flat we were in, or any of his friends, but Paul was talking intensely to them the whole time we were there. Don't get me wrong, I didn't sit there with a face like a slapped arse, wishing to be home the whole time. Oh no, I did enjoy myself.

In the small living room, the music was turned up, and rather than sitting on the sofa, I needed to dance. I danced with the short woman with long blonde dreadlocks. I danced with the tall man with the shaved head. I danced with a couple of other guys who kept giving me their cigarettes and didn't mind when I complimented them on their bodies—they had taken their T-shirts off and were dancing topless, pecs and abs glistening with sweat, on full beam pointing towards me, with low-hanging combat trousers exposing their pants and navels a mere few feet from me. I had to concentrate on not staring at them.

One of the topless guys asked how long we'd been in Ibiza, and how we'd got our big break. I explained about Slinky Simon, who both the topless guys had heard of. I told them about the orbital parties, and they both nodded, telling me stories of their best nights while rolling themselves and me more cigarettes, which we smoked together dancing in a circle in the middle of the living room. One of them asked how long me and Paul had been together; I counted on my fingers and told him it was a year—a whole year—but we'd known each other before that, explaining about the shops where we had both worked. It was all sound, wicked, sorted and brilliant, as we danced together.

"My mate told me about the DJs to look out for. Before we came out here. They mentioned you and Paulie Paul. Said you were the ones to come to for the best party. The best tunes. Songs that would grab us by the Balearics. You know what I mean?"

I didn't know what to say to that, so I leant forward and hugged him as we both danced. I pulled back.

He smiled, a black hole where one of his front teeth was missing. "It's sound. You two. I don't have a problem with it. It's so laid-back here, innit?"

So I suppose that was why the time passed quickly, once I had got into being at the afterparty, once I'd realised we weren't going back to the leather sofa in the office at Spaced. I glanced across the room at Paul talking to one of the girls, gesturing with his hands as he explained something.

Paul caught my eyes; he blew me a kiss.

I caught it and pressed it to my heart, winking back at him. This was one of our things we had developed from the many nights in clubs together. If one of us caught the other one's eyes, we would blow a kiss and catch it. It made us feel connected, close, in love; even if we were at opposite sides of an aircraft-hangar-sized club, talking to other people, we both knew how much we loved each other.

Sometime later, as the sun turned from an orange glow to bright white streaming into the living room, I opened the curtains and stepped out onto the balcony. I watched people making their way home, others leaving their cars, their flats, bags over their shoulders, heading for the little supermarket on the other side of the road. Behind the row of shops and houses opposite the apartment was a stretch of yellow sand, covered in beach towels and people, and beyond that the deep-blue sea and the light-blue, cloudless sky. I felt a kiss on my neck and hands round my waist. I knew it was Paul; I recognised his smell: a mix of his favourite CK One scent and sweat.

Facing him, I pointed at the view. "Beautiful, eh?"

"You are, yeah." He smiled, then kissed me. "Shall we make a move?" He nodded to the door.

"Thought you were never gonna ask."

As we walked to the door—and said goodbye with hugs and kisses to the others, our friends for the night, the people we'd shared philosophical thoughts, theories, the best creative ideas ever, all now forgotten, disappeared into the blue sky where the clouds weren't—we took each other's hands to shouts of "Laters" from the others.

"Where now?" I asked once we were outside.

"Let's go home and fuck like rabbits." Paul winked.

"If you put it like that, and you insist, then who am I to disagree?"

Back at ours, we lay naked under the covers, facing each other and kissing like horny teenagers. Paul grabbed me, and I responded to his touch, stiffening more than I already had from the warmth of his body so near to me. He squeezed me.

I kissed his lips, then moved down via his nipples, his chest, his navel, down until I was completely under the warm duvet, the musky smell of our bodies filling my nostrils. I pushed him onto his back, licked his inner thigh and, using my hand, squeezed him, expecting him to respond by pointing towards my mouth. After continuing for a while, I licked him and took him in my mouth, and got stuck in, expecting him to quickly stiffen as usual.

After a while, Paul pulled my head up. "Sorry. It's not happening."

"What's wrong? I'm bursting. Look!" *He doesn't fancy me anymore. I'm a useless lover.*

I pulled the covers back and sat astride his chest, pointing ceilingwards. As I leant forward to kiss him, I pushed my stiffness on his chest, hoping it would reignite his passion.

"I dropped with that guy in the kitchen." He paused, avoided my eyes. "We were dropping partners. Said he's coming to our next set. Said he wanted to come out when we have a night off."

I pulled the covers round myself; a sudden chill came over my whole body. "When?"

"Next time we're out. When is that? You've put it on the calendar, haven't you?"

"No, when did you drop with him?"

"Not long before we left. It's not really touched the sides, to be honest. It's flogging a dead horse, I think. Can't feel anything. It seemed like a good idea at the time. He offered me one, so I just…" He shrugged. "Give it a while. I'm sure it'll come back."

I wanted to come and go to sleep, but even though I didn't know what to say about what he'd told me, I knew saying that wasn't very sexy or loving, so I said nothing. I moved to climb off his chest, noticing how my excitement had obviously subsided too in the wake of his news.

"It's nothing you've done. I really want to fuck like horny rabbits, in here—" he tapped his head "—but down there, it's a bit all over the place at the moment. Normal service will be resumed soon, I promise. You're gonna ache if you try to sleep now, after that." He stopped me climbing off his chest. "Stay there and I'll do you."

"It's all right. Moment's passed now. Cuddle up and we can go to sleep, see how things are in the morning." I leant forward and kissed him, then lay on his chest, my legs still astride his waist. The warmth of his body, the hairs on his chest, the gentle stroking of his hands on my back, all conspired to defeat my intentions, and soon I was just as excited as I'd been before.

He kissed me, pushing me backwards so I was pointing at his head, in between his nipples. He grabbed me and, using both hands, pulled at me with one and pressed me underneath, with his thumb, exactly how I liked it. He smiled as his pace quickened and his thumb pressure increased.

I reached behind me, grabbing him so I could reciprocate, so I didn't feel like I was the only one benefitting from the sex, but despite my efforts, he remained soft and unresponsive.

"It's all right. Later." He smiled, his thumb pushed harder, his hand pulled quicker.

I arched my back and pressed down on his pecs with my hands, the wave of pleasure building up through my legs, into my groin, more and more. With a gasp and a shudder, I finished in a shower covering his chest, up his neck and on his face. Once I'd got my breath back, I apologised; I didn't like it in my face.

Paul pulled me forward and kissed me, his lips covered in my stickiness. "I love you."

"I love you too, you fucking pill-head."

And we lay like that, under the covers, me on top of him, until, with a few gentle movements, we adjusted our positions to drift off into a warm, fuzzy sleep together.

CHAPTER 12

PAUL HAD MANAGED to arrange for us to play Amnesia midweek during the day. This was a prestigious slot as it generally attracted a classier sort of clubber, a less full-on messy, more chilled Balearic clubber. Apparently, that was the audience we needed to chase—subtly, of course.

The room where we were playing, if you could call it that, had a frame of fake Roman columns at each corner, with a horizontal ornate carved cornice around the top of the four columns, green plants and flowers winding around the stone, if it was stone. I doubted, really. I'd knocked it as I walked to the DJ booth on its raised stage in the middle of the room. The stone thudded and felt quite light, probably polystyrene, but with its carvings and stone colour, it did look pretty realistic from afar. That was all that mattered.

Paul and I were trying out some lighter, more chilled sounds for the daytime crowd, and in the middle of this set, Paul explained he'd be back and not to worry. He disappeared into the crowd, leaving me alone in the DJ booth surrounded by sun-drenched clubbers in colourful shorts, T-shirts and vests, some wearing their swimming trunks or bikinis, all waving their hands above their heads at the crescendo of the music and swigging water with great enthusiasm.

I felt like I was having as near to a religious experience as I'd ever had. The only catch was the lack of Paul.

I played two more songs and checked the time. He'd been gone for half an hour. I couldn't leave the booth and had no way of getting in touch with him, so I lined up the next record and played on, plastering a smile on my face, waving my hands in time with the dancers, debating whether to neck a pill to take the edge off the anxiety but deciding it was best to remain straight, in case anything kicked off and required sorting out.

Just as I was about to lose my cool, the sweat pouring down my face, cursing myself for not wearing a hat in the sunshine, Paul reappeared, wide grin, arms open for a hug.

"Where the fuck you been?"

"Here and there. I'm back now. Let me do the next track." He took the headphones from me and stood between the two decks, mixing into the next song to a cheer from the crowd.

Once we'd finished our set, we walked to the bar. I turned to ask if he wanted water as usual, but he'd gone again. I looked around, walked back to where we'd just come from; no sign of him. My heart rate rising, the sweat on my brow dripping, I walked round the whole of Amnesia, checking the bars, the dance floors, pushing my way through thick crowds of dancers, asking bar staff if they'd seen him, returning to the DJ booth and asking the next DJ if she'd seen him, but everyone shook their heads.

Desperate for anywhere else to look, I checked all the toilets, calling his name as I stood by the door. Then I went to the manager's office, explained the situation and asked if he'd seen Paul. Another shaken head. I was out of ideas. The 'he'll turn up, he's a big boy' from the manager as he sat at his desk didn't really help either.

I had wanted to go home over an hour ago, and yet I was still out, looking for Paul. I left the club and did the only thing I could think of: I reported him missing at the police station, using my broken Spanish, with the help of a female police officer's rudimentary English.

With a sympathetic tone, the police officer said, "He is not gone for long enough. He is not missing. I'm sorry. He is an adult."

"Yeah, but he's gone," I pleaded, pointing to the form she'd taken from the drawer before I explained when he'd gone missing and how old he was.

She shook her head. "This happens all the time. He will be back. I am sure."

Without even a case reference number to show for it, I returned home and tried to sleep alone in our enormous double bed, feeling like it was mocking me every time I turned over.

***

The next morning, I woke with a start to a ringing noise that filled my head. I rolled over, reaching out for Paul's body and finding only empty space, and then remembering what had happened. The ringing was the phone. It would be Mum calling for her regular chat to see how things were going, make sure we hadn't gone too far off the rails, and tell me how her and Dad were getting on. *It'll finish in a bit. I'll just roll over and it'll go away.*

I rolled over in bed and the ringing stopped. The apartment filled with silence, the glorious noise of nothingness, only the quiet background chatter from the world outside beyond the balcony. I put my pillow over my head, but the ringing started again.

Eventually, after three more sets of rings, I picked up the receiver. "Yes?"

"What sort of a way's that to greet your old mum, eh?"

"What do you want?"

"A bit less of the bloody attitude, thank you very much. I'm only ringing when we said I would. Don't you remember?"

"I've been busy. It's been all go. Didn't get in till late last night."

"Still having more fun than you can manage, then?"

"Something like that."

"What was it this time? Beach party as the sun comes up? Dancing in the bones of a hollowed-out beached whale? Four-day bender in a volcano crater?"

I told her about Amnesia and the daytime set. As I stared at the empty bed, I bit my bottom lip, then lit a cigarette, my hands and lips shaking and making the cigarette jump all over the place until I'd taken my first drag.

"Me and your dad was thinking about coming over to visit you. See how you're getting on with this new life of yours, you know, in person, not just on the phone."

I was still staring at the empty bed. I swallowed hard, tried with all my body to hold down the cry of fear and worry that was building from the pit of my stomach.

"You still there, love? You listening?"

"Yep," I let out with a yelp.

"Big comedown, is it? Feeling a bit sore, are you?" She paused as she lit a cigarette. "I can call back later if you want, when you're feeling a bit more human. Although I'd have thought daytime clubbing, by now you'd be back on your feet, but then again, what do I know?"

The thought of the silence in the flat alone was worse than the tortured conversation I was in the middle of, so I told her to carry on, that I just needed some caffeine.

"Dad didn't know what to do with himself since giving up work, so he's gone back. I tell you, that week he retired from the council was the longest week of our lives. He wouldn't get out from under my feet. Sat about moping, asking what to do. I almost killed him. Who'd have thought money would cause so much stress? Not that I'm complaining, mind. No, but it's just something to get used to, to adjust to, I suppose. No way he'd have upped sticks and moved abroad like you did. Getting him to eat a curry or French toast were big enough battles without persuading him to move abroad." She paused.

I was *still* staring at the empty bed, twiddling the phone cord round my free hand, pulling it tight so it left a red mark on my wrist.

"You still listening to me?"

"Yep."

"So can we come over, visit you, like? Both of us. I doubt he'll come if I'm honest, but we'll cross that bridge as and when."

"Fine, yeah, whatever."

Mum was talking about if they could stay at ours, or if they'd have to book somewhere else, and saying she'd prefer staying with us, and then asking which airport to fly from and whether or not they'd have to drive on the wrong side of the road, on the wrong side of the car, and how the hell we'd got used to all that palaver. At the point where I thought my stomach was going to drop through the floor into the flat below us, the door opened with a click and the chatter of a group of people.

"Mum, gotta go. Something's come up." I put the phone down, walked to the door and hugged Paul tight. Then, once I'd established he wasn't a mirage and was indeed stood in front of me, grinning and twinkling those beautiful eyes of his, I said, "Where the fucking hell have you been? I've been worried sick. Thought you were dead, in a ditch, kidnapped, taken by the Mafia. All sorts."

Paul said, "You do worry, don't you? Have this." He handed me a pill. "Catch up with us lot. Come and let me introduce you to everyone. I've told them all about you. They'd heard of us on the posters and flyers, and when they met me, they were made up—they wanted to meet you. I said they could as soon as we got back here." He paused, smiling at me. "Come on." He twirled round and danced into the middle of the room in time with the quiet music floating through the open door.

The room filled with dancing strangers, and the music became louder when Paul inserted a clubbing mix CD into the player and resumed his position in the middle of the room, hands in the air, eyes closed, hips gyrating.

It all happened so quickly, I hardly knew what to feel, never mind what to do. I was so relieved he was back, safe, alive, but now he was with a group of randoms wanting to have a party in our living room, *my* living room. I didn't know how to broach those two facts at the same time. I pushed past a few dancing strangers into the small kitchen where I put my head under the running tap and closed my eyes, drinking the water and enjoying the cooling sensation as it soaked my hair and face, wishing when I opened my eyes again I would find something different from when I'd closed them.

I shook my head, spraying water all around the kitchen, and turned to face the living room. Same random people, same random music, same random situation. Same random fucking life.

Fuck it, this is my life, my living room, my boyfriend, I'm going to talk to him.

I strode across the room, knocking a few people over. The crowd parted like Moses with the Red Sea until I reached the middle. The core of all this. Paul. My Paul.

He was gyrating in time with the music, staring at me, arms stretched far either side of his body. "All right?"

"Can we have a word?"

"Now?"

I nodded, grabbed his arm and led him to the balcony. Once there, I said, "What the actual fuck?"

"Come on, it's a party. It's a laugh. It's fun. Remember fun?"

"Yeah, I do, as it goes. But unlike you, I know when I've had enough, when I have to return to earth to get on with my normal life."

"We're not working for a while. I checked. I think I did." He looked out the corners of his eyes, screwed up his mouth, then looked back at me, smiling. "I think."

"Not the point."

"Let's go higher and higher. Together." He took my hands and tried to lead me back into the room. I resisted.

I twirled Paul round so his back was against the balcony rail, walked across the living room, switched the music off, turned the lights on, clapped and said, "That's it, everyone. Party's over. Home, please."

A chorus of "No!" and "Why?" and "Do we have to?" filled the room, but I stood resolute.

Paul walked into the middle of the floor, next to me, his eyebrows furrowed as he took in the guests gathering their things and slowly walking towards the door. "He's only joking. Stay. Dance. Come on." He walked to the CD player and pressed play. The room filled with music.

A few people started dancing again, but I unplugged the CD player. "Off you fuck, please, everyone." I clapped.

Once all the randoms had gone, I sat next to Paul on the sofa. His legs were shaking in time with some imaginary music, and his hands tapped in time to some beat on his thighs. "All right?"

"I've had better nights."

"What you have to go and do that for?"

"What did you have to go and disappear for? You had me worried sick! I thought you'd died. I thought I was never gonna see you again. I went to the fucking police station. Politzie, or whatever it is in Spanish. I was worried. What the fuck happened to you? You just disappeared."

He shrugged. "I forgot."

"What did you forget? Being at Amnesia and forgetting— that's pretty poetic, isn't it?"

"Yeah." He smiled awkwardly. "Funny."

"It's anything but funny, actually. It's scary. Terrible. Worrying. Me not sleeping. Me not telling Mum you'd gone missing cos I was embarrassed. It's me going to the Politzie station and reporting you missing. That's what this is. This fucking mess. So don't say it's funny. Don't you dare say it's funny to me, with your big smile and your big, wide, innocent eyes. Cos it's not gonna work. I'd kill you if I hadn't already thought you were dead."

He shrugged. "So I went off for a bit. You knew I'd be back. I know where we live. I've lived here as long as you. I'm a big boy, I can look after myself, you know."

I leant forward so my face was inches from his. "I can hardly look at you. I can't believe you've done this. Why would you just disappear?"

"You know I'd never cheat on you. You can trust me." He held my hand and started stroking it.

I pulled my hand away. "But sticking together, always sticking together, all night, that is our thing. That *was* our thing. Why the change?"

"I didn't think. I wasn't thinking. I got swept up with everything. I didn't think."

"That's just it, isn't it? I don't know who you are anymore. You're disappearing before my eyes." I left the flat, slamming the door on my way out.

I had to leave him alone when he was like that. There was no point trying to have a sensible conversation with him while he was totally off his face and I was on a comedown. I walked along the nearby beach, found the shade under a tree where we sometimes had picnics together. I lay on my front and—using my arms as a pillow and with the background chat of people, the splash of the waves and the cool breeze on my face—fell asleep.

***

Sometime later, I was woken by a tickling sensation on my nose.

Paul knelt in the sand by my head with a bag in one hand and a feather in the other. "Thought I'd find you here."

"What do you want, a prize?" I rolled over, my back to him.

"I brought lunch. Chorizo, bread, manchego cheese and olives. The green ones you like. An apology picnic."

I did like olives, especially the green ones. And the cheese and chorizo was our comedown lunch that we'd had dozens of times before on the beach, each mouthful of crunchy bread, red spicy sausage and creamy cheese gradually revising us back to our usual human-being levels of functionality.

"Sparkly water too."

That was what we always called sparkling water to each other. Our little joke. I sat upright, legs crossed, elbows resting on my thighs. The sun was low in the sky, and it was no longer too hot to sit out of the shade. "Do you want to sit in the sun or is it too bright for you?"

"That sounds perfect."

We moved a few steps into the sun.

Paul sat opposite me, putting his hands on my legs. "What did your mum have to say?" He unwrapped the cheese, sausage and bread and laid them on the bag.

"When?"

"You said you'd spoken to her and hadn't told her I'd gone missing. See? I do listen. I was listening. I wasn't totally bollocksed." He was assembling a sandwich with the separate ingredients.

"You were pretty bollocksed. You were well beyond having a sensible, well-reasoned conversation."

"I wasn't. I got a bit over-enthusiastic, inviting all those people back."

"I'm not arguing about it. I can soon walk home alone."

Paul handed me a cheese and chorizo sandwich on crusty bread. "Please don't. Please stay."

I bit into it. The oily paprika of the sausage mixed with the creamy cheese encased in the crispy bread were, as always, the perfect combination. I chewed thoughtfully for a while.

Paul handed me the bottle of sparkly water.

"Thanks." I took a swig. "I sometimes wish we were back to working in the shops, living in that flat in Catford, doing this at the weekend. Things were simpler then, don't you think?"

"It was your idea to come here. It wasn't all me. 'It's what Auntie Luella would have wanted,' you said. 'It's the perfect timing just as we're about to be thrown out of the flat,' you said."

I had. That was exactly what I'd said; there was no denying that. "Aren't you eating?"

He tapped his stomach. "I'm not hungry."

"You made all this for me and you don't even want any?"

"Yep." He smiled. "Sorry. Shouldn't have brought the randoms back with me. Shouldn't have disappeared, sorry."

"It was always us two. Together. That's our thing. No matter who we bump into, who we talk to, where we end up, we stay together. We knew I was going home with you, and you were going home with me. No matter what else was going on, that was our thing. And this sort of threw all that out the window. I don't know what's happening to you."

"Nothing's happening to me. I'm still me. Nothing's changed. Promise." He kissed me.

I offered him some of my sandwich. It was too delicious to not share.

He waved it away. "Not hungry. Not at all."

I stared into his eyes; the pupils were pretty large for sitting outside in the afternoon sun. "Did you go to sleep after I left? Or did you just carry on partying on your own?"

"What does it matter? The randoms left, I'm here now."

I put my half-eaten sandwich back on the bag with the rest of the food. "Are you ever going to tell me where you disappeared to yesterday?"

"If I knew, I'd tell you. I sort of lost myself. I'm sorry. I'm back now." He stared at me.

Are you? I felt the sickness welling up from the bottom of my stomach, rising into my throat as the smallest thought about whether this new life in Ibiza, thanks to wonderful generous Auntie Luella, was actually pushing him farther away from me. Farther away and into what, I wasn't quite sure. Even though he was sitting a few inches in front of me, I still wasn't a hundred percent convinced he was back; not all of him, anyway. And a little bit of me worried I'd never quite get him back if things continued as they currently were.

"I didn't mean to disappear. I got talking to some people, they suggested I come back to theirs for an afterparty. I went back to find you in the club and you'd gone. They were just about to leave so—"

"You left without me." I stared at him.

He nodded. "Not good. But I wasn't thinking. I just…did it."

"Same with this morning, I suppose?" I asked.

"Pretty much. More of the same. I remember thinking when I arrived with everyone that you'd missed out on the party last night so you'd want to join in with this one."

"I can see your logic. Kind of."

"Not thinking. Again. Sorry. Very sorry." He paused and took a bite of the crusty bread sandwich he'd made me. "Shall we walk home, cuddle up on the sofa, put some chill-out music on, watch the sunset from the balcony? How's that sound?"

Because I was exhausted from lack of sleep, from a busy week of working, from the conversation we'd been having, from the worry, from the night at the police station, from pretending to Mum everything was OK, I just nodded, and we tidied up the picnic and walked along the beach, as the sun set, holding hands, saying nothing.

Once back in the flat, I felt an urgency from him, a desperate need to be with me, to show me he still loved me, that he was still him, to do what we'd always done so well together, how we'd always had such chemistry, fitted together so well in bed. He grabbed at my clothes, kissing my face, my chest, my stomach. With the balcony windows open, he knelt in front of me and made love to me, taking me in his mouth as I stood, stroking his head. Although I enjoyed it, there was a tinge of desperation in his actions, like he was giving me a blow job as if his life depended upon it, not coming up for air, not pausing to look up at me like he usually did, just keeping on with his head bobbing up and down.

Sensing something wasn't quite right, I pulled back and lifted him to stand in front of me, kissed him, enjoying my taste in his mouth, turning myself on even more than I'd been before.

"My turn," I said with a smile. I knelt and unbuttoned his combat trousers, pulling them down with his underpants. His musky smell hit me strong in the nostrils, and I felt myself stiffen, reaching to pull on myself.

He hunched forward, saying he was OK, and he wanted to carry on where he'd left off.

I told him I wanted to make love to him, and for him to relax. But it wasn't until five minutes of licking, squeezing, rubbing and teasing later I realised something wasn't right. He was having a serious case of Mr. Floppy, and nothing I was doing with my hands or mouth was having any effect.

He pulled his trousers and underpants up and sat on the sofa, arms folded. "Said I wasn't bothered. You should have let me get on with it. I'm all right."

I tucked myself back in and joined him on the sofa. "You're not all right. What's up? Am I doing it wrong?" I knew I wasn't, but I didn't want to go in all guns a-blazing with accusations of him being off his tits still.

"No."

"When did you last drop?"

He counted on his fingers after looking at the wall clock. "Four hours. It's not that. I dunno what it is. It's nothing. Stand up and I'll do you."

"Someone mentioned something about a chill-out album and the sunset. Does that offer still stand?"

"After." He tried to undo my trousers.

I held his hands and shook my head. "It's all right. There's other times. I want it to be both of us, when we're both in the mood, so we can click together, like we always do."

"I'm sorry. I didn't mean to. It just happened. I don't know what's wrong with me. This never normally happens to me. I didn't want to let it spoil things for you. Let me finish you off."

I stood and put a chill-out CD on. "Mum said she wants to fly over, see the setup for herself. Reckons Dad might come too. That's OK with you, isn't it?"

The room filled with a slow song, floating through the air, wrapping us in its comforting noises.

He leant his head on my shoulder. "Suppose so. Bit serious, isn't it? Parents visiting us?"

"Why?"

"Showing them we're together. Pressure, that's what it is."

"Is it?" I hadn't thought about it like that before and told him so. "It's just Mum and Dad wanting to spend time with us in the sun. Doesn't mean anything more."

"OK, then," he said quietly. "I don't like all the talk about future intentions."

"Mum was joking. Anyway, never mind future intentions. What happened to you last night?" I sensed he wanted to change the subject.

"I don't know where I went. Honest. If I did, I'd tell you. Some people's flat a taxi journey away. But I do know I didn't cheat on you. Cross my heart and hope to die." He crossed his heart.

"I believe you." *Because I have to. Because I'm pleased you think I'm not useless enough to cheat on.*

We stared out the window at the orange-red sunset as it descended over the buildings, disappearing into the sea beyond.

***

Later that evening, once we were in bed, he spooned me from behind, reaching round to pull me at the front, kissing my neck.

I leant back to kiss him, pushing myself backwards, anticipating his hardness pressing into me, into where he pushed his thumb, but as I pushed myself backward, backward, backward, there was no hardness to meet.

He continued pulling me towards the finishing line. I reached behind, trying to grab his hardness, but was met with Mr. Floppy again.

His hand frantically pulled at me, quicker and quicker.

I asked what was the matter, and did he want me to do him? He could lay back and I would fill him—that was something he usually loved, something that would awaken his sexuality, reignite our spark. But he stopped me talking, pushed my lips together with a kiss, and continued pumping away at me with his hand until I finished.

"Where were you?" I asked quietly, trying to stroke him behind myself.

"I'm here. I'm always here," he said, closing his eyes.

I'd never felt further from him before. Even when he was missing in the club, he'd felt like the possibility of returning to me, but in our bed, him lying behind me, his breath on my back, he was nowhere to be found, and I didn't know why, or what I could do about it.

CHAPTER 13

A FEW WEEKS LATER, we took Mum to a daytime Spaced dance party on one of our rare nights off: something laid-back, something chilled out, something we felt would be a good introduction to the whole Ibiza clubbing scene. We wanted to take it easy. We agreed we'd not go mad, not get completely mad out of it, and would ease Mum into the whole scene.

Mum had wanted to visit us for ages and finally we'd managed to make it happen. She'd also been on about dropping with us since we'd agreed the dates she was visiting us.

In fact, she'd been interested in it as a new drug since the first time I'd come home with eyes like bin lids, having a one-man disco in the kitchen, throwing shapes in time with the little kitchen CD player.

She'd stood at the door, arms folded, and asked what I was on and could she have a bit for herself, just to take the edge off the shitty week she'd had. I'd explained it was this new party pill called ecstasy, and if she imagined the best, most wonderful warm feeling filling her body, making her want to dance, that would be about half of the effect.

She used to enjoy chatting to me when I came home the morning after, still pretty on it, chatting, making me tea, giving me cigarettes and asking about how my night had been, what the dances and songs were like nowadays. But we'd never actually got round to her dropping with me. I knew she would have done, eventually, and I preferred she do it with me and Paul, with stuff we trusted, rather than some random guy in a club. So as soon as Dad said he wasn't coming to Ibiza, I could feel the excitement crackling down the phone from Mum, and the plan was hatched.

The *clubbing in Ibiza dropping with Mum* plan.

Now, on the way to the club, me on one of her arms and Paul on the other, she said, "I weren't born yesterday. I lived through the seventies. When I say lived, I mean I did a shitload of acid and danced my arse off around fires and stones with no bra on, camping in a field. So no need to bleedin' well babysit me, all right, lads?"

Paul got our drinks as we settled on some wicker chairs on the edge of the outdoor room. I asked why Dad hadn't come and Mum said he'd got so worried about relaxing for a whole week he'd come out in a rash, so he'd cancelled the holiday from work and was now resurfacing part of Lewisham's High Street for the council.

I shook my head. "Instead of this?"

"He's as happy as a pig in shit. Honest to God, he is. He's never been one to relax, has your dad. Not since he relaxed a bit too much in the seventies—let it all hang out a bit too much, if you know what I mean."

"No...what do you mean?"

"Acid's a funny thing. Not funny ha-ha, but funny strange. They say every time you take it, there's this risk the crossed wires it makes in here—" she tapped her head "—don't uncross when you finally come down. Your dad had a mate who was doing it every weekend. Actually, not just every weekend. Every night, I think it was. And one day he lost himself." She let that hang there in the air between us.

"What do you mean, lost himself?"

"The crossed wires never uncrossed themselves and he couldn't get back to the man he was without drugs. He literally lost himself."

"Is that what happened to Dad too?" This was all news to me.

"No. Nothing so dramatic for your dad. He was the one who saw his mate when he lost it, close up, slowly at first, then not so slowly. Said it was awful sad. Terrible, it was. And since we had you, he's not touched anything. Didn't want to lose it with a baby to look after, see."

"Except pot."

"Yeah, except pot." Mum lit a cigarette, offered me one, looked around, asked where the hell Paul was, then sat back in the chair.

"And alcohol."

"Right, and alcohol."

"And tobacco." I smirked at her.

"Yeah, except, pot, alcohol and tobacco, he's totally clean. Look, point is, he's not touched anything like the hard stuff, not since you came along. He didn't say to me, but I think he was worried he'd come here, get on it and risk losing himself all over again."

"Pills are nothing like acid. Not that I've done acid, but honestly, nothing like each other. Speaking of which, when do you want to drop?"

"I'll follow your lead, love. It's your home, whatever. And where the fuck is that Paul of yours with our frigging drinks?"

Paul arrived, handed us each a bottle of water, sat on the coffee table between our chairs and explained he'd got sidetracked. He'd been talking to one of the barmen we were friends with, who'd told him about a DJ who was flying back to the UK, leaving an opening two nights a week in one of their bigger rooms. The barman reckoned we should give it a go.

Mum tutted. "I've never seen you two work so hard. There was me thinking you were here on holiday, and here you both are, working your little arses off."

"Wicked," Paul said, winking at me, which was the sign we always used.

I checked for bouncers, then necked a pill with a swig of water, indicating for Mum to do the same.

After a quick look round, Mum put hers in her water bottle hand and as she took a swig dropped it in her mouth. It was done.

Dropping ecstasy with my mum. It's hardly an everyday occurrence for most people, is it? I'm sure some of you are thinking how wrong this was. How odd it was. How dangerous. But I didn't feel any of those things. It was something we'd spoken about on the phone—in code, obviously—before she flew over and discussed again since she'd arrived. I'd explained what it felt like, and Mum had used other experiences to gauge whether she'd enjoy it or not.

We had a really friendly guy who sorted us out for party prescriptions, Jose, he was called. How can someone who's a drug dealer be friendly? Well, having met lots of other dodgy fuckers, Jose was a pussy cat in comparison, and he only ever served up the best quality ecstasy tablets. One of those and most people would be flying and dancing all night.

Mum had taken half of hers, just to be on the safe side; we didn't want a puking mother on our hands, did we? So, on balance, it was pretty well considered, pretty well organised, and not going to turn any of us into heroin addicts.

Mum said, "When do we start dancing our tits off?"

I said, "You'll know when you wanna dance. You won't be able to stop yourself, trust me."

"Safe."

Paul asked how she was getting used to the money and if they were thinking of moving. Mum said she was trying to be sensible and not spend it all at once.

"No plans to come and move out here with us?" he asked with a smile. "You'd be very welcome."

"Not at the moment, love. How's this place work, then? The rooms and the daytime/nighttime? When you said you wanted to take me to a daytime club, I thought you was joking."

Paul explained how the different clubs had various types of music, and how within the clubs there was an assortment of rooms for different subgenres of music. The clubs had become so busy with people wanting to party at night, they had to turn a lot away due to their licensing laws and maximum capacity, so they'd started opening during the day, to attract a different type of clubber, to give everyone more hours to dance during their hedonistic holiday.

Paul finished with, "Clever, huh?"

"Something. It's definitely something." Mum squeezed his cheek. "You know what? I think I fancy a bit of a dance. How about you two?"

Paul had been dancing on the coffee table while talking to Mum, and my foot was tapping in time to the music. I could no longer resist it.

We all made our way to the dance floor, holding hands, Paul at the front, Mum in the middle and me at the back, nodding in time with the music. We found a comfortable bit of the dance floor with plenty of room, and got stuck in.

Paul kept checking if Mum was OK, asking if she wanted more water and if she felt light-headed or sick. She shook her head and continued dancing. He turned to me, asked if I was coming up yet, and I told him to calm down and just enjoy the moment. He flicked his eyes to Mum and nodded, in an obvious sign he was worried about her.

I mouthed to him, *she'll be fine*, and on we danced.

After a long, sweeping, up-tempo 130 beats to the minute Euro-trance song still showed no sign of ending, Mum shouted into my ear, "Does it, you know, have a chorus? Or is this it?" She waved her hands in the air like the whole club had been doing a few minutes earlier to the crescendo.

"This is it, I'm afraid. You not feeling it?"

She shrugged, her hair nodding in time with the music. "Dunno what I'm meant to feel. Dunno what I'm looking out for. I keep waiting for this big rush to hit me like a train. That's how you described it, innit?"

It had been, exactly that. "Stop worrying about feeling it, waiting for it to happen, and just get on with your night. That's the best way. You'll know when you know."

"I'm gonna sit and have a fag. Coming with me?"

"I'm staying. I like this one. It's nice to be able to dance, not worrying about other people. Having a night off. You gonna be OK?"

Nodding, she kissed my cheek, shook her cigarette packet, then said, "And now you're worrying about your old Ma, eh?"

"It's..."

But she was gone, swallowed by the throbbing crowd.

Paul danced opposite me, his trademark wide grin plastered across his face, his big twinkly eyes open, smiling back at me. Not everyone can do that, smile with their eyes, but Paul could. Oh yes.

He blew me a kiss even though he was only feet away and I caught it. Pulling me towards him, he pressed his hard body against mine, and I felt how turned on he was, which, considering he'd dropped a while ago, was pretty impressive.

I continued dancing, letting myself lean into the moment, the physical pleasure of the music, the heat, the love. I shouted into Paul's ear, "Hope she's all right."

Paul held a hand up to indicate he'd be back shortly, then danced towards where we'd left Mum.

I continued dancing, closing my eyes and getting lost in the music.

Shortly afterwards, he returned. "Dancing away. Fine. She's brought you up and lived with your dad for twenty-odd years, she'll be fine. Besides, I'll nip back in a bit to check on her."

I nodded.

"Wicked." And then he reached into his pocket, pulled out a pill and, with one movement, swigged from his water bottle and swallowed the pill, all with his other hand dancing in time with the music.

"What the fuck you doing?"

"I'm feeling the music. Come on, live a little. Relax." He tried to grab my wrist.

166

I pulled away, shaking my head. "We said. We said we'd take it easy. Someone's gotta be together enough in case anything's wrong with Mum. That's what we said."

"Relax. She's having a great time. I've just seen. Want one? I've got more."

"But...but..."

"I'd given it a good half an hour and wasn't feeling anything. Reckon these must be duds. Won't go back to that guy again."

"Same guy we always go to. Same as always." I took a deep breath, a swig of water from my bottle and reached out to steady myself on my legs as I was just coming up. I was at the start of the crescendo of the pill; the moment when everything in life was as it should be, every molecule in the world was exactly where it should be and doing exactly what it was always meant to do, giving me the deep feeling of contentment and happiness. It was an all-encompassing happiness that wrapped me up like a blanket, making me want to move every muscle in my body simultaneously in time with the music.

The having-to-move urge is so strong I have seen people dancing in McDonald's when they'd dropped too early before their night out. They'd be surrounded by their friends quietly munching Big Macs and cheeseburgers while they're throwing shapes after the leg-shaking and hand-moving have become too much for them to sit still.

I held Paul's shoulders, took a deep breath to compose myself, said to him, looking straight in his eyes, "Well, I'm absolutely fucked. Don't know what's wrong with yours. No more drugs for me at the moment."

He smiled, lifting his hands above his head, shrugging off my hands, closing his eyes in that unmistakeable display of pleasure he was feeling. "Maybe me too. Good, isn't it?"

"So why another one?" I furrowed my brow, which, given I was coming up on the best pill I'd had for the last few months, was a huge achievement.

"If one's good, then two's better." He shrugged. "It was there. I didn't want to wait."

And with that, my argument disappeared. My argument and my boyfriend, who turned, dancing, walking deeper into the crowd of sweating, dancing bodies, whistles round their necks, glow sticks in their hands, heads shaking, arms waving, legs twitching, they both disappeared.

I realise now, that was the day I lost Paul, but at the time I didn't know the significance of what he'd done.

I left Paul to find Mum. Shortly afterwards, he returned and suggested we all dance near Mum.

She was in the house music room, dancing on a table, hanging from an air-duct pipe above her head. "All right?" she shouted as she saw me.

"Working, is it?"

"Fucking 'ell, love, if we'd had this in the seventies I'd have never come down off it. I feel so happy." She massaged her head with both hands while continuing to dance on the table.

"What about the music?"

"What about it? This is all I'm gonna listen to now. Dad'll go fucking mental." She hadn't thought she'd like the music, preferring instead more acoustic songs with lyrics she could hum along to, with a normal verse-chorus structure.

After dancing for a while, we sat in the chill-out room smoking cigarettes and drinking tea from the bar—very popular with many of the patrons. We found Paul getting right involved in the trance room, stood by the DJ booth chatting to the queue of others waiting to put in a request. Then all three of us danced in the trance room, arms round each other's shoulders, leaning in for a group kiss, eyes closed in time to the music. Mum and I left Paul there and went to the outdoor room and danced under the stars, not a cloud in the sky, staring upwards as we danced and felt the music.

Mum turned to me and said, "It's like religious or something, this, innit?"

"Having a good time?"

"Fucking right."

Later, as we stood by the bar getting another bottle of water each, Mum asked where Paul was as we'd not seen him in a while.

I checked and it had been an hour. Since the time when he'd gone missing, I'd changed my tack when he did a disappearing act in the clubs. We'd had a long and very emotional discussion where I'd explained I was worried he was cheating on me, and he'd said, promised on his life, and his mother's—I found that less convincing than his life—he wasn't cheating. He just wanted to float about on his own as well as sticking with me. He explained he would always come back to me at the end of the night, that he'd never leave me as long as the last time, and it would only ever be me he went home with at the end of the night.

Despite my asking why he wanted this, why the change, why now we were away from home, he hadn't quite been able to explain apart from a vague "I want to float around, but I'll always come back to you." Which, for wont of any better explanation, and satisfied he wasn't cheating on me, I had accepted. I felt somehow more at ease with the whole situation, knowing I didn't have to run around the club frantically searching for him if he wandered off, that he would inevitably find me and all would be well.

As I started to explain this to Mum, he appeared at my side, put his arm round me and squeezed my bum, grinning widely.

He kissed me, then whispered into my ear, "I want you so much right now. How thin do you think the walls are in our place?" He placed my hand on his groin.

Mum turned her back to us and carried on dancing as if her life depended on it. In all fairness, at that point she probably did feel that was the case.

I kissed him back, slow, tongues, mouths open. "Shall we go?"

He nodded to Mum, who was back on a coffee table throwing shapes, blowing a whistle and waving a green glow stick. "Maybe let's leave it till she's come down a bit. Imagine her in our living room." He laughed.

I giggled. "Where did you disappear to?"

"Bit of a wander around. Checking out the other dance floors. Seeing if there's anyone I know in tonight."

"And?"

"Nice wander. This is the best room. Nope. Sorted."

Sorted.

We joined Mum and all was well. Paul's double-dropping at the start of the evening was forgotten; nothing happened to Mum that night. Contrary to what the media would have you believe, the world didn't come to an end; she didn't become a junkie or suddenly move on to crack cocaine. She continued with her life, with her holiday in Ibiza with us. OK, so the next morning she was a bit weepy, complaining how Dad wasn't there, and how she missed her mum—who'd been dead ten years—and how she'd never been as close as she'd have liked with her mum, or her dad now she thought about it. But really, honestly, that was all standard comedown operating procedure. Nothing that some sleep, a decent brunch of Spanish omelette in the sun and a walk along the beach didn't cure.

At the end of her ten days with us, Mum looked round our apartment one last time and said, "Looks like you got it all sorted here. I'm so happy for you both." She touched the handle of her wheelie suitcase. "If I was twenty years younger, or if we'd got the money twenty years ago, I think I'd have joined you. No chance your dad's gonna leave London, though. Still, plenty of holidays out here with you two, eh?"

A beep outside signalled her taxi had arrived.

"Right, that's me. It is all right I come here every now and again, isn't it? Break from the rain and your dad. See you both, bit of sun and whatever else?"

I picked up her large suitcase. "It's our home. You can visit any time you want. No invite needed. All right?"

She nodded, wiping her face with the back of her hand. "What am I like? I blame you, pouring those naughty disco biscuits down my throat. I'm all at sixes and sevens."

The taxi beeped again.

"Come 'ere." She hugged me, then Paul. "You, look after each other, all right?"

***

We had a few weeks without guests until Slinky Simon and his mate Rob arrived 'on business stroke pleasure' to check how we were doing with the clubs where he'd arranged our tryouts.

When we met them at the airport, all baggy neon T-shirts and cutoff jeans for shorts, Paul reminded him it was only Amnesia he'd set us up with. "Or did you forget?"

"Boom! Boom!" Slinky Simon hugged Paul and me.

Rob stood back, playing with the handle on the sports bag slung over his shoulder. "All right?" He winked.

Paul said, "Sure you don't want to stay at ours? Plenty of room. Well, there's room, I'm not sure about plenty of it."

Slinky Simon strode off towards the exit. "Hotel's only round the corner from you. I think we'll leave you two, renowned DJ couple of Ibiza, to yourselves."

That was the first time I'd heard someone say it out loud to me. I sort of knew we were well-known, since we were getting top billing on the club promotion and regularly pulling in crowds of ten to fifteen thousand to our nights, but somehow when he said it, it made it real, more real than turning up night after night, playing song after song, as we'd done. It didn't feel that amazing because experiencing it day to day, as we were, it didn't seem much. It had happened gradually—bigger room, bigger crowd, additional nights to appear—until now, we were working four or five nights a week.

I shrugged it off when Rob asked if we were moving to one of the white two-storey haciendas on the outskirts of town.

***

Slinky Simon had invited us to meet with the father of the island, a sort of British ex-pat friendly uncle known as Jessie, no surname, who knew everything about the British who made Ibiza their home.

If he's such a father of the island, how come I've not yet met him? was the first thing that sprang to mind when Simon suggested it, but now, sitting opposite him at a restaurant in Ibiza Town, I smiled and politely ate my food. Paul had said we must take the meeting; if we'd been summonsed, we must come to it to see Jessie in person.

Whatever, was what I thought, but I hadn't told Paul that.

Jessie was a large, round, short man with a bald head and ginger beard. He wore a short-sleeved shirt and tie, with tailored grey trousers. Both, in my opinion, fashion disasters.

"I'm sorry it's taken so long for me to meet you both face-to-face. I've had people looking out for you—they've been combing the island. I like to meet all the British people who choose to move here—make them welcome, see if there's anything else they need. Be kind, like." He smiled broadly, revealing a mouthful of large, yellowing, wonky teeth.

I had never wanted to be somewhere else more than in that moment. Probably.

I was about to point out we were fine, now we'd lived there for nearly a year, and his offer of anything else we needed was about as useful as trying to find a virgin in Ibiza Town on a Saturday night, but I didn't think it was best. Slinky Simon's warning about Jessie rang in my ears: something about him pulling the strings of the island and having his finger on the pulse and not saying no to Jessie. Some load of old crap, anyway.

Slinky Simon said, "As you know, I'm here to see how these two are doing and if there's any other areas of business we can work on together."

Jessie picked up a flyer Slinky Simon had been showing him, turning it over in his fat fingers that reminded me of raw sausages.

The two of them talked about how we'd been taking over the island and how Jessie couldn't turn up to a club without seeing us on the list of DJs. It was all very flattering, but I knew very much a load of old flannel.

Paul lapped it up, hanging on Jessie's every word, asking if there were any other club nights he could get us into.

We'd finished our lunch and the waiter cleared the plates. A silence fell over the restaurant.

I checked the time and, contrary to what I believed, the last two hours had actually been twenty minutes.

Jessie said, "I do have an opening in one of the clubs on the other side of the island. I wondered if you'd be interested."

Slinky Simon banged his hand on the table. "We'll do it."

Paul agreed; another bang on the table.

"Hang on," I said, looking around at everyone. "We don't even know what it is yet. And Simon, as much as I love you, you're not part of us." I pointed to myself and Paul. "You don't live here, so unless you're going to move out, it's us two who are going to be doing all the work." I turned to Paul. "Am I right?"

Jessie explained he was taking over a club in Ibiza Town, one of the venues the British package-holiday companies for the under-thirties used on their bar crawl, so it was always busy, always profitable, and always full of people wanting to party.

I knew exactly the sort of party people he meant. Kids flying over for their week of sun, sand, sex and shitloads of everything else, finishing the night upended in the gutter outside a club, passed out on the beach, red like a lobster when they flew home. Exactly the sort of clubbers we tried to avoid by playing the bigger clubs with the higher door prices. It wasn't because we were snobs; it was just the way the island divided. We'd chosen to live and work on the other end of the island, for better or worse. And let's be honest here: I, too, had been that person flying from the UK for my week in the sun and going more than a little bit mad. Who hadn't? Twenty-somethings like us were discovering cheap sun in Ibiza in their droves every summer.

I had zoned out for a while but looked over and realised Jessie's lips were still moving: "I'm looking for someone to serve up for me. At this club. Last owner had it closed down. Police were worried about underage drinkers, and when they came to look around, they found all sorts. We'd need to be a bit more subtle, do you know what I mean? Bar staff walking around squirting foamy drink into punters' mouths, and it wasn't just piña colada. You know what I mean?"

I didn't quite know what he meant. As I'd reached my boredom threshold with this man and the entire lunch, and I had a square of beach, a paperback and not much else all afternoon with my name on it, I said, "What *do* you mean? Sure it's not just me who's thinking it." Then I added, "Sorry," for effect. I wasn't remotely sorry.

"They'd laced the drink with MDMA powder and sprayed it into punters' mouths, walking around the club. Blatantly."

Paul shrugged and sniggered. "Yeah, that is rather blatant, isn't it?"

"As I said, they were closed down. And now I'm taking over. It's all still there, just needs someone to run it. How do you guys fancy managing it for me?"

Slinky Simon said, "Hang on, I thought you said something about serving up. What was that about?"

"I'm trying to look at it in the round. In the widest sense. Obviously, I'll need someone to serve up, but I'll need someone to manage it first. A manager." He looked at me and Paul.

And then, slowly, quietly, aware that I'd been told by Slinky Simon and Paul that you didn't say no to Jessie, I said, "I think we're gonna have to say no, I'm afraid." I looked for the waiter. "Busy, see. In fact, I've got to go. I have to get back for a beach thing I have planned."

Paul kicked me under the table. "He's joking."

"I'm not. It's with the woman. The woman I said I'd help. She fell asleep and woke not knowing where she was, and she was in this house with these seven little men. Each of them was doing something different to her. Anyway, she's escaped now."

Rob, who until this point had said nothing but at my blatant bullshit obviously couldn't resist saying something, jumped in with, "Did she blow the house down? Or was she asking your help to get away from a wolf who was trying to blow her house down?"

"Yes, that's it. She was homeless. Her house was swept away in the storm. She needed somewhere to stay and I said I'd help her, and I'm meant to be meeting her now." I stood, sensing my lie was well beyond its best-before date, especially since there hadn't been any storms for months and months.

Paul threw some money on the table as he stood and apologised for having to leave suddenly.

Jessie folded his arms. "Best go and sort out Snow White or Little Red Riding Hood or whatever this damsel in distress is called." He waved dismissively for us to leave.

Paul grabbed my hand, waved quick goodbyes to everyone at the table and we left. Once outside, he said, "What the fuck are you doing? That was an offer we couldn't refuse. That was the person not to refuse. Slinky Simon told us before. And what do you do? You fucking well refuse him. Why?"

"He was dodgy as fuck. He's icky. I don't like hanging around icky men. Did you see how he looked at me when he realised I was sitting next to him?"

"Like a man sitting next to him for lunch?"

"Like a hungry dog looks at its breakfast. And he kept touching my arm, commenting on which things to order. Not to mention he stuck his fingers in my flies and had a good root around."

"He did not."

"OK, so I made up the last part, but the rest is true. He also rested his hand on my thigh until I removed it. I got a feeling from him. He gave off a feeling, and I'm not talking about his body odour that was making the plants wilt, or his bad breath that made my eyelashes curl. I'm talking about a feeling, a sense."

"Managing the club could be good for us. Give me a chance at the event-planning stuff. I liked that. I was enjoying it, but now they only want me as the DJ, nothing to do with the decorations and stuff. I miss it. I wish we could go back to the parties in fields off the M25, don't you?" Paul stuck out his bottom lip.

"In some ways, yes, in others, no. I wouldn't swap a damp December in a field in Bucks for a pink sunset over the sea here. No way. And that's why I said no to him. Well, why I walked out with my fairy-story lie. He's dodgy. It's one thing asking us to manage the club, but sorting out drug dealers, all that? Does he think we came down with the last bloody shower?"

"You knew what he meant—serve up?" Paul took my hand.

"'Course I did. Have you met my mum?" I blinked.

"Then why the big show, the innocence, the problem with it?"

"I don't want to lose all this." I gestured to the white buildings, the beach, the deep-blue sea, the light-blue sky. "Why would I risk all this, risk ending up in some Spanish prison for serving up for some weird man?"

"Does this mean you're going to stop dropping yourself, now you've come over all legal and puritanical?"

"I wouldn't go that far. There's a big difference between a bit of recreational use and dealing, or managing people who deal. And as far as I know, the law sees dealing or being involved with people who deal as pretty much the same. Intent to supply, dealing, all that."

"Wicked." He took my hand and we walked towards the beach.

"Where we going?" I asked.

"You said you had a beach meeting with a woman. Poor Snow White, sounds like she's fucked without you."

"She so is. She's fucked without me. Totally fucked."

As we reached the beach, we took off our shoes and walked towards the water. The sand between our toes, we sat a few yards from the sea.

Paul took off his Global Hypercolour T-shirt, darker colours at the armpits, and stepped out of his white shorts, revealing his boxers. "What?" He stood with his hands on his hips, and it was all I could do to stop myself jumping his bones there and then.

"Nothing. Well, it is something."

He sat cross-legged in front of me. "What? I am all ears." He bent his ears towards me.

"Do you think we're maybe doing a bit too much partying? And maybe we should ease off a bit? Just a little bit?"

"I don't know if you're a bad influence on me, or I'm a bad influence on you," he said.

"Neither do I. That's why I'm asking."

"Maybe. But nothing to worry about. Not as much as how we're going to sort out the Jessie mess we've left back there. He's important. He can uninvite us to clubs. He has connections. He is the father of the island."

"Yeah, and doesn't he ever stop telling us?" I'd been thinking about something for a while and decided now was a good time to mention it. "Why did we stop our date nights when we moved out here?"

"Dunno. Do you miss them?"

"I used to love them. Highlight of the week. Just us two."

"It's more freestyle now. Plus we don't have those crappy jobs where we need something midweek to make us feel better." He laughed.

"I thought it was more than that. Besides, I didn't think our jobs were that crappy. Let's bring date night back, shall we?"

"Whatever you want," Paul replied and kissed me.

CHAPTER 14

A WHILE LATER, WE'D all gone out with Slinky Simon and Rob, who'd apparently spent the intervening few days "Clearing up the fucking mess you left with Jessie," Slinky Simon said.

Despite the music being just the right mix of uplifting and repetitive beat dance, and the fact I was flying on my one pill of the evening—I didn't want to overdo things and had told Paul one each tonight would be enough—my sense of not wanting to be there overtook all the other feelings swirling round my stomach and brain.

I turned to Slinky Simon, stroked his sweaty cheek and said, "Have fun, I'm done. We're going home. See you later. You can let yourselves in, can't you?"

"It's early. It's not even two. What you going for? Look, if it's about Jessie, I'm sorry. I didn't mean to go on about it. I was just saying, that's what we'd been doing, sorting stuff out for you. That's all." He grabbed my arm.

"It's nothing. Don't worry. I'm done. It's fine."

He leant forward, hugged me, kissed my cheek and told me he loved me and didn't want to end things on a bad note.

Even in my somewhat mind-altered state, I thought this was a bit over the top, but judging by his quickly chewing mouth and wide black pupils, he was much further gone than either me or Paul, so I agreed with him, kissed his cheek and said I'd see him later.

Paul and I walked the short distance back to our flat, surrounded by crowds of scantily clad people dancing, drinking from bottles, some leaning forward and throwing up in the street, pausing behind rubbish bins to relieve themselves, not showing an ounce of worry about anyone seeing them. This, I would not miss when I left Ibiza. This, I wouldn't hanker after when the crowds left for the summer and the island returned to its usual sleepy Spanish chilled-out self for people who called it home and not just a fairground ride for a few weeks of summer.

Paul was making us a cup of tea while I rolled us a cigarette each and the CD of chill-out tracks filled the living room—our usual coming-down routine—when the phone rang.

At nearly three in the morning, who the hell would be ringing us?

I let it ring and busied myself with the rolling of the cigarette paper, and the inserting of the filter tips, and the licking of the paper to finish the job, but the phone didn't stop.

Paul shouted, "Can you get it, please? It's doing my head in."

I stepped across the room, mumbling to myself something about so much for the love drug, and picked up the phone. "Mum, if this is you, I hope someone's dead," I said with a smile to myself.

Rob's voice filled my ear, babbling quickly, repeating himself, saying something about the hospital, and the ambulance, and just after we'd left it had all gone wrong.

"Where are you?"

"At the hospital, the nearest one. Can't pronounce how to say it. Can you come? It's Simon. It's not looking good."

"On our way." I put the phone down.

Paul stood next to me, holding two mugs of steaming tea. "What's up?"

"You all right to drive or shall we taxi it?"

"Where we going?"

"Hospital. It's Simon." By Rob using Simon's real name, omitting the Slinky part, I knew this was serious. No one ever called him just Simon, it was always Slinky Simon—a nickname given to him years before any of us had met him, relating to how much of a wheeler-dealer he was, always slinking between groups

180

of people, trying to cook up the next deal, sort out the next party. Now, in the hospital, if Rob's blurted message was anything to go by, he was anything but slinky.

In the car, I told Paul what I knew from Rob's call. "Twenty minutes after we left, Simon asked Rob to sit down cos he felt faint, his legs were wobbly. Then Simon started shaking, threw up all over himself and went into a foetal ball with his eyes rolled into the back of his head. Rob called the security staff, who got an ambulance, and now he's in hospital."

"Shit," Paul said. As we walked into the A&E, he asked, "Is he still conscious?"

"Rob didn't say he was, but he didn't said he wasn't." At the reception desk, in my best schoolboy, picked up in little pieces Spanish, I asked if I could see my friend Simon Stephens.

Paul furrowed his brow. "Stephens?"

I shrugged.

The receptionist told me in very quick Spanish something about family and no visitors, then pointed to the rows of chairs behind us.

I tried to explain we were expected and we needed to see the friend he was with; my friend had no family with him on the island.

She shook her head, pointed to the seats again and turned back to her computer screen.

Defeated, my stomach churning and Rob's words echoing in my mind, I joined the rest of the average-night-in-a-hospital flotsam and jetsam on the chairs.

Paul sat next to me. "What now? Can't you at least tell Rob we're here? He must be going mad."

"I tried. She's having none of it. Feel free to try yourself." I wiped my sweaty hands on my shorts and clutched my stomach, willing everything to be all right.

Paul left, walking quickly past the reception desk through the double doors where nurses had been taking patients from the chairs since we'd arrived.

Alone in my thoughts, I remembered Mum's drug horror stories from the seventies. There had been something about orange juice and acid, I struggled to recall. And something about just leaving it, and another something about usually people came back, found themselves again, and it was someone's way of giving them a little warning shot across the bow. *Yes, that's what this is, surely. Slinky Simon's prone to overdoing it every now and again, isn't he? This'll show him. He'll leave here and have an amusing story to tell everyone when he gets back home to the UK. Stupid fucking idiot Slinky Simon, with his big grin and his bottomless appetite for more and more of everything.* A hand on my arm brought me from my spiralling thoughts.

Paul was with Rob, both staring at me, neutral facial expressions; not a smile, not a frown, but exactly in the middle.

Rob gestured. "Follow us."

"What about…" I flicked my gaze to the receptionist, who was staring deeply into the computer screen, tapping loudly on the keyboard with her clackety nails.

Rob grabbed my hand and led us through the double doors into a room filled with curtained cubicles. He pulled back one of the curtains, pulled us through and closed it behind us.

Slinky Simon lay, head raised, in the bed, his eyes closed, an oxygen mask on his face and a stand of clear liquid with a tube going into his arm. A grey kidney-shaped bowl rested on his chest as the blue and white sheets rose and fell.

"He's breathing." I stared at Rob.

Rob squeezed Simon's hand. "'Course he's fucking breathing. That's why he's here." In a whisper, he continued, "Might not be if he wasn't here."

I asked what had happened, why he wasn't awake, what the doctors had said, and Rob tried to explain, saying he hadn't really followed what the staff had said as his Spanish was a bit rusty—

"Well, a bit non-existent to be honest." He laughed quietly.

"You're fucking laughing. He's almost dead and you're fucking laughing?" I grabbed Rob by the throat. "Is it you? Dodgy fucking pills, is it? I fucking told you. I said don't get 'em from the dodgy fuckers in the club. But would you listen? I said we'd had enough, but no, you went off and scored some more. What I had wasn't enough. You're one greedy fucker, you. Laughing. It's not some fucking joke. He could die."

Paul separated us, said it wasn't helping anyone and there was no point blame-storming at this stage; best we waited for the doctor, to hear what the prognosis was.

Rob, tidying up his stretched T-shirt and standing in the furthest corner of the cubicle, said, "Yeah, prognosis. That's what we want. Prognosis."

Willing my whole being not to jump across the bed and over Slinky Simon, I clenched my fists and asked, "Do you even know what a prognosis is?"

There was an enormous silence, the only noise Simon's breathing.

"I'm going to fucking kill you."

At that, a junior doctor not much older than we were, pulled back the curtain, stood next to the bed, looked at us three, then said, in slow English with a thick Spanish accent, "You are not his family, I think."

I explained he was over for a holiday business trip and his family were in the UK; we were his friends on the island, so could he tell us how bad it was, please?

"It helped when we knew what he'd taken. When your friend—" he looked at Rob "—told us he has taken ecstasy."

Rob crouched forward and made a shushing noise.

I rolled my eyes and said, "I think that ship's sailed." I turned back to make eye contact with the dishy doctor.

"He is very lucky, your friend. He fainted because he was not drinking enough water. He danced and danced and did not drink." He pointed to the clear bag of liquid on the stand. "This will help."

Rob said, "So it wasn't a dodgy one?"

"What does this mean?"

Rob mimed swallowing a pill.

"We do not know. We cannot know without more tests, which is cost for you. I have worked here since the start of summer and this—" he pointed to Simon in the bed "—is normal. Water will fix it."

Looking at the doctor with a frown, I said, "Will he be all right? Nothing permanent, no brain damage?"

He shook his head. "No. He can leave in a few hours when the fluids are in him."

"Why's he not talking?"

He explained they'd had to lightly sedate him so they could give him the fluids and settle his heart rate, which was very high when he'd arrived. He'd be awake soon.

"Thank you."

"The receptionist will settle your account." He left.

Rob, his head in his hands, said, "Fucking payment? What's that about, eh? How we meant to pay for it? I've not got any money. I'm out here on his credit card. I'm sponsored by Slinky Simon Air. All the time. Couldn't have come otherwise. It's all my fault. I should have never said to him to get more from that geezer in the club. You'd already sorted us out. I think Simon was a bit put out, as it goes, you two knowing more people here than he does. That's why he asked me to get some more. Should've said no."

I put my hand on his arm. "Calm down. It's easy to say that now. Hindsight, always with crystal clear vision. He'll have travel insurance, or a credit card, or both. Let's focus on what went right, not what went wrong. OK?"

We stood, silently, like three not-so-wise men around the bed of baby clubbing Jesus, staring at Simon as he gradually got his Slinky back.

**

Once Slinky Simon woke, they sorted out payment and I rang his girlfriend to say he was fine; she didn't need to fly out to see him, but he wanted me to tell her what had happened.

"Fuck! Is he dead?" she asked.

"No, he's alive. Talking to Rob now."

"I'll fucking kill him myself. No, actually, I'll kill Rob, then I'll kill Simon. I told him he'd do this one day. I said law of averages, he's gotta overdo it one night."

I said nothing.

"I'll get on the first flight tomorrow. Thanks for ringing. He's in so much trouble when I see him, fucking reprobate." She cried quietly down the phone. After a few moments, she said, "It'd be so much easier if I didn't love him. You know?"

"I do."

"Bye." She put the phone down.

As I caught everyone up on the girlfriend phone call, Rob and Paul tutted.

Slinky Simon listened, a small smile spreading on his face. "I suppose I deserve it, really. She loves me."

We left Rob and Simon talking about arrangements to meet the girlfriend the next day.

Paul and I drove home in silence, well into the next normal day of people going about their business—buying food, going to work—like ordinary people who didn't stay up all night. The madness and debauchery of last night well forgotten, I reached across the car and grabbed Paul's hand, squeezing it tight. "I love you."

"I love you too."

We drove in silence for a few roundabouts and sets of traffic lights. As we approached our building, I couldn't stop the thought leaving my body any longer. "I love you and I don't want to lose you."

"I know. And I love you too. I take care of myself. Plenty of water, no dodgy dealers."

"There are other ways I could lose you." I couldn't look him in the eyes as I knew I would crumble, end up in a pile of tears and snot. I stared straight ahead now we were parked just outside our building.

"I'll never cheat on you. I promise. I cross my heart and hope to die."

From the corners of my eyes, I saw he was crossing his heart. I wiped a tear with the back of my hand. "I don't want you to become another casualty of clubbing."

"You know I won't. I don't. It's nothing to worry about."

"There's other ways you could lose yourself." I swallowed hard, blinking my eyes quickly to stop the tears rolling down my cheeks.

He leant across the car, kissed my cheek and said, "I love you. That's all you need to know." He got out the car. "I might go for a walkabout to blow the cobwebs away because sometimes everything feels a bit close. But you know I'll always come back to you."

I nodded and trailed after him, wondering why he had to go away, why I made him feel like everything was 'a bit close', but he'd already told me he'd never had a long-term boyfriend before. The longest relationship he'd managed was three months and Paul had ended it because the other guy was too clingy, always in Paul's face.

Turning to me, he said, "Let's close the blinds, wrap up in the duvet and go to sleep."

I followed him to the apartment where we did just that, but I couldn't stop one thought floating around my head: whether it was already too late and I'd already lost Paul to clubbing.

***

I later found out that Slinky Simon's girlfriend stayed for three days. She bollocked him, saying if he ever did anything like that again she'd never forgive him and it would be over. She slapped Rob and told him he should have known better, I wasn't sure why. Slinky Simon tried to laugh it off, saying it was an occupational hazard of club promotion, but his girlfriend wasn't having any of it. A few days later, we waved the three of them off at the airport with promises they'd return later in the season, but it was highly unlikely.

A few nights later, as we were getting ready for a set at one of our clubs, I asked Paul if he could take it easy tonight, just for once. Maybe we could do something the next morning have a brunch picnic together on the beach.

"Might do. Why you asking?" His back was to me as he busied himself with something in our box of records and CDs.

"Don't disappear in the middle of the set, all right?"

He turned to face me, all sleeveless vest and big pocketed shorts. "Once. I did that once."

"Twice, actually—three times if you count when you were pulled out by that guy you said you knew but didn't and then came back half an hour later as you were coming up on a pill you'd dropped with him." Quietly now, I said, "Three times."

"I didn't realise you were my mum."

"I'm not your mum, not that she'd give a shit. I'm your boyfriend. I love you. I'm trying to say you need to take it easy or one of these nights the wheels are going to fall off."

"You look after your wheels and I'll look after mine. All right?" He turned away, his back to me again.

"We're a team. Me and you. The gay DJ couple of Ibiza. People ask for us to come. They know if we're there, it'll be a party. We *are* the party, they reckon. But I don't want to become the party at any expense. Why would we throw all this away by being stupid?"

"I'm not being stupid."

"We start getting shit reviews of our gigs, we'll soon be dropped by the clubs. Don't think they'll keep us on. This shit is fickle. Slinky Simon told me. You're only as good as your last gig. A few shit ones and we'll be out, back to London working in some shop. How's that sound?"

He turned to face me. "We came here to escape all that dull grind, didn't we? And look what we've made for ourselves. I can't believe you're talking about going back to that. That's the last thing I want. Don't you understand that?"

"That's why I want to protect it. Make sure we don't lose it from some stupid mistakes."

"I'm just enjoying myself—enjoying the euphoria, enjoying the lack of routine, living for the music. If we're playing it or dancing to it, it doesn't really matter, does it? We don't need the clubs, we could stay out here and work as waiters, whatever. It doesn't matter. Your auntie Luella made sure of that." He reached into the wooden box on the bedside table, pulled out a small, clear plastic bag of white pills, took out two, handed me one and necked one himself.

"We're not even there yet! It's not even eleven and you're dropping. How the fuck are you meant to play the set we planned if you're permanently fucking banjaxed?"

"Take a chill pill." He offered the remaining pill to me.

"Not yet. That's not the answer to everything, you know."

"Depends what the question is." He shrugged, his hands facing upwards either side of his body.

"What's that even meant to mean?"

"Nothing, everything. Something. I dunno. It'll be fine. They love us we can do no wrong. We've got the latest tunes to include, it'll all be fine."

"Yeah, cos I went to the only record shop on the island that sells this sort of music and made sure I bought them. And why did I go on my own?"

"Can't remember. You getting dressed?" He stared at me, looking me up and down.

"What's that got to do with what we're talking about? And don't you go bringing Luella's money into this. That was for me. To enjoy, to make good use of, not so we could lay around all day in the sun slowly spending it on partying."

"She'd have disapproved?"

"Not of the drugs. You know that. But the laying about, the not getting on, yeah, I reckon she would, as it goes." I put my hands on my hips, puffing up my chest, not quite believing I was having this same conversation with him.

"It won't come to that, trust me. It'll be fine. We've got the new tracks, we've got the crowds, we've got the promotion—I did some wicked flyers for tonight, did I show you? And I am the number one party-planning go-to guy on Ibiza." He smiled.

"Who said that?"

"People."

"Yeah, but who, though?"

"Jessie."

"I said I didn't want anything to do with him. He's a dodgy icky fucker, and I'm not having anything to do with him."

"You did say that, but I sort of bumped into him, and he asked me to help him with the promo and club decorations for the opening night of his new club—the one he talked to us about. He's paying me loads-a-money!"

"Is there anything I can say to stop you doing this?"

"You don't own me, Tom."

"I know that, Paul." I knew we were in trouble when we both started using each other's names in speech. "But we're a partnership, a couple. It's about compromise and checking in on each other for stuff like this. Isn't it?"

"I thought you'd be happy for me. You know how much I enjoy the party planning. This is my big chance, a launch of a new club under new management. Everyone's gonna be there. It's gonna get, like, ten thousand or more. It'll be like those orbital parties we used to go to, only much slicker. That's where I come in, see?"

"That's all he wants you to do? Nothing dodgy? Nothing about serving up or any of that shit?"

"I promise." He turned up the *getting ready to go out* music on the CD player, took my hand and we danced in the middle of the living room. He kissed me, pushing a pill into my mouth with his tongue like we sometimes did on the dance floor of crowded clubs to avoid the eagle eyes of bouncers.

I swallowed the water he handed me, wishing there was another set of eagle eyes looking at our relationship; someone who could help me look after Paul, ensure he didn't move any farther from his tether, any farther away from me than I feared he already had.

***

We played our set. Paul stayed with me in the DJ booth the whole time, but he did take another two pills. I joined him for half but refused any more, wanting to keep a clearish head for mixing and changing the records so I could watch the reaction of the club as I responded to their collective mood, manipulating them like a conductor does his orchestra; my tools were the records and music I chose.

We walked home. I walked slowly while thinking about how another night's work had gone; Paul ran around me like an excited puppy on a lead. He was chatting at twenty to the dozen about some guys and girls he'd met at the bar who were going to ring to meet up later for a beach party, and how Jessie had said if he did well for this club night launch, he wanted him to be in charge for all his club promo and interior dressing, and wasn't that great, wasn't that wonderful...

Because I was one and a half pills behind him, I trudged along listening to his chatter, watching his eyes as he ran around me. I knew half of what he was saying would never come to anything; it was just codshit clubbing banter. I wondered if what he was saying about Jessie was true too. I didn't want to piss on his fire as I knew how much this meant to him, and how he'd wanted something of his own rather than just another thing he'd latched on to me for, like the DJing had been. Not that anyone in Ibiza knew that's how it had started, but as Paul had said, *he knew, and he always would.*

PART 3

CHAPTER 15

Y<small>OU KNOW WHEN</small> you reach the final straw? The thing that makes your mind up: that's enough, you have to get out of this situation and can't put up with it any longer? Well, the first time I had one of those moments was the night of the fire.

A month or so later, we were having a rare night off. Since Paul's club launch had been a triumphant success and Jessie had done as he'd offered, Paul's club dressing had taken off. When we weren't DJing together, he was usually busy doing that, but that night, fancying a change, we'd gone to a large club in Ibiza Town, a taxi ride from our place: somewhere we could go out and not be recognised at every turn.

We were in one of the smaller rooms that radiated in a circle off the main dance floor, dancing to some happy house, waving our hands in the air and we definitely didn't care, when a bell rang accompanied by water spraying from the ceiling.

Having been to a fair few foam and outdoor parties, where this sort of thing was usual—except the bell, now I think about it—we carried on dancing.

Paul pulled me closer, kissed me, pushing himself into me as the water soaked my hair and body.

It was cool water, and many people jumped onto tables to get closer to it.

The bell continued ringing, and it occurred to me everything may not be quite as it was meant to be. Pulling Paul with me, I walked through the doors to the balcony above the main dance floor. The black smoke hit me as I opened it. Water sprayed from the ceiling in there too, and men in black suits were pushing

193

screaming people towards the exit. The side door opposite ours, which led to another small niche dance floor, had smoke billowing from the gap under the door.

Paul was dancing behind me. "Wicked."

I coughed, put my T-shirt up to my mouth. "No, not wicked. This place is on fucking fire. We need to go. Fucking now!" I grabbed Paul's hand and walked back into the small room we'd come from. It had emptied of people, the floor covered in water, beer bottles, plastic cups of discarded drinks and bits of clothing. But at least the air wasn't smoky in there.

I followed the trail of footprints to a small door in the opposite corner, which I'd not noticed before. We walked down three flights of stairs to some back part of the club and were deposited in an alley full of coughing, wet, dirty clubbers and large wheelie bins overflowing with rotting, sweet-smelling rubbish.

A bouncer pointed to the crowd of others and clicked something in his hand twice as we passed. He asked me in Spanish where we'd been and why hadn't we come out until then.

I explained about the balcony, and he shook his head. I asked what was happening, and he said there had been a fire in a toilet next to one of the smaller dance floors. I asked what had caused it; he mimed a cigarette and crossed his eyes.

I leant against the wall and turned to check Paul was OK. He was dancing to some unheard beat, a wide grin on his face as he talked to other wet, disorientated clubbers.

I pulled him nearer to me. "I don't want to be dramatic or anything, but we just nearly died."

"'S fine. Never been in a fire before. Shall we see if we can find the fire brigade? Wonder what they wear out here? Bet it's not the same as back home." He started to walk away, towards the flashing blue lights coming from round the front of the club.

I pulled him back. "Aren't you worried? We could have died and all you can think about is checking out if the firemen are cute."

He shrugged. "Why wouldn't we?"

"Do you take anything seriously anymore? Or is it all a joke to you?"

"Good job we weren't working tonight." He ran off towards the flashing lights.

Following him, I shouted his name and told him to wait for me.

Who is this person I'm running after? is what I would think to myself later in a quieter moment of reflection. *Why does he not take anything seriously? What will it take for him to realise life isn't all fun and debauchery and feeling the music and partying with strangers?*

At that point, I had no idea, and it took another few final straws before I reached the real proper, ultimate, final, final straw when I knew what I had to do to get him to pay attention to me. But then, as I ran after him in search of the hunky firemen, I was still pretty far away from that place.

The firemen turned out to be mostly middle-aged, dark-haired and nothing to write home about, except the last one who ran past us carrying a water-gun contraption. He was pretty easy on the eye, we both agreed on that. We stood watching them put out the fire, carrying people from the smoky building as flames filled the windows of the floor we'd been dancing on not half an hour before. Without anything else to say—I didn't know where to go, what to do, what I should say to Paul, the man I loved so much, but knew I was losing—we walked up a hill and sat under a tree to watch the sun rise over the town.

Paul turned to me as the sun came up. "Wicked, eh? The beauty. The sun. Nature. The redness. Everything, really."

And because I didn't know what else to say, because I couldn't deny that beauty in front of us but couldn't quite get my head around how he was ignoring all the chaos and ugliness and destruction and danger we'd seen earlier that evening, I simply said, "Shall we get a cab and go home?"

"That's a wicked idea—the best idea ever. I love you so much. I'm so happy with our life together." He kissed me.

The next day, I came home from the beach—Paul hadn't wanted to be in the sun—and found he'd made dinner and tidied up our very messy apartment.

"What's this in aid of?" I asked, surveying the clean room and smelling the chorizo and meat casserole with beans he'd made.

"Thought you'd be tired after an afternoon in the sun. I didn't have anything to do. Remembered how you liked this. We had all the stuff, anyway. Just sort of threw it in. That Spanish cookery book your mum got is…very handy."

We ate dinner with the balcony windows open, listening to the sea as the sun set, and I thought life could have been much worse; in fact, I thought how lucky I was.

As we finished eating, I stood to collect the crockery and Paul told me to leave it.

"Later. Let's snuggle," he said, leading me to the sofa where we watched one of my favourite films, me sitting in between his open legs and leaning back on his chest.

***

The next final straw happened when we were in the hotel room of some men and women we'd met in the club after we'd finished our set. We'd danced with them; we'd drunk with them; we'd taken more drugs with them. It was all going to be *wicked, sorted, brill, safe.*

We'd shared a cab with Matt? Mike? Melvin?—the leader of their pack—and had chatted about the UK and how wicked living in Ibiza must be, and he'd said he was going to move there too, that was definitely his plan. We'd ended up in their hotel, and there had been much talk of them coming back and staying at ours. We were going to visit them in Birmingham, Burnley, Blackpool, wherever it was they came from, next time we flew back. They were going to be our new friends.

As the sun came up, streaming into the window of their two-star hotel room, I looked round at the heaps of sleeping bodies on the floor, on the beds, people I'd talked myself hoarse with, sharing cigarettes and drugs and opinions about very important things, none of which I could remember now. And now they rested.

"Anyone fancy a tea or coffee?" I asked.

A few hands went in the air, and some people mumbled, "Yes."

With the enthusiasm of a condemned prisoner, I walked to the kitchen and started arranging mugs and things for the drinks, then was suddenly struck with a feeling of wanting to be anywhere else but there. Of realising everything with these people would inevitably come to nothing and wondering why I was wasting any more of my time on them, when essentially the party had been over a few hours ago and all we were doing now was eking out the final hours before the real world took over, with its light streaming through the blinds, once again.

I walked back to the kitchen, grabbed Paul's hand. "No sugar. I'll go to the shop."

"Yeah," came one lone voice from under a duvet on the sofa.

We ran downstairs, out onto the street, closing the door behind us, and I held my hand out for a taxi.

Paul pointed over my shoulder. "Shop's there. Where we going?"

"Home. Bed. I'm done."

We got in the taxi together and sat in silence, went to bed in silence, until, after four hours of sleep, we woke and I told him, "I just couldn't be there any longer. I don't need a whole new set of friends for a week, never to see them again."

Paul said nothing.

"I want to try and make more friends—friendships with people who do things other than partying all the time." I stared at him.

"But we don't know anyone like that," Paul replied.

"Exactly."

***

Despite denying it would ever happen, the day finally arrived. The day Marilyn and Roger, Paul's parents, flew to stay with us for a week. I knew intellectually that it was coming. I had it marked on the calendar in the kitchen for weeks and weeks, but even though, day by day, we crept closer to the actual day they would arrive, I still denied it, like those people who deny the holocaust or the moon landing happened.

I had been denying Saturday.

We met them at the airport, a bright sunny day in the low thirties; I wore a vest and shorts, and Paul wore a T-shirt and tailored shorts.

At first, I couldn't see them, only their trolley of seven Louise Vuitton dark-brown suitcases hiding Marilyn as she glided across the floor in her white cotton trouser suit, blue blouse and chunky gold necklace and earrings. Her eyes were obscured by square gold-framed Gucci sunglasses the size of small portable TV screens that covered most of her face.

I knew she was disapproving of me, my clothes, my hair—everything really. I felt it beaming at me from her eyes through the sunglasses. It was a shame they didn't diffuse her disapproval, I thought to myself as I briefly kissed her cheeks.

"Roger, I told you, get someone from the airport to do that. I don't understand why you insisted on pushing it yourself. It's so—" she waved her hands "—undignified, unnecessary, inappropriate, working-class." She turned to Paul, brought him close into a tight hug and whispered something in his ear.

Paul pulled back. "It will all be fine. Trust me. Ready to see Casa Tom and Paul?"

Marilyn flicked her stiff wavy blonde hair, threw her shoulders back, pointed her nose to the sky and said, "If you insist."

"I insist, Mother. I'm not having you staying in a hotel when this is where we live. It's just not right."

Roger leant on the luggage trolley and lit a large cigar, allowing the plume of smoke to fan over his head, his eyes shut while grinning subtly.

"Glad to be here, Father?"

"Glad not to be on that bloody plane. They say it's business class, but in those tiny planes, it's not much different from cattle class. Precious little extra elbow room. One lukewarm glass of not-champagne and a decidedly mediocre meal does not business class make."

Marilyn strode ahead. "Where do we get a driver? Where's the queue for those services?"

I kept well back, feeling my car keys in my pocket.

Paul leapt in with, "A taxi? No need. I said we'd drive you to ours." He pointed towards the car park sign. "Follow me."

She turned to face her son. "Yes, but I wasn't sure you really meant it, like the offer of us staying at your apartment. I thought you'd gone native, taken on some of the local customs somewhat too much. There really is no need to do any of this. We're perfectly capable of staying in a hotel."

We were approaching the car park ticket machine. Paul fiddled with the ticket and some change. "You came here to see us, didn't you?"

She nodded, looking either side at the other people waiting to pay for parking.

"Then you'll stay with us, travel with us, holiday with us." Paul held the ticket aloft and led us towards the car.

It was a bit of a squeeze with their luggage filling the boot and resting on Roger's and my laps in the back, while Marilyn clutched tightly her LV handbag on her lap and complained about how small the car was, and why couldn't we have bought something larger, and why were we still insisting on driving her ourselves?

I sat quietly in the back, squashed under too many suitcases while making small talk with Roger about the wonderful weather and how the flight had been.

Eventually, after three trips up and down the stairs, his parents sat in our living room while I made them drinks and Paul pointed out the open balcony to the sites: the beach, the town centre, one of the clubs we worked in.

Marilyn held on to the door frame of the spare room Paul had shown her would be theirs for the stay. She tutted and shook her head. "Is this really the best you could do housing-wise? I imagined you in a large villa with sweeping grounds, a gardener, little shaded spots, a pool round the back, a sun terrace. Shame."

Paul said, "Where were we living in this fantasy? A special part of Ibiza called your imagination?"

"Don't be rude. It's so unbecoming."

We ate a lunch of cold meats, cheeses, olives and bread with a bottle of local wine.

Roger asked how the party planning and the DJing were going. I explained we were too busy, we'd been turning work down, and with Paul's party work taking off since the successful launch night, he was even busier.

Marilyn wiped her mouth with a paper napkin. "No cotton ones, I see." She didn't wait for a response and ploughed on instead asking what Paul was actually doing at these party nights. "I've read your letters, and I do so look forward to them coming every month. Although I wouldn't mind them being a little more frequent. But we won't dwell on that, will we, Roger?"

Roger shook his head, stared at the plate and filled his mouth with a piece of ham.

"It was all so much more romantic, so much more glamorous in my imagination. I know you sent us some pictures, but I really wasn't convinced they were the actual place you were living in, was I, Roger?"

"She thought you'd played it down so we wouldn't get jealous of what you have, didn't you, Marilyn?"

She helped herself to another glass of wine. "I wouldn't quite go that far. I'm very happy in our place, and with the holiday homes in Biarritz and Monaco, I'm in no fear of you outdoing us, darling, but I would have thought, with Tom's money, you'd have been living...well, rather better."

There was a bang and then a child screaming from the flat above, followed by another bang and two voices shouting loudly in Spanish as footsteps thumped on our ceiling.

Since I'd been mentioned by name, and so had my money, I decided to break my *keep well out of it* rule and said, "It's set us up here. Without Luella's money, we'd still be in Catford."

"Yes, I heard about that little episode. Mercifully, I managed to avoid visiting in person since you were there so briefly, it seemed."

"Six months. We're being prudent. We're using it for things we need. Paul's promotion work needed some setup money, and now look how well he's doing. The flights, the deposit for this place. At first, when we didn't have much work, we used it to live, but now, we don't need it."

"The car," Paul added optimistically.

"Useful. Practical."

"Utilitarian and sparse is how I'd describe it." Marilyn turned to Paul. "And will we be able to see one of these so-called parties you put on?" She looked at me, her eyebrows raised. "And the DJing—is that what it's called? Will we hear some of that? Assuming it's something one hears, rather than sees."

"Of course you can." I cleared the plates and handed round bowls of fresh figs with goat's cheese and honey. "All from the market. All from the island."

Everyone ate in silence for a few moments until Paul said, "I could take you to the club during the day. Less crowded, you'll get to see the decorations and the stuff I do to make the party really memorable." He collected some flyers from our bedroom and handed them round the table. "I design them, work with the club, work out which sort of clubbers they're aiming it at."

Roger and Marilyn looked at the flyers with a combination of interest and bemusement.

Marilyn dropped the flyer on the table as if it were a bag of dog poo. "There are different types of clubber, are there?"

Paul took the flyer back. "Oh, yes. All the different types of music, various scenes, a variety of clothes, all sorts of other stuff, yeah." He opened the leaflet and showed her pictures.

"Foam party? Wearing swimming costumes? To a club? What on earth is that about?"

Paul explained how the warmth of the island suited water and foam parties, which, for many of the holidaymakers, was exactly why they'd come to Ibiza in the first place. "Among other things."

"Yes, my neighbour said it's all sand, see and sex here. Her daughter went on holiday with a group of friends and came back with the most terrible itching and a rash downstairs. She'd gone on a diet beforehand to squeeze into the bikini. Now I understand why that's so important if you're expected to go out in a bikini too. She was on some special diet to lose the weight and said she'd come back on the F-plan diet, whatever that means."

I suppressed a laugh.

Paul shot me a look that said *don't even think about telling her more about the seedier side of the island.*

Roger clapped his hands. "Sounds great. When do you want to take us? What do you have planned for today?"

"I thought you'd want to take it easy after the flight, have a walk along the beach, check out the town with us."

"And go to one of these clubs, see you in action." Marilyn glanced around the room, gently shaking her head in disapproval.

"You sure you want to go to the club at night when it's full of people? Sweaty, dancing, drinking, jumping-up-and-down people?"

"I'm sure I've got something I can wear that's suitable. You may not believe this to look at me now, but when I was younger, I was rather racy."

Roger nodded. "And me. We grew up in the seventies, and I don't remember much of it, If you know what I mean."

***

We took them around the town, to a supermarket, where I offered to buy them anything they had particular requests for, to which they responded they thought we'd be eating out mostly, so not to worry. We walked together along the longest beach on the island; Paul pointed to our apartment building a few hundred yards from the beach.

"Yes, I can see the appeal," Marilyn replied airily.

As we reached a bar, Paul said he had to go in to talk to a man about some business and he'd catch us up at our place on the beach.

I walked close to Paul, out of his parents' earshot, and said, "Please don't be long. It's like wading through treacle. Why's she such hard work?"

He hugged me. "She can't help it. She wants everything to be the best for me, for us, and anything that's not up to that standard she feels she has to comment on."

"Yeah, everything. Every fucking thing. Right down to our crockery being too plain and the bed in her room being a bit small and offering to talk to the landlord on our behalf."

"She's well-meaning." He waved. "Half an hour, tops." And he was gone, disappeared into the darkness of the club's interior.

Then there were three. I was on full-time parents-in-law entertaining duty. "Let's go to the beach, that's where we're meeting him. We have a special place we always go there. You'll love it." Keeping a positive note in my voice, I led them away from the bar.

***

We sat on the rocks under our tree, enjoying its dappled shade, the water a few yards away while people played volleyball and read or chatted all around us. A speedboat pulled waterskiers, and another boat pulled groups of tourists on a yellow inflatable banana skimming through the water. There was an *I Love Ibiza* air balloon floating across the sky, full of waving tourists.

I explained to Marilyn and Roger how much the island had to offer for holidaymakers, more than its reputation for clubbing and debauchery: the beautiful scenery; the shops full of local artists' paintings; the markets of local produce; the restaurants with authentic Spanish cuisine.

A man ran towards us from a group of people who were dancing to a portable CD player on the beach. He leant on the rock, took a few deep breaths and turned to face us with a smile, eyes like bin lids, pupils enormous, deep and black, his jaw clenching with chews. Facing the sand, he threw up, wiped his face with the back of his hand, then turned to face us again.

"Sorry. Coming up, like, really strong, you know." He walked back to his group while moving in time with the music.

Marilyn said, "What do you suppose is wrong with him?"

I stared at the group he'd returned too, all now waving their hands in the air and cheering to the music, and because there was no answer I could give, I said nothing.

We made small talk between bouts of awkward silence, each commenting on how long it would be until Paul returned, talking about the weather being warmer than the UK, how golden the sand was and how the sea was a particular shade of blue they'd not seen before.

Time ticked on. Very. Slowly.

After a while, Roger said, "Full of drugs, that's what I was told when I said my son and his partner had moved to Ibiza. That's the first thing everyone told me. Drugs—full of them. Drugs for breakfast, drugs for lunch and drugs for dinner, that's what it's like there. Judging by that little party, I don't think they were too far wrong."

Marilyn took in breath sharply. "Is that what it is? Is that what he meant, coming here and being sick all over the beach. What do you suppose it is? Heroin? Cracker? Marijuana? LSD? Or maybe it's one of those new drugs they're all taking at the acid-house parties—acid, I presume? I read something about it in the *Daily Mail*, but I lost the thread after a while, all these new terms."

I checked my watch. Paul was, undeniably, half an hour late. My shoulders tightened and raised themselves so they were near my ears.

Marilyn tapped my shoulder. "I say, Tom, are you listening to us? The drugs, it's terrible. Don't the police do anything about it? Spoiling it for people trying to get on with their days surrounded by cracker addicts and people out of it on smack or heroin. It's liberalism and progression all to blame. You mark my words. It wasn't like this in my day. No, there were some people who may have had a little bit of marijuana, and even then only for medicinal purposes, help you to sleep, that sort of thing, and everyone simply got on with their lives. Now there's designer drugs, manufactured drugs, it's like a Glaxo for illegal substances. I mean, honestly how did this happen? And, more importantly, why did you choose to live here, amongst this filth?" She gestured to the group of people dancing on the beach, hugging one another, laughing and kissing cheeks.

"Shall I see where Paul's got to?" I stood. "I'd better see. Won't be long."

"What about us? What are we to do? Alone, on this beach, near the smack and cracker addicts?" She pointed towards the group of dancing people.

"Honestly, I don't have time to explain to you how wrong you are about pretty much everything you said, but maybe tomorrow I will. Just for now, I'll leave you with this: smack is heroin, and it's crack, not cracker. None of those people are on anything remotely like those two. They're just enjoying a dance from an ecstasy tab. And alcohol and tobacco kill more people than drugs every year. You're more likely to die from a bee sting than an ecstasy tablet."

Marilyn opened her mouth, poised to respond, but I had gone.

I walked to barman in the bar where I'd left Paul and asked where he was.

The barman shrugged and pointed to the door with 'Management' written in Spanish across it.

Once inside the dark room, I was confronted with the last person I'd wanted to see: Jessie. I tried my best to charm him, to apologise for leaving so suddenly last time, and thanked him for the work he'd given Paul, and then asked where I could find him.

"He's gone. He's gone a long time." Jessie shrugged, reaching into a wooden box on the table to retrieve a cigarette and a small clear ziplock bag of white powder. "He has gone a long time to do me a little favour." He grinned and licked his lips. "You want some?"

Briefly, I thought *in for a penny in for a pound, might as well have some Dutch courage to go on the hunt for Paul*, then very quickly afterwards realised that was a terrible idea, especially given I was parents-sitting.

It wasn't that I'd not tried cocaine before; I had. It had its place, it was all right, when it was actually cocaine and not huge mountains of dextrose powder doing nothing of any note. The instant high—the chattiness, the feeling of being the king of the world and the most interesting person in the room and having to tell everyone how amazing you were—had been quite fun, in the right situations. But the comedown. Fuck me gently, the comedown.

Once, after a particularly bad coke binge when me and Paul had worked our way through two grams of the devil's dandruff—that's two of the little bags like Jessie held now—we'd stayed up for two days, at first at an afterparty with others, then back to our place alone, just chatting, drinking, smoking and sniffing. Each time you do a line, you think you're almost at the point of discovering the most interesting thing ever, uncovering an amazing thought you must share with everyone else, whether they'll listen or not. Inevitably, that's not the case, and you just do another line to stave off the comedown. That time, I had lain in our bed for twelve hours in the foetal position, crying in a fitful half-asleep, half-awake state, my whole body aching and crying out for just another bit of coke to make it all right. I realised how people become seriously psychologically addicted to coke, and since then I'd avoided it except in very small moderation if offered at a party, to be polite.

Instead, my drug of choice was and always had been ecstasy. Nothing could beat the floaty feeling, the strong impulse to dance, to make the world at peace—the way it made you feel, not as if you were the most interesting person in the room like coke did, but that you wanted to open up your innermost emotions to your friends and new friends for the night, because you experienced a deep intimacy and empathy with other humans. Those three things made ecstasy my drug of choice.

Now, I thought of Marilyn and Roger sitting under the tree on the beach. I thought of Paul being fuck knows where, leaving me alone. I thought of the conversations we'd had about him disappearing at the most inappropriate moments. I banged my fist on the table. "Fuck it, yeah. I'll bite."

Jessie cut out two long, fat lines of white powder on the dark wooden desk and handed me a rolled-up note.

I stood, blocking one nostril, put the note in the other and hoovered up half the line, swapped nostrils and finished the rest. The chemicals immediately hit my bloodstream through the inside of my nose. I felt my head swell and my heart race. *I am Tom, here me fucking roar.* "Giz a fag, will ya?"

"What did you say?" Jessie leant backwards, rubbing his nostrils after snorting his line.

"A fag. A ciggie. Can I have one?" I mimed a cigarette, while putting my feet up on the desk. I was Tom, I needed a ciggie, and I wasn't afraid to ask for one.

In fact, at that point I wasn't afraid of anything.

He threw me a cigarette and a lighter.

I lit it, inhaled deeply, the smoke filling my lungs like the chemicals that were filling my brain. This was good. This was a good situation. This was a fucking brilliant situation, and only I knew why. I started babbling about Jessie's clubs and what Paul was doing for him, and whether Paul had said where he was going.

Jessie listened for a few minutes then interrupted me. Puffing on his cigar, he told me where he'd sent Paul: "On a delivery errand."

"Nice." I nodded slowly. I was enjoying this. I could stay here all afternoon; sit in this small, dark room with this fat, icky man and sniff fat lines of his beautiful white powder as if my life depended on it. And it would be fucking amazing. *But why did I come here? Ah, yes. Paul. His parents, the beach, the tree. Yes, all that.* "Write it down."

"What you ask?" Jessie poured some more white powder onto the table.

"Where Paul has gone. The address, please."

"Tell you what, you write it down and I'll do us another one of these. Do you want another one of these?"

No, I said inside my head. But I nodded and said, "Yes," out loud.

CHAPTER 16

EMBOLDENED BY A few more lines of coke, I stormed out the bar into the bright light and heat; I'd forgotten what time of day it was. Drugs can do that to you, I've found. I checked the address on the piece of paper and strode off in what I thought was the right direction.

Eventually—after much asking of directions, going back on myself, swearing and calculating how long I'd left Paul's parents on the beach under the tree—I arrived at a white house with a blue door: number 73, matching the number on my bit of paper.

I knocked and waited.

A voice in Spanish spoke over the intercom, asking who it was. I told them my name and that I was looking for my boyfriend, Paul. My throat was dry, my jaw clenched, I heard my blood racing round my body, and my too-fast heart felt as if it was about to explode from my chest like some terrible over-the-top scene from a horror film.

The door buzzed and I let myself in, up two flights of narrow stairs into a room with a tiled floor, a white sofa on the far side and a large TV on the near wall. Paul sat on the sofa next to a man who looked like a slimmer and more attractive version of Jessie, surrounded by little bags of white powder and white pills.

"What's this?" I asked, staring at the two men and the drugs between them.

Paul laughed. "What's it look like, sweets?"

I grabbed him and led him to the far side of the room. "Don't you fucking sweets me! You said you'd be half an hour. It's been an hour and a half. You said you wouldn't get involved in any of this shit—just the party promo work, you said. And look at you. Caught with your pants round your ankles. Your parents are still on the beach under our tree and here you are, getting high with whoever this is—one of Jessie's henchmen, I assume."

"Sorry. It was meant to be a chat about the parties this week, and he said while I was there, could I drop something off for him? I should have come to tell you."

"Drop something off... You're not the fucking Royal Mail dropping off a Christmas present. It's drugs. Which are illegal. And if you get caught with that much on you, they'll put you in prison, none of this personal use shit. Intent to supply. Bang. Spanish prisons are meant to be lovely this time of the year. Do you know what they do to cute, posh, British boys?"

Paul stared at me, pursing his lips. His eyes darted to the man on the sofa, then back to mine.

"I don't know who you are anymore. You say you've not changed since we got here, but you have. This isn't you. You wanted to show your parents a good time, and look at what you're doing." I stared into his large, black pupils. "Been sampling the merchandise, have we?" I pointed to his face, my hand trembling.

Paul looked up and down my arm, then stared into my eyes deeply. "You know what they say, don't you? People in glass houses shouldn't throw stones. Looks like you've been having your own little party without me too."

Banged to rights. Realising this had seriously weakened my argument, I hung my head and looked away. "I didn't know what to do. He was there. It seemed like a good idea at the time. I needed something to keep me going while I looked for you. However, I was so fucking angry, I think I'd have managed to get here on pure, undiluted fury without any chemical enhancements."

He held my arms. "It's all right. No harm done. I'll tell these guys I can't do the delivery. We'll have some water, get our heads straight and walk back to meet my mother and father. We'll say we got caught up with some work—Father would approve of that. He has a strong work ethic. And we'll take Mother to a nice four-star seafood restaurant tonight—she'll forget about all this once she has a cocktail in her hands."

"Sometimes, and this is definitely one of those times, I don't know if I'm a bad influence on you or you're a bad influence on me." It was usually Paul who said that to me, but in this instance, I'd repeated it back to him. With hindsight, I realise this showed we were both in so much trouble.

A small cough sounded from the other side of the room, breaking the silence. Paul said he needed to sort something and he'd meet me outside by the door.

"Like you were going to meet me on the beach with your parents? You must think I'm fucking stupid."

"Promise. Cross my heart." He crossed his heart.

Because I had nowhere else to go and no more strength to argue at that point, I went along with his suggestion. Leaning against the wall outside, I lit a cigarette and thought about how this afternoon had suddenly began to resemble the plot of a Quentin Tarantino film rather than a Richard Curtis rom com as I'd originally hoped.

After a short while, Paul appeared at the door. "I didn't realise it was drugs when they first said deliver something. Then I worked it out. I dunno why I said I'd do it. Stupid."

"Very." I scoffed.

"Got carried away with Jessie. One minute we were chatting and he's telling me all the stuff he has lined up for us. Then casually he mentioned the delivery. The pick-up point. No big deal."

"You're either very naïve or very stupid, or both. And I bet he gave you some coke so it seemed like a good idea."

"Idiot. I thought if I did as he wanted, he'd get us a big break— even bigger clubs, more money, everything."

I was satisfied he was sorry, and although the execution was idiotic, I understood the intention behind it. *I don't want to lose him.*

We slowly walked back to the beach to meet his parents. On the journey, we worked out a story to explain what had happened involving a promotional emergency and an irate club owner worried about having an empty club tomorrow night.

Paul said, "I don't think you're a bad influence on me. And I hope I'm not one on you."

I shrugged. "Maybe. I worry I'm losing you. Losing you to all this. Every time you disappear, I worry you'll not come back again. You hear about it in the news—clubbers found drowned in the sea, dead in club toilets."

"That's not going to be me."

"It's not just that. I worry I'm losing myself, doing drugs during the day. I worry you're losing yourself too—the boy who wanted to impress his parents, show them how proud he was of his new life, and you disappear like this. That's not you. I worry we're both becoming untethered from ourselves. The longer we stay here, the more we're pulled into this world."

Paul said nothing for a few moments, then said, "This world we wanted for ourselves. This world we came out here to pursue. This world we used to love back home. This world was the only thing that kept us going from one weekend to the next. And now you think it's destroying us?"

"There is such a thing as too much of a good thing. Having to get up for work meant we kept ourselves in check, always tethered to reality. But out here, there's none of that. We can party and stay up as long as we want. And we sometimes do."

"What's wrong with that? We're young, we're enjoying ourselves. We've got the rest of our lives for serious commitments like mortgages, responsibilities—all that bread-head stuff. What else should we have used Luella's money for? It's what she would have wanted."

"Don't say that. You never met her. Don't just say that and think it makes it all right. That's a sneaky thing to say. It's not that, it's when *sometimes* turns into *often*, and soon it's *usually*, and that's only a hop, skip and a jump away from *always*. That's what I worry if we carry on together like this."

Paul shook his head. "You're overthinking things. I don't see the big deal. Even if you hadn't come to find me today, I'd have still come back to meet you on the beach—on our bit of the beach. Or I'd have gone back to the apartment. Eventually. You would have seen me again. Trust me. I just don't need to be tied down. Besides, I wouldn't have actually done the drugs delivery."

I raised my eyebrows. *Tied down?* "It's not just physically missing you, it's how it's changing us. How everything here's making us different people."

We were approaching the tree and Paul's parents.

Paul said, quietly now as we weren't far from where his parents were lying on sun loungers, "I don't understand what you mean. 'Course we're different here from back home. We're doing different jobs. We have different friends. Family is further away. It's inevitable."

"Is it inevitable you change so much you can't see the change because you don't recognise the person you used to be, and I don't recognise the person you—both of us are becoming?"

But Paul hadn't heard that. Or if he had, he'd chosen to ignore it because now he was hugging his parents, apologising for leaving them for two hours, and offering to take them to a beautiful seafood restaurant round the corner, and asking how they'd got the sun loungers and parasols and did they want an ice cream?

And so, in a bundle of hugs and money for ice cream and scrabbling to get more sun loungers, everything Paul and I had been talking about was put to one side. Again.

***

That evening, Marilyn, Roger and I sat on the terrace of the seafood restaurant that Paul had booked. It was only yards from the gently breaking waves.

I was making small talk with Marilyn and Roger about how wonderful the weather was and whether to go for the raw oysters or the cooked ones. After a pause, we all looked around to see if Paul had arrived yet.

Marilyn said, looking at her watch, "Where is that son of mine? To disappear once is unfortunate, but to do it twice in one day is definitely approaching carelessness." She pursed her lips. "Does he often do this?"

I shrugged, not wanting to say anything for fear of it all tumbling out. "The promo work is a fickle beast. It doesn't exactly keep office hours. When he's needed, he's needed."

"Quite."

Roger picked up his menu. "Shall we order, or give him another fifteen minutes?"

It was already twenty minutes past the time he'd said he'd *definitely, absolutely without fail* be with us. I shrugged from both the inevitability of it all and not wanting to make a big scene with his parents. It would spoil their holiday, their chance to see their son.

The waiter arrived, asked us if we were ready to order.

"Not quite," I replied tightly.

And so the evening rolled on, and on and on, without Paul, with just me and his parents.

It had all seemed so innocuous when we'd left our apartment together and Paul had said he needed to see a man about a club and he'd be twenty minutes, half an hour tops. After the performance he'd put on to make up for leaving them earlier, his parents had no reason to think otherwise. He'd been the very model son, telling them about his life on Ibiza with me: the DJing, the promoting, the friends he'd made, the beautiful sweeping long beaches, the sunsets and sunrises that he'd stopped photographing after a month because they just kept getting more and more beautiful, the Spanish food he loved so much he doubted he could eat at their favourite Spanish restaurant in Kensington again now he'd tried the real thing. They'd both laughed at that. They'd laughed a lot at what he'd said, while showing them the clubs we worked, the restaurants we ate at, the market we shopped in and the beach we flopped on.

It had all seemed like a long video for the Ibiza tourist board, and his parents had lapped it up, asking questions, turning to me, checking we really were this happy, did we really love it that much? I'd nodded, smiling, because mostly it was right. Except for one small matter he obviously failed to mention to his parents: his increasing appetite for party drugs and partying, to the exclusion of almost everything else—sleep, eating, work, friends and, it seemed, parents.

Now, I wished he'd bought one of those mobile phones that were starting to appear in some of the club managers' hands. Maybe that would have been a good use of dear Aunt Luella's money. At least I'd have known where he was, rather than him simply disappearing into the morass of Ibiza.

Marilyn folded her hands in her lap. "Is there no way of getting in touch with him? Roger has one of those mobile telephones. It's marvellous for tracking him down. Finding out where he is. Expensive to use, or so I gather, but worth it for peace of mind, I feel."

I shook my head, turned to the menu, blinked a tear from my eye. "Think we'd better go ahead without him or we're never going to eat." My stomach rumbled.

***

Later that evening, after a meal of elaborate tactfulness where none of us had mentioned Paul's absence and instead had stuck to topics bound to cause less controversy—the poor summer weather in the UK, the strong Catholicism of the island and its effect on how Paul and I were received—we returned to our apartment to find him asleep on the sofa. He was lying on his back, his arms folded across his chest like he'd been laid out for a funeral viewing.

My heart jumped, thinking he'd done what I'd often warned him about: overdone it to such an extent his heart had just given up and stopped beating. But then I heard his familiar loud, gruff snoring; I breathed normally again and shook him awake.

Hand on hip, I said, "Where have you been? Did you forget the meal you booked with your parents?" I crouched in front of him and whispered, "They're going the day after tomorrow and you've hardly seen them. Be fair. Make an effort, would you? I'm left entertaining them. Every. Bloody. Time."

He yawned and stretched, chewed on nothing in particular, rubbed his eyes, then said, "I think I sort of lost track. One thing and another. Came back here for a rest. To, you know—" he stared at me "—get my head straight. I must have nodded off."

Get my head straight meant one thing and only one thing. Yet again. "I'm going to bed." Clenching my jaw, I hissed into his ear, "I've had enough. I am so done with tonight."

"You handled it OK, didn't you? You're better at all that serious-parents thing. I fancied doing something else."

Unbelievable. Sometimes Paul's *free spirit, playing things by ear, not being tied down* nature was really bloody irritating. Still whispering, I said, "Something else other than being with your parents?"

"Yeah, and?"

There was no answer to that, and I didn't want to have a massive row in front of Marilyn and Roger. Instead, I walked to our bedroom, calling back to his parents, "Paul's going to make you drinks, anything you'd like, make up for lost time. You can fill him in on our dinner conversation. Night." And I was gone, behind our bedroom door, only able to hear muffled voices, the clatter of cups and swoosh of water as Paul filled the kettle and played the doting son once again.

When he eventually came to bed, he said, "I'm—"

"Don't say sorry. You say it like you're breathing in and out. It's meaningless. They're your parents and I was left with them. You can be so selfish sometimes."

He climbed into bed next to me. "I apologise. I was so tired when I came back here, I closed my eyes and then... I knew they'd be asking what my plans were, what we were going to do about staying out here. All that. Plans, commitment, being sure of the future—it gives me the creeps."

Does that include our future? Us together? Keeping my back to him as he spooned me from behind and kissed my neck, I said, "You make it really hard to like you sometimes."

But I still loved him. And I believed him. Which was why I forgave him. Again. Stupidly.

***

The final days of Marilyn and Roger's visit passed in a miasma of tactfulness, neither of them broaching the topic of his disappearance and me biting my tongue so hard and for so long I drew blood when we finally dropped them at the airport two days later.

As they walked towards the departures entrance, Paul turned to me. "That went well, don't you think?"

I swallowed the blood that had filled my mouth. "You are fucking joking, aren't you?"

"No. Why?"

"You were hardly there. You disappeared at least four times in one week. Not just half an hour, but whole, entire, sprawling afternoons and evenings with you AWOL and me left playing the enter-fucking-tainer with your bloody parents."

A horn beeped from behind the car.

"Best move on." He tapped the dashboard.

I clasped the steering wheel tightly, my knuckles white. "I wonder myself if I should move on, you know."

"What's that supposed to mean?" Paul frowned.

"You must think I've got mug written across my forehead."

The horn beeped again. Paul tapped the dashboard impatiently.

Swallowing the bitter bile that had risen up my throat into my mouth, I put the car into gear and nipped out into the flow of traffic outside the airport, narrowly missing an oncoming taxi.

Paul stamped the car's floor with an imaginary brake pedal. "Watch out. You nearly killed us!"

"That makes two of us." I stared straight ahead, concentrating on the traffic, trying to assemble the words carefully in my mind before releasing them.

Paul babbled on about how his parents wanted to return soon, and he'd told them we'd take them to the other side of the island to explore more of the scenery and culture, not just the restaurants and beaches, because there was much more to Ibiza than its reputation.

Finally, in a gap in his stream of consciousness, I said, "I think we should both take it easy for a bit on the old Persians." Persian rugs—drugs.

He was staring out the window. He waved his hand dismissively. "Definitely. Besides, it's the end of the season soon. Once we've got that big closing party over and done with, it's blissed-out Balearic until next May. Most of the clubs shut, or go down to one night a week. They've already said they won't want me in low season. The DJing will be the same. Slinky Simon said it's not like the UK where you can guarantee crap weather all year round. People come out here for the whole shebang—the weather, the beach, the dancing…and the Persians, obviously."

I wanted him to have his say, to complete his reasoning, because we had already talked about the low season and what to do then. "You abandoned your parents. You abandoned me. Not once, but four times in a week. Can't you see the problem here?"

"They'll be back. You're here still, aren't you?"

"Your reasoning of more always being better is wearing a bit thin. Partying is taking over from everything—from you, from your personality."

He patted his legs and smiled. "It's all me. I'm still here. Very much so."

"Can we just agree we'll take it easy for the next few weeks? Both of us. I can't remember the last time we had a drug-free week, can you?"

He shrugged. "Three weeks, six weeks, three months—what difference does it make? It's not heroin. It's not smack. It's not doing anyone any harm. Relax, will you? It's just a bit of fun. You wanted this lifestyle. That's why we moved out here, isn't it? Would you prefer to be back at the shops in cold, grey London, going out at the weekend to grab a little slice of fun between all the greyness?"

We'd arrived at our apartment. I turned off the engine, wondering if I could articulate how I felt, then thought *fuck it, I'm gonna give it a try.* I turned to face him. "Sometimes, yeah, I do."

"What? Wanna go back to that?"

"Yep. We were different then." I meant *he* was different but couldn't quite allow the words to leave my brain through my mouth. I wasn't sure why. Maybe if I said it out loud, it meant it was true, and the thought of me going out with a different Paul from the one I'd first fallen in love with was too much to cope with so I didn't quite let that out of Pandora's box.

"OK, we'll take it easy on the Persians. Shall we go up? Nice to have the place to ourselves again, eh?" He winked. And smiled. And squeezed my leg.

I was in so much trouble. I was helpless to resist those three most Paulest of Paul gestures. Because, deep down, I still loved him. He was wonderful. We were wonderful together...most of the time. My life, *our life*, on paper sounded perfect. And a flash of his beautiful, wide, toothy smile made me forget all my worries because my heart had overtaken once again; my love for him overruled my head's worries, my brain's logic.

We slammed the car doors, walked upstairs to our apartment, holding hands as we climbed the three flights, and we made love for the first time since his parents had arrived. Then we tidied the apartment together, made a big pot of coffee and sat on the sofa and listened to the beautiful sounds of the town floating up to us through the open balcony doors. Once again, I told myself all would be well; all would work itself out in the end. There was nothing to worry about, nothing to discuss in that *we have to talk, head angled to the side* way I'd tried in the car.

CHAPTER 17

September 1996

T HEN THERE WAS the straw that well and truly snapped the camel's back in half after it had been strained for so long.

Unsurprisingly, despite the little conversation we'd had in the car on the way back from the airport, Paul hadn't changed. Well, he had changed; difficult as it is to admit now, he actually became worse. He was partying longer and harder and disappearing more than he had before.

Despite me trying to talk to him about how I worried he was over-clubbing himself and disappearing into the scene, the drugs, the music and all that it entailed, Paul just waved it away like it was nothing. Kept telling me he'd be fine, that he had it under control; he wasn't taking anything except party powder and disco biscuits, and I should stop worrying.

I didn't know what to do, until The Straw happened, then I knew I had only one option.

We were headlining the end-of-season party at Space, and it was all going so well. We were the DJ pair in the main ten-thousand-strong dance floor, which, thanks to Paul's party and promotional skills, was at capacity and full of sweating, dancing, hand-waving clubbers all screaming for us to play the last song again: Paul Van Dyke's 'For An Angel'. This song, as Paul and I had predicted, turned out to be the song of that summer, and we'd already played it twice.

As I mixed and blended so the track could start again, before it had faded to the end too dramatically, I turned to Paul. He had one ear covered by headphones, was nodding in time to the music and grinning widely.

"All right?" I asked.

"Wicked!" He nodded.

As the track began from the start, the crowd jumped up and down, clapping above their heads and screaming.

Paul said, into the mic, "Who's ready to make this the closing party to end all closing parties? Who's here to have a wicked time?"

The crowd replied with a shout and more jumping and dancing.

A few hours later—after we'd finished our set, and the manager had thanked us and asked us to stick around for an afterparty, and we'd said we might but we'd definitely call round later that week to see what their plans were for the low season—we left the club.

Leaning against the wall in the warm evening air, I was ready to go home, but Paul had disappeared, promising to be back in five minutes.

I lit a cigarette, closed my eyes and allowed myself to just experience everything around me: the chatter and shouts of clubbers; the music, the traffic noise; the smell of late-night restaurants, the whiff of diesel fumes from taxis.

Maybe it isn't so bad. Maybe we'll get through this season in one piece and then things will calm down. Paul will return to the man I first met, to the man I fell in love with, and we'll go back to the less hectic lifestyle we had before we moved out here.

Right on cue, Paul arrived, arms around a woman and a man in swimming costumes, eyes wide, mouths chewing, glow sticks in both hands and said, "These guys know where the real party is moving to. We can tag along."

"I thought we were going home. Said you were tired, didn't you?" We'd deliberately not brought any of our own pills out with us, agreeing we'd do the closing party, stay to the end and then go home. Paul had stayed with me after our set, so I knew he hadn't scored while in the club. It had all been worked out.

"I was, but then I met these guys. Well, him—" he nodded to the man to his left "—in the gents' and he sorted me out. *Us* out. And now we're all set for the afterparty."

"Really?" I asked, thinking about our abandoned plan.

"Come on. It's the last night. We won't be doing this for another six months at least. You know you want to."

And then—with an inevitability and a flow all of its own, enhanced by the man and woman next to Paul and their mates, and their mates' mates who had gathered around us, all wanting to have our autograph—we piled into a few taxis and soon arrived at a white three-storey villa with a pool and a view of the beach on the edge of the town.

But that wasn't The Straw.

That was actually good fun. I was talking to our new mates, who asked me how we'd started the DJing, what had made us come to Ibiza, why I wanted to go back home for winter, what I thought would be the next wave of dance trance songs for the next season, which artists to look out for.

I asked them where they'd come from—"Little village in Lincolnshire, mate"—what they did for work—"I'm in sales, mate"—if they'd been to Ibiza before—"First time and it's well wicked, innit?"

We made all sorts of plans to see them when we came back to the UK, *if* we came back, because that hadn't quite been decided between me and Paul, and in a moment of ecstasy-induced madness, I said they could stay at ours next season if they came back.

"Definitely, totally, absolutely, I'll give you my number," I said with a smile. And at the time, I really meant it, like you do with everything you say when you're banjaxed on the love drug.

Then, like the two sensible people that we were, high as kites that had been dropped from an aircraft, we tried to have a reasoned, sensible discussion about what to do now the season had ended. Because of the state we were both in, it was a somewhat circular argument. I'd been long campaigning for us to return to the UK, see friends and family, have a bit of normality back in our lives, just rest for a few months—"Take it easy, chill out, calm down."

Paul wanted to stay in Ibiza—"Experience it from all four seasons, see what it's like when the tourists fuck off and leave us locals to it."

"What about your parents?"

"They'll come back. They said so, didn't they?"

"Not sure why, after your last little performance, but yeah, they did."

"What's that meant to mean?" He stared at me, chewing quickly.

"You know what it means. You disappeared into thin air four times while they were here. I was left making excuses, making awkward conversation about anything but you. And somehow they didn't want to talk to you about it either. Do you have some sort of magic mind tricks on them or something?"

"They'll come back. What other reasons are there for leaving all this beauty, this weather, this food, for cold grey London? Living with my parents or yours again, having to stick by their rules, telling them when we're going to be home, if we want dinner or not. All that shit again. How can you want that?"

"I happen to think it's not all that shit, actually. I think we could both do with a bit of structure, a bit of calm, after all this."

"That's where we don't agree." He folded his arms resolutely.

"That's why we're having this conversation."

"Again and again and again."

Desperate for us to move on when neither of us was prepared to compromise our position, I said, "I don't want to lose you. And that's what I'm worried will happen if we stay. You know why."

He threw his hands in the air. "*This* is the closing night. The end of the season. A one-off. Don't have a go at me for wanting to let off steam tonight, of all nights."

"I'm not. I'm just saying, it's been going in one direction, and I want it to come back in the other direction. I want you—" I coughed "—*us* to come back to the old us we used to be before we moved here, before one of us goes so far they can't come back."

"You'll never lose me. I'll never go. I love you and I'll never let you go."

"That's not what I'm worried about." I took a deep breath.

"What *are* you worried about?" He stared at me.

"You losing yourself." I stared back at him, unblinkingly, willing him to really listen to what I'd said, despite my having said it many times before, willing this to be the time it would really sink in.

Before he could reply, in a flurry of new people—cars, motorcycles, a rubbish truck and a white van that could have been an ambulance, pointing, waving flyers about another afterparty we must go to, all led by a man in a zebra-print jacket and white jeans, who I think was called Paulo—we were swept far, far away, into the next part of the evening's proceedings.

There, things shifted when somehow, in a way I can no longer remember, we moved onto the after-afterparty in the basement of a disused hotel four streets from the sea front and well into the bit of the town we'd never ventured into before. Although Paul was still with me, I felt like I was in a gritty public-safety broadcast about the dangers of taking drugs.

The room was filled with people I neither knew nor cared to get to know. The 'mates' from the first afterparty had long since disappeared, to be replaced with a collection of people we'd somehow become attached to, who were the human equivalent of a box of broken biscuits: half covered in ripped clothes and bits of swimwear, piercings through noses, lips, eyebrows and tongues, whole arms covered in blue and green and red tattoos so I wasn't sure of the ethnicity of a man a few feet away until he revealed his skin-coloured back.

Paulo and his zebra-print jacket were long gone. I couldn't remember seeing him after we'd arrived, not that I had any idea of how long ago that had been. Time had taken on that elastic quality it did at that time of the morning, at that stage of proceedings, when that many Persians had been consumed.

A pile of white powder was making its way around the room on a square mirror with a rolled-up two-thousand-peseta note.

The woman sitting next to me had fallen asleep, resting her head on my shoulder.

I felt my body go limp, and my eyes started to close as I settled into the soft, squashy comfort of the broken sofa where I'd been sitting since arriving. Just before I properly drifted off to sleep, I pressed my stomach with my hand and realised the trip to the toilet I'd been promising myself for the last half an hour of listening, chatting and smoking with these strangers couldn't be put off any longer. I stood, searching for a room that may be a bathroom. I walked past Paul, deep in conversation, crouched at adjacent corners of an upturned wooden fruit box with a mirror and white powder on top, talking to a white man in this thirties with long dreadlocks interlaced with colourful ribbons.

I wobbled slightly; the effects of partying for six or seven hours had well and truly taken their toll. "Where's the toilet?"

The dreadlocked man laughed and pointed to a door in the far corner of the room. "The alley, out the back. Where we came in."

That option relied on me remembering how we'd come in and unfortunately wasn't an option right then. I tried to catch Paul's eyes as I clutched my stomach.

Paul looked up from the white-powder mountain, stood. "You all right?"

"How much longer you wanna stay? I could, you know, do with going home." I rubbed my stomach. "Feeling a bit rough."

"Have a piss, drink some water, you'll be fine." He pulled me down to his level, kissed me, pushing two pills into my mouth, then handed me some water.

I was a bit sleepy, and anything seemed preferable to how I felt at that moment, so I took a swig of the water and double-dropped with as much thought as I'd give to adding another sugar to my tea.

Paul said, "I love you so much. I don't think I could love you more."

Despite all his faults, and because I meant it, I said, "I couldn't love you more either." I walked to the door at the far corner of the room and pushed it open.

The smell of piss and shit hit me, along with an acrid, rotting stench from inside what once would have been a small toilet and hand basin, but since the water had been disconnected to the disused hotel for a while, the toilet was filled to above the brim with shit and toilet paper, the floor covered in a mixture of piss and water.

I slammed the door, dry-retching, trying to be sick but nothing coming up. Suddenly my bladder wasn't so full. Suddenly the alley out the back of the hotel looked like a better option, and while I thought of it, being outside the hotel would be a few steps closer to being away from all this and on my way...*our* way back to our apartment.

I returned to Paul and the dreadlocked guy and explained what had happened. "Paul, do you want to come out the back with me for a minute?" If I got him that far, I'd stand a better chance of whisking him away with me. Instinctively, I felt for my wallet in my trousers pocket.

Nothing.

I tried the other pocket—the one I never used for my wallet, but given events so far that evening, anything was possible.

Nothing.

I ran back to the flies-infested, stinking, acrid toilet.

Nothing.

I searched the sofa where I'd installed myself when we'd arrived, rifling behind the cushions, moving the sleeping woman, pulling all the cushions at the back and base, throwing them on the floor.

Nothing.

Back at Paul's fruit box, I said, "Some fucker's nicked my fucking wallet. I'm done."

"Chill out. It can't be that bad."

"Chill out? That's what you're telling me? To chill out?"

"What was in it? About ten-thousand pesetas and some cards you can cancel." He shrugged.

"I don't know any of these people. The woman sleeping next to me, I've no idea who she is, how she got here—how I got here, actually. What about this guy you're sniffing coke with? What's his name?"

Paul turned to the dreadlocked man who was cutting out another two lines on the mirror. "Begsy? Gigsy? Joaksey? What are names, anyway? Just things we call ourselves. It's like age, it's a social construct. It's all bollocks. We need to make sure we are moving towards getting away from all that shit."

"Have you heard yourself? You don't even make sense. I don't know who you are."

That was The Straw that broke the camel's back.

That was the moment I knew I had no choice but to do what I should have done a long time ago.

"I'm leaving."

"All right. See you later. I shouldn't be long. Not much left in this party, anyway." He gestured to at least another six hours' worth of cocaine piled on the mirror.

"No, Paul, I'm leaving you, Ibiza, everything."

Paul stood, grabbed my arms. "Can't you just stay here a bit longer, carry on with the party?"

I indicated around the room to the piles of resting bodies scattered among the broken furniture. "I'm done. This isn't fun anymore. This party, this relationship." Before Paul could say anything else, I walked out the disused hotel, and walked back to our apartment, not even stopping to have a piss round the back of the hotel.

I threw my clothes and a few things I didn't want to leave into my suitcase, picked up some cash from the wooden box of magic tricks, pushing the small, transparent bags of white pills and white powder onto the floor as I collected my passport from the bottom of the box. Then I hailed a taxi outside the apartment and told the driver to take me to the airport.

This is the right decision to make. This is the only decision I could have made. This is what I need to do, I told myself again and again during the taxi ride.

I was quite pleased with myself when I arrived, marched up to the customer-service desk and asked how I could book a ticket for London ASAP. I was directed to the bank of check-in desks for various airlines.

It wasn't until I'd tried a few different airlines for very much last-minute seats, finally found one willing to sell me a ticket, waited in the queue to check in my luggage, aware of the familiar tingling along my arms and the tight, sick feeling growing in my stomach... It wasn't until after all of that, I realised I didn't feel quite so clever anymore. I was massively coming up on the pills I'd double-dropped just over an hour ago, and now I had to pretend to be straight, flyable and composed for the duration of the flight home or risk sleeping it off somewhere in the airport and Paul finding me and talking me down from the one perfect decision I'd made.

I took a deep breath, cocked my head to the side and slowly, one word at a time, one movement at a time, concentrated on acting normal until I was on the plane, on my way back to London and normality, far from the madness of the Ibiza party crowd, back to the bosom of my family home.

CHAPTER 18

Home—Far From The Mad-Out-Of-It Crowd

I ARRIVED AT THE reception of The Friary, a squat Edwardian building with modern extensions added to each of its four corners. Nestled in the New Forest, it was surrounded by acres of lawns and trees and a yellow, crunchy gravel drive that swept you from the bypass to its front gate.

Fuck only knew why Paul had been checked into The Friary—what was wrong with similar places in London?—but I was sure Roger and Marilyn had their reasons.

I waited for the receptionist—a perky, birdlike woman in a white uniform similar to those worn in health farms—to finish her phone call.

"How can I help you, sir?" she asked, bright eyes twinkling, hand of long red nails hovering optimistically over the keyboard.

Can you type optimistically? Can someone sit optimistically? I was definitely reading too much into everything since I'd decided to make the journey to Hampshire and see Paul after all that time. Even the traffic on the M3 had signalled something; I wasn't quite sure what, but it had definitely signalled *something* to me on my journey. And the sign welcoming me to Hampshire at the top of the M3 had resulted in me wiping a few tears from my face.

Madness.

Idiocy.

She repeated her question.

I apologised and said, "I'm here to visit Paul Stockton. Mr. Paul Stockton, please." I held his letter, offering to show her he'd requested my presence. My boyfriend—ex-boyfriend really—requesting my presence, and me calling him Mr. *Could this get any more bizarre?*

She waved away the letter, explained it was on the system and directed me to a visiting room a few doors and corridors away behind her. "You must wait there, and Mr. Stockton will be summoned. No visitors are allowed in residents' rooms."

So it is going to get more bizarre. OK. I took a deep breath and soon found myself facing a sign on a door:

Visiting / Group Therapy Room

I pushed the door to find the room arranged with twelve tables, each with plastic seats at opposite sides, and a row of chairs along the far wall. These were in front of a row of windows that overlooked a green-filled courtyard with a fountain in the middle.

A few of the chairs were already taken by people twiddling their thumbs, resting elbows on the table or reading a book. No one spoke.

I sat at the nearest table and waited. I checked under the table for a rabbit hole or any signs on the wall reading *Eat Me*, or *Drink Me*, but nothing.

Time passed so slowly I think I noticed my nails growing.

A matronly woman in a dark-grey nurse's uniform, red collar, white nurse's hat and puffy white sleeve appendages appeared at the door with a clipboard. She announced each resident by their surname as they entered, noticed their relatives and joined them at the tables. She ticked off her list as each resident sat, then turned to the next in the queue behind her, looked them up and down, sometimes issuing little pep talks about remembering last time, or making sure no tempers were frayed, then tapping the clipboard and gesturing them to sit.

Paul waited patiently for the matronly woman—Sheila O Something, her name badge said—to pep talk and tick him off.

His hands hung limp by his sides, his head slouched forward. He appeared smaller than the Paul I'd known—the Paul I'd known and loved—but as I caught his twinkly blue eyes when he looked up to see where I was, I knew it was my Paul.

He arrived at my table where we did a half hug, half kiss on each cheek performance, then we shook each other's hands. This was something we'd not done—ever, probably—but for some reason, in that room in The Friary, nothing felt like quite before.

We sat, our hands resting on the table where his crept towards mine, held them and he said, slowly, his eyes filling with tears, "Thank you. Thank you for coming." He took a deep breath. "I'm sorry. Like, really sorry. For everything. So sorry."

I said nothing. It was a small word to excuse a lot of crappy behaviour. He certainly looked contrite.

"Sorry isn't enough. I know that now. That's why you're here."

I leant forward, whispering, "Seen any celebs?"—something I'd wanted to ask since I knew where he'd been admitted but hadn't wanted to put it in the letters we'd been exchanging.

He mirrored my movement, whispered, "Not as many as I'd thought. It's been one of the most disappointing factors of coming here, to be honest. Mother was well put out when she arrived, expecting it to be a Who's Who parade, having got more dressed up than usual. She was very much let down."

We let that hang in the air for a moment. I was desperate for this to be comfortable, normal, for it to be like Tom and Paul chats had been before. But *before* was a long time ago. *Before* was another lifetime. A lot of stuff had happened between *before*, and *now*.

He smiled, those beautiful twinkly blue eyes crinkling at the edges as they always had done. Underneath the crumpled shirt and old jeans, and three days of stubble, he was still Paul, my Paul.

OK, so not my Paul, but still Paul.

Swallowing slowly, I asked, "How are your parents?"

"Fine. I think they're regretting admitting me here rather than somewhere in London. I never did get out of them why they chose here. Mother complains about the M3 every time they visit."

"But they are visiting regularly? I'm not the only person you've seen?"

"They are visiting. Father wants to see what he's getting for his money, I suppose. And Mother seems to have been holding hopes for the sauna, steam room, Jacuzzi and pool facilities."

"Isn't she confusing a rehab facility with a health spa?"

"She said in the brochure it was very glamorous. Fluffy white towels, bathrobes, fresh fruit and vegetables, and a spa, it said in the brochure."

"Like those hotels in Ibiza—they all look good in the brochure, but when you get there, the hotel's not been built."

We both laughed quietly at the shared memory.

After an awkward silence, I spoke first: "What do you do all day? And is there a spa? For patients, I mean, not guests, obviously."

"Residents, we're called. There's a pool. They encourage exercise. It's all about mind, spirit and body here. That's their mantra or something. Says it in the brochure, apparently."

"No celeb spotting and no treatments. Sorry to be annoying, but really, what do you do all day? Or is that why you've so much time to write me huge long letters? Not that I mind them. It's wonderful to hear you're all right, honest, it is. But all day sitting in your garret writing letters—it's a bit, I dunno. Dickensian, isn't it?"

"It's peaceful. It's to encourage us to just be. When was the last time you saw me *just being*."

"Being what?" I frowned at this new concept.

"Being myself, sitting alone, no distractions and just being."

"What, not watching TV, listening to music, talking to someone, nothing?"

He closed his eyes. "Yes, just being."

234

I pursed my lips and racked my brain. "Can't say I remember that specifically. And now?"

"Yesterday, I sat in my room, being, reflecting, praying, for three hours."

Three? Fucking? Hours? I can't sit and just be for three minutes! "I'm pleased you've found God. Someone's gotta find him, I suppose. It's nice. It's good you have a hobby. Everyone should have something, and now you've got God. I'm happy for you."

He shook his head. "It's not God. It's spiritualism. It comes from in here." He tapped his chest. "You shouldn't expect the world to constantly keep you occupied and expect stimulation twenty-four hours a day. That's where I was going wrong."

Blimey! Who is this man sitting in front of me?

"That and the addiction, of course. I've got an addictive personality, haven't I?"

"Have you?" I'd not really thought about it before.

"Always looking for the next party, the next high, the next bit of fun, never wanting it to end once it's started. If one drink or pill or line is good, then ten is fucking fantastic? Sound familiar?"

I bit my lip, choosing my words carefully as I didn't want to fall out with him, I couldn't go without having him in my life at all again; that had been far too hard. This new relationship, like New Labour everyone else kept banging on about since I'd been back in the UK, seemed to be working out all right and I didn't want to scare it away. I wanted to be *the relationship whisperer.*

It had taken me a long time to reply to Paul's first long letter. Mum had told me I was best off getting rid, staying well away, but something had encouraged me to read the letter, and then pulled me to see what he was like in person now he was going through the rehab process. To see if there was any of the Paul I'd first fallen in love with left.

"Maybe sometimes," I said.

"Thanks for agreeing to this first visit."

I shook my head. "It's nothing. Who doesn't want a trip to the New Forest?"

"You realise why you're here, don't you? It was in the letter."

"Closure, apologies, witnesses to your addiction, it said, didn't it?"

"Didn't one of The Friary staff explain it to you?"

"Were they meant to?" I sat back in the chair, my legs fidgeting, as Paul called the matron over.

She explained that part of the treatment programme involved admitting wrongs, apologising to those the residents had wronged and how difficult it often was for all involved. She added that they'd tried to think of other people Paul could have asked to fulfil this role but hadn't come up with anyone else suitable—"Or anyone whose details Paul has so he can contact them. His parents are out of the question. They only witnessed things at the end. It needs to be someone who saw things as they worsened."

Paul avoided my eyes.

"All right. Tell me more about what's involved."

The matron explained Paul would put everything in a letter inviting me for the first group session, which I was under no obligation to attend, even though I'd agreed to participate now.

"First?"

"It's a series. We can't go too far in one session, it's very tiring for all involved. We can space sessions out as you wish, to suit you and the resident."

She went over the details, then left us alone in the visiting room. Well, I say alone; sitting in the corner was a man in a white tunic and black trousers who looked like a nursing-bouncer mashup.

Paul said, "It's to stop anyone smuggling in anything to give us." He rolled his eyes. "Thanks for coming. It means so much to me. Even though we're not together, it's kind of you."

"What happened for you to end up here? What did you do?"

"No." He looked away. "I've not come to terms with that yet. I'm going to bring it up in group this week, then I'll put it in the letter I'm sending you. It'll all be in the letter, everything about what you need to do when, if, you come back here to help me."

He shook my hand. "Sorry. Please read the letter. Some people's relatives return theirs unopened. Just read the letter and give me a chance, OK?"

"'Course I will." *Come to terms? Bring it up in group? Who is this person?* "There's no *if*. I will come back."

I left feeling like I'd agreed to do my good deed for the season, dismissing it all as a trivial series of talks with Paul in the glamorous country spa where he'd been staying for a while.

Piece of piss.

Simple.

It seemed like a good idea at the time.

***

Paul's letter arrived a short while later, in a thick, A5, brown envelope, his familiar, twirly, copperplate handwriting leaning to the right and reminding me of every Victorian person's letters I'd seen in museums and archive collections. I knew it wasn't a bill; since moving back with Mum and Dad, I'd been mercifully saved from those.

I didn't want to open it on my own in case it contained terrible news, so I handed it to Mum, who was smoking, leaning against the kitchen sink.

"Terrible news? What, worse than going off his nut in Ibiza?" She took a drag of the cigarette, holding it in her mouth while she opened the envelope.

I shrugged. "He could have died." It had been one of my biggest worries when his partying had got really out of control, with no sense of ever being able to put the brakes on it.

"Writing from the grave, is he? Very impressive." She glanced at the letter. "It's dated a few days ago, so I think you're all right on that count, love. Besides, you only saw him last week. What's going to have happened to him since then in that nuthouse?"

"Read it, will you?" I wiped my sweaty hands on my grey combat trousers, fiddling about in one of the enormous pockets for my cigarettes. I lit one and tapped it on the ashtray before any ash had accumulated.

Mum rifled through the letter. "It's pages and pages. Fucking War and Fucking Peace. I'm sitting down for this. And I'm having a new cuppa tea. You?"

Because I knew it would delay the inevitable letter reading, I agreed and waited while she made it. I stared at the pile of his handwritten words fanned out on top of the envelope. *What will they contain? Why has he chosen now to write to me? Should I have just thrown it in the bin and ignored him?*

Mum sat opposite me, handed me my drink, clipped me round the head lightly, told me to chill the fuck out and began reading Paul's letter.

> *Dear Tom,*
>
> *I'm sorry. I'm sorry for what I put you through. I'm sorry for forcing you to leave. I wasn't myself. I don't remember you leaving that squat party. I got home sometime later, and when I found you not at the apartment assumed you'd gone to work. It took me three days to realise you'd definitely left me.*
>
> *THREE DAYS!*
>
> *That's how off my box I was. And had been for some time.*

Mum paused. "I didn't know he was this bad. Bless him. Bless his little heart, writing all this to you. I'm filling up, I am. I take back what I said."

I coughed. "When you're ready. Let's get to the end and then we can discuss it, all right?"

Mum saluted, took a drag on her cigarette and continued reading.

I don't know what happened after you left. I sort of carried on as best I could, but the promo work dried up as the season ended. Most of the clubs didn't want me to DJ on my own, said we came as a package, like French and Saunders, Morecambe and Wise. It was great at first. I thought I could do what I liked with no one saying I needed to stop, needed to be ready for work or anything, nowhere to be in the future. No one else to think about. No commitments. There was no work, so I just carried on and got right into it.

It was like a fortnight-long party, moving from one closing party, birthday party, anniversary party, party for Wednesday, anything, to the next, going to squats, hotels, people's apartments to carry on. Once, I forgot where I lived. I'd ended up in someone's flat on the other side of the island, and when everyone drifted off to fly home, I was left in this flat with this woman I didn't know, and she said she had to catch her flight as the holiday rep season had ended and she had to leave.

She turfed me out on her way to the airport, and I was alone on the other side of the island with no money and no memory of where I lived. I slept on the beach for a few days, then gradually it came back to me, piece by piece, like a ripped-up newspaper as the pieces blow into a room.

I assembled the pieces of my newspaper until I remembered the town where I lived, so I walked there, and the memories of our apartment came back to me. I walked into our place, the door left open, bodies of sleeping people I'd never met strewn across the floor, the music playing too loudly, the window left open.

A girl stood to hug me, said she'd been expecting me and wanted to know where she could get some more pills – could I sort her out.

And do you know what I did?

Did I chuck them all out, tidy it up and straighten my life out?

No, I raided the wooden box in our bedroom and dished out some party sweets to everyone and carried on partying until sometime later when we'd really run out of drugs and the sun had risen and set once more.

It always still felt like our place, our bedroom, our apartment, even after you'd gone. I somehow hoped you'd come back. I didn't really understand what I'd done that was so wrong. Why wouldn't you want to join me for more partying? I tried calling your parents, and your mum said she'd pass on the message. I didn't hear back, so I assume she didn't.

Mum looked up from the letter. "Bloody right, I didn't. Fucking cheek of him. You was in bits. I wanted to protect you. Last thing you needed was him begging you to come back, saying he'd change when he didn't even fucking know what he'd done wrong." She coughed, then continued reading.

It wasn't until I woke in hospital that I realised I had a problem. The bills piling up, the unpaid rent, the lack of money to buy food – none of that really bothered me because I was off my face most of the time.

I found myself at a party in a derelict apartment building due to be pulled down as it was filled with asbestos or something, with a group of people I barely knew and who all seemed content to stay there as long as they liked. None of them seemed to have anything to get back to. It was the early hours of the morning, you know the time that feels like it belongs to the clubbers, the party people, as everyone else is sleeping, the streets are empty of cars.

I walked to the balcony overlooking the pool, filled with dirty grey-green water, white plastic chairs and tables and bits of clothing from when we'd thought it a good idea to swim in it when we first arrived at the hotel. A group of grubby men and women with wide red eyes sat cross-legged by the window. As I leant on the wall, lighting a cigarette, wondering if I had anything that needed doing in the day in front of me, I noticed someone pulling at my shorts.

I woke from my not particularly deep thoughts to find a greasy-haired woman proffering a small plastic bag of light-brown powder. She said, "Want some?"

"What is it?"

"H."

Without even thinking, I nodded, joined her on the floor and watched as they chopped lines of the powder onto the back of a CD case, handing it round as the group leant over it, sniffed, and it disappeared up their noses.

Since then, I've thought back to what I was doing at that point. I knew H meant heroin. I'd not done heroin before, but somehow, as they were snorting it rather than injecting it like I'd seen on the films, it seemed the same as snorting cocaine or crushed ecstasy pills, like I sometimes did at the end of the night when there weren't enough left to go round.

Just writing that makes me feel sick. The thought of a group of near strangers crushing white pills and snorting them to make sure there was enough to go round at the end of a night, to stave off the inevitable end of the party, makes me feel sick. But that was me. That was what I used to do, just like I would make you a cup of tea. In that space, the strange time before the day starts, while last night's party continues, in that time, all this seemed normal, usual, the done thing.

The others around me were lying on their backs, grinning in pleasure, or curled into a ball. That looked like just what I needed at that stage of the party. A bit of fluffy, cuddly sleepiness. That's how someone had once described the effects of heroin to me, so why should I question that?

I picked the larger of the two lines left on the CD case, because, well why not, fuck it? I blocked one nostril and sniffed through the other. I pulled my head back.

Fuck me, but I woke up in hospital, with my parents at the bedside.

Eventually—as she watched a removals company box up my things because she didn't let me out of her sight while she flew home with me—I got the full story out of Mother.

She told me I'd been dumped at the doors of the hospital. She told me my heart had stopped at least three times. She told me if I'd been lying on my back during the journey to the hospital, I would have choked on my own vomit. She told me I was in a coma in the hospital for three weeks. She told me the first she knew about it was a Spanish doctor in broken English telling her on the phone he thought he had her son in hospital and if she wanted to see him before he left, she had better fly over soon. She told me she wasn't at first sure what the doctor had meant by left, until he explained what had happened. She'd screamed and dropped the phone. Father had taken the details from the doctor, and they had jumped on the first flight to Ibiza.

I asked, joking, was it a budget airline and how had she felt about that?

She slapped my face so hard it left a hand-shaped bruise for days.

She told me she loved me, but as I'd already technically died three times, she wasn't taking any chances and the only thing that would kill me now was her if I didn't come home and take up the place at The Friary they'd booked for me.

We went straight from Heathrow airport to The Friary. I didn't pass Go, didn't collect £200, didn't stop at home first. They didn't want to let me out of their sight.

They signed my papers and left me at the reception where I was shown a tiny, cell-like room with a bunk bed against one wall and a small window in the far wall.

A rotund, smiling man uncrossed his legs as he sat at the table by the window, introduced himself with a limp handshake and a smile as "Harold. Overeater. And you are?"

Harold? Really. I'm sharing a room with a man called Harold who eats his feelings and looks like he could do without food for at least a month. I put on my grey tracksuit bottoms and grey sweatshirt with a green tree logo of The Friary and jumped onto the top bunk.

"What do we do now? Can we watch TV or listen to the radio?"

"You need to get your schedule from the resident who's on orientation this week. It shows you the group therapy, lessons and free time you have scheduled. Time flies. It's fun."

Fun. Just what I needed. I lay back on the bed and closed my eyes.

Harold continued talking. He'd been there for two months and still had another month to go and said we might be in the same groups together as they usually paired people with their roommate for at least some of their timetable.

Roommate. I rolled my eyes, even though they were still closed.

Harold said, "What was your name? I didn't catch it."

"I didn't throw it. Can I just have a moment, please? It's all a bit too holiday-camp for me – orientation, schedules, timetables, bunk beds. I thought I'd be here for a few weeks, stop taking drugs and then go back to real life."

He snapped his fingers. "Thought so. Thin ones are always drugs. What was it?"

I sat up, hitting my head on the ceiling. "What was what?"

"Your drug of choice? Mine was teacakes. And jars of golden syrup."

"That's not drugs." I sighed, realising this was to be my lot for at least the next few weeks so I might as well make nice with Harold. I held my hand out. "Paul. Drugs."

Harold shook my hand. "More than pleased to make your acquaintance."

I rolled my eyes again. Bet he's an estate agent, I thought to myself. "So, teacakes and golden syrup, what's that about?" Throwing him an open-questioned bone, I hoped he'd run with it and leave me to think about my new situation from the relative isolation of the top bunk.

"Biscuit base, filled with marshmallow, all covered in chocolate. They come wrapped in foil in packs of six."

"I see." I didn't, but I wanted to show willing. Despite trying to sit still, my skin itched and I found myself having to jump from the top bunk to stand in the middle of the room, my hands thrust in my pockets. I stepped from one foot to the other.

"All right there, Sparky?"

"Fine. Go on. Teacakes."

"I was up to thirty a day towards the end. It got worse when they sacked me at work. I couldn't fit in my car or walk more than a few steps. I'd started getting taxis and asking the customers to see themselves round the houses."

"Estate agent?" I huffed under my breath.

"You?"

"DJ and party planner."

"Get you!"

"Thirty teacakes a day, that's quite a habit." I laughed to myself quietly.

"Thirty packs of six a day." He stood, his arms resting on his wide hips. "Never mind laughing at me for what I've done to bring me here. I suppose what you were doing was brain surgery or something, wasn't it? You've still not told me what your drug of choice was."

"Sorry. Ecstasy. And cocaine, I liked that too. Sometimes a bit of hash, to take the edge off, when I needed to get to sleep after a big night. You know."

He shrugged.

I told him how much I loved drugs, how they made me feel so good I couldn't really believe how that could be wrong, how I hankered after the perfect moment of coming up on the first pill of the night at the start of the evening, when everything and anything was possible, when the music filled my head, when I was stood next to my boyfriend, my ex-boyfriend Tom—I couldn't really believe we weren't together anymore—in the DJ booth, with a crowd of 10,000 in our hands, manipulating their moods with the songs we played. How nothing had ever beaten that feeling.

"Who's your significant other for the admitting-the-problem session?"

I had no idea what he was on about.

He explained after the first few sessions, when they make you admit you have a problem—I snorted at that, saying it was just a bit of recreational drug use and nothing to worry about—he asked what brought me there if it was all so under control.

I stared at the floor, clenched my fists, tried to stop myself hopping between feet and said, "Had a teensy-weensy bit of an accident with a bit of heroin."

"That'd do it. I was making myself sick so I could eat more. When I couldn't get upstairs to use the bathroom and started using a bucket, I thought I had it all under control. Even when I ordered taxis to buy food and deliver it. Still under control. It wasn't until my friend from work visited me. She told me how wrong I was and called my parents. I was here soon after. Sometimes it takes someone else to point out how abnormal your normal behaviour is."

"Whatever." I hated him. I wanted the earth to open up and swallow his smug, fat body.

When I first arrived at The Friary, I had lost myself, completely come untethered from who I was.

Tom, I am no longer that person. I now know I am an addict. I have had weeks and weeks of group therapy to get to the reasons behind my behaviour. I have an addictive personality, and if I'd not become addicted to drugs, it would've been food, sex, shopping – anything really.

I used the drugs because I'm scared of committing to things: events, careers, people. Drugs meant I was always focusing on them rather than my future.

It feels good to write that down after saying it so many times. I am what the therapist called a sensation seeker. I find a sensation I enjoy and I want it never to end. If one tab of ecstasy is good, five is amazing. If partying for three hours is good, partying for thirteen is perfect. If ecstasy and cocaine are fun then heroin will be even better. Except when it isn't. Except when I end up in hospital.

Although I lost myself, I knew I could find myself again. When I lost myself, I lost you too, and I wanted to try and see if I could get even a small part of you, as a friend, back.

You're probably wondering why the big long letter. Well, as I said when I saw you, part of the therapy is to invite someone you care for who's been affected by your behaviour and to hear them talking about how it made them feel. I know what Mother and Father felt. It's all I got on the journey home and every time they've visited since, reminding me I nearly died and how they'd have died of broken hearts if I'd actually gone and bloody well died. But the only person I could think of who's put up with my behaviour again and again until enough was enough and they left, is you.

So what I'm asking, dear Tom, is can you come to my next group therapy session to tell me what it was like, how my behaviour affected you? There will be a counsellor. She'll ask some questions to me and you. She's a bit of a hippie hangover, but she knows what she's talking about. Some of the things she's said have made my eyes water. It's not fun. Some of the others have been really hard to watch even from the sidelines, so being the people at the centre of it won't be a picnic, but it would really help me if you could come.

I know we're not together anymore. I know I've fucked that up right royally, but I was hoping we could maybe, after all this is behind us, behind me mainly, if we could, if you wanted, we could be friends.

Paul xxx

Mum stuffed the letter into the envelope, lit a cigarette and took a deep drag before saying, "So, what do you make of that?"

"Who'd have thought I'd be back here, single, no job, no boyfriend when six months ago I had everything. I sometimes think it was all a big long dream, you know? Ibiza, the DJing, everything. And I've woken up, and all along I was sleeping here, upstairs in my bedroom where I grew up, and Paul was never anything more than my imagination." I folded the envelope in half and put it in my pocket. "I don't know what to do."

Mum sat next to me at the kitchen table, putting her hand on mine. "Do you love him, love?"

I nodded. "Stupid, innit? After all this, after me leaving him, I still love him."

"No taking account of love. Makes you do stupid things. For instance, I married your dad." She laughed to herself. "No, seriously, why else would we do most of the things we do for people if it's not love?"

"I should move on. Find someone else. Plenty more fish in the sea. That's what they say, isn't it?"

"It is."

"Fuck him. I'm not going through all that shit for him. Bastard, after what he did. After how he treated me. After all the chaos and mess I tried to keep him from, he finally stepped into the abyss and ended up in hospital. Well, it's not my fault. Not my fucking problem." I banged my fist on the table.

We sat in silence for a while as Mum made another pot of tea, clattering and banging on the far side of the kitchen. "That's that, then."

"It is." I took the mug she'd handed me. "Except…"

She offered me a cigarette. "Except what, love?"

"Except I don't want another fish. I want the fish I had. I don't want to go fishing again. Christ only knows what I'll catch."

"Have you had a look?"

"Went to some gay night in Brixton, got chatted up by someone Dad's age. Met someone who's opening questions to me were 'Are you a top or a bottom?' and 'Do you like water sports?'"

"Like swimming and water polo?"

"No, Mum." I stared at her.

Her eyes widened. "Sex, is it?"

"Yeah, sex."

She pulled her chair closer to the table, sipped her tea and asked me to spill everything, about what water sports meant.

Because I hadn't the energy to talk about Paul any longer, I indulged her and revelled in the easy, slightly too close for comfort, too cool relationship we had.

Should I visit Paul at The Friary?

What do you reckon? 'Course I did.

Obviously, I spent the next five days umming and aahing about it, rereading Paul's letter, crying, remembering our time in Ibiza before things had got too bad, crying some more, checking the date, crying again.

There was a lot of crying involved, until finally, after I'd gone round in circles about whether I should visit Paul or not, my main reasoning being that we'd split up and why should I do him any favours, Mum said, "If you don't want to go, fucking well don't go. I'll call The Friary now for you, put Paul out of his misery. But I don't think you really don't want to go. If you'd made your mind right up, we wouldn't still be talking about this.

"And love, I mean this with love and affection, but I've had this conversation up to here—" she indicated above her head "—going round and round the same bloody argument again and again. I don't think I can have this conversation another time. Just go. See him. Worst that can happen is it's fucking hard, but you're not exactly jumping for joy and going to Disneyland now, are you?"

Her reasoning and logic were undeniably persuasive. I felt my body go limp. "If you're saying I should go, I'll go."

"I…" She paused. "Yeah, love, that's exactly what I'm saying. Now get the fuck out from under my feet, I'm trying to catch up on my soaps while your dad's out, and I can't get on with you rabbiting on like some big gobby...rabbit."

"I'll do some CV handing out. Just local, like."

"Yeah, you do that, love. Just piss off and leave me in peace. Want me to call, let 'em know you're coming on the date he asked in his letter? Poor soul, Paul."

"Yeah, if you could." I walked to the door. "Thanks." I left, without the copies of my CV I'd printed, without any clue of where I was going to walk, but for some reason feeling clearer, more in possession of a direction than I had since leaving Ibiza months ago.

CHAPTER 19

I WORE A WHITE sleeveless T-shirt and white combat trousers with clean new white high-top trainers. My bed was covered in piles of discarded clothes I'd tried on before finally settling on the rather angelic ensemble. I wasn't sure why I wanted to make such an effort when seeing Paul. After all, we were just friends— not even that anymore. Definitely miles away from boyfriends. I wasn't going to get back with him, not after what he'd done, no way. I told Mum this when I walked into the kitchen in my white outfit.

"Fancy dress, is it? Where you off to?"

"The Friary. Seeing Paul. Having the talk. He's going to hear my side of the story."

"Is that today? Come round quick, hasn't it? Where is this Friary business? Is it on the Tube somewhere?"

"New Forest, bottom of the M3." *Bottom.* My mind flashed to the man in the club in Brixton. I shuddered briefly.

"Gonna be all right driving afterwards?"

"Fine."

"Only they said, the receptionist lady, she said it can be quite traumatic. She went on about closure and some other stuff I didn't quite understand, but I definitely picked up it would be traumatic. And shitloads of hard work. Promise me you won't drive if you're too fucked afterwards. If one of us needs to pick you up, we will. Or get a train and we'll get your car. Whatever, just don't drive miserable. It's as bad as driving drunk, I think. This psychotherapist was on about it one morning on the TV."

"Gotta go. Wish me luck."

"Good luck." She tapped her cheek.

I kissed her cheek, and she held me in a hug, tighter than usual, longer than usual.

"Call me before you leave."

"How?"

"The mobile phone. Have you brought it?"

I ran to my bedroom to collect the new gadget I was still getting used to having in my life. The concept of not having to tell people where I'd be and which number they could reach me on was still new.

Mum hugged me again. "Go. Be fabulous. Be brave." She waved.

***

At The Friary, I was led to a large room with chairs around the edge, one wall of windows looking out to the expansive lawn where people walked alone or sat with magazines, smoking in desperation. No sign of any celebrities, though, I noted with disappointment.

Three chairs stood in the middle of the room, Paul in one and a small woman with short, brown hair, a disconcertingly wide smile and a purple medium-length kaftan worn over flared jeans. *Brave choice with those hips.*

She gestured for me to sit opposite Paul and took her place in between our chairs, facing us. After an introduction about the purpose of the first of up to six sessions, as Paul had explained in his letter, she said, "I'm Barbara, a trained psychotherapist, and if at any time you feel unable to continue, you must communicate this to me and we will stop the session."

Up to six! Is that what she just said? "Like a safe word?" I quipped, instantly regretting it.

"What do you mean?" she asked slowly, breathing through her nose after every word.

"When you do…there's a safe word, that means stop."

A few people in the chairs at the back laughed quietly.

A part of my soul died. I closed my eyes, willing myself not to be there, not to have said what I'd just said. I opened them, and everything was, sadly, as I'd left it. "Stop, do I just say stop?" I tried, optimistically.

"Yes, that would suffice. Now, can you please tell Paul how his addiction made you feel?"

"Lost."

"Can you tell us a bit more about that, please?"

"Like…you wanted to live life as it if was one long party. But it isn't. It can't be. You have to get back to reality, don't you?" I was getting going now, it was flowing out of me. I rubbed my hands together. "You didn't know when to stop. You just carried on and on and on until I couldn't take it anymore."

"Feeling words, please, Tom," Barbara said.

"I feel that you didn't listen to me when I said we had to stop. I feel you thought I was spoiling your fun. I feel sad everything we had was built on feelings that aren't real, feelings that are from chemicals, drugs." I stopped myself. The reality of what I'd just said hitting me in the face, taking the breath out of my body. *What the fuck am I doing here? What's the point?*

Barbara turned to Paul. "How does that make you feel?"

Paul avoided eye contact. "Sad. It must have been real, what we had together…wasn't it? Chemicals can't have kept us going that long, surely? When I lost you, I didn't just lose my boyfriend, I lost my best friend. After you left, I had no one to balance me, my addiction, to keep it in check. That's why I did what I did." He paused, biting his lip and rubbing one hand with the other.

"What do you mean, Paul?" Barbara asked.

"What happened," he said quietly.

"Can you talk about that a bit more, Paul?"

I started to say something, but Barbara silenced me. "It's time to hear from Paul now, and you'll get your turn later."

Paul said, "I thought I had it all under control. I thought I'd done it all before, nothing could harm me. OK, so I'd had a few

close scrapes, but nothing that wasn't a good story down the pub."
He laughed.

I didn't.

He put his hands in his pockets. "It wasn't until you'd gone I realised how much you did, how much you balanced me out."

I narrowed my eyes at him. "Stopped you having your fun, more like."

Barbara said, firmly now, "You'll have your turn, Tom. Paul. Can you say more about the balancing?"

"I used to enjoy the sensation of the drugs, the unreality, the dislocation from the everyday, the floaty feeling they gave me. I loved how I felt like I was floating away like a kite from myself, standing on the ground. And every time, you used to bring the kite back, back down to the ground. But when you'd gone, the kite just flew higher and higher until the me that was standing on the ground, he just let it go." Paul paused. "And then I woke up in hospital."

I looked at Barbara. "Me now?"

She nodded.

"You can't live in the sky like the kite. You've always gotta come back to earth, get on with life. That's all I wanted you to understand. Do you get that now?"

He nodded slowly.

"I don't like how you're trying to make me feel guilty for leaving you; like it was my fault you ended up in hospital. I had to leave. I had no choice. I'd tried talking to you, but you didn't think you had a problem."

"I'm an addict, with an addictive personality, I understand that now. But then, you had no chance of me understanding that, not without all this to help me." He gestured to the room. "You did what you did because it was what you had to do."

"Yes."

"And I'm sorry. Sorry for making it your last resort, the only thing that got through to me. Sorry for being a selfish arsehole.

I didn't want to feel tied down by anything. Turns out that's not such a great way of living. Anyway, I am not that person anymore."

There was a pause as we stared at each other. His twinkly blue eyes still shone brighter than the sun beaming through the window.

"Can you forgive me?" He held out his hand for me to shake and flashed that familiar smile—the one I'd fallen in love with way back with the record shop in London, in the prehistoric age of our relationship.

"I forgive you." I shook his hand. In the face of an apology like that, and the fact that he was in rehab, and the small inkling of feelings that I didn't deserve someone to love me, I thought it would be unkind to throw it back in his face.

He pulled me towards him into a hug, and he whispered in my ear, "I love you. I always will, until the day I die."

I pulled back from the hug, his words ringing in my ears, deflating all my anger and frustration at him.

Barbara said, "This was very good work today, both of you. There's a long way to go on this road, but this is the important first step you've taken." She clapped and was joined by the others in the room. She nodded to me, mouthing *thank you.*

I was led out the room by a man in a white tunic and black trousers. At the door, I caught the eyes of a woman in her Sunday-best clothes—black pencil skirt, pink blouse and matching pink chunky necklace—eyes wide and wet, mouth pursed with pink lipstick and hands clasping a pink handbag across her stomach like a protective shield.

Good luck, I mouthed to the woman.

She looked past me, pushed her hair behind her ears and strode into the room as one of the men from the outer circle joined her in the middle.

The white-tunicked man led me to the waiting area in reception and offered me a drink before I left.

"Is that it?" I asked, assembling myself and my thoughts as I sat.

"Until next time."

"Next time?" My body wilted like an old cut flower.

"It's ongoing. Your friend's lucky. Lots of relatives don't want anything to do with it. Takes months to move through the stages without them."

"I think I will have a tea, please. Strong, four sugars."

"Sometimes they send the letters back, torn up. Your friend wants to count his lucky stars." He left.

This wasn't part of the plan when I'd agreed to Mum's suggestion of visiting Paul. This was not meant to happen. I was going to do my bit, play my part in his rehabilitation, help him get back to who he was before he floated into the sky like a lost kite, and then maybe we would be friends.

And if I only saw him as a friend, if that was the only thing I saw for us in our future, why was I now wanting to run back into that room and ask him if it had all been imagined, if our love was all just down to chemicals, or if what I was feeling for him now was the same as what he felt for me?

***

I walked to my car, crunching the gravel, noticing the birds tweeting, the trees rustling. I leant against the car, dialled Mum's number. "Mum?"

"Yes, love, how did it go? You all right to drive?"

"Can you make yourself stop loving someone, or is love something you can't control?" And then I cried. Sobbing. Big, sploshy tears rolling down my cheeks. Bolts of pain escaping from my chest which felt as if it was being pressed down with a heavy weight. I gasped for breath as the sadness and loss coursed through me.

"Stay there. I'm coming to get you, love. I repeat, do not drive. This is not a drill. I repeat, this is not a drill. Do not drive. I'll be with you as soon as."

***

We travelled home in silence. I had no words to express how I felt. It was like I'd emptied myself of everything during the therapy session and now it took all the strength I had to stay upright.

In the kitchen, waiting for the kettle to boil, Mum said, "You gotta do this malarkey again, have you?"

"So they said."

"I can soon give 'em a ring, tell 'em to stick it." Her fingers were poised over the numbers on the white cordless phone she'd treated herself to after the Luella money came through.

"I don't hate him. Not anymore. I think I still love him. I thought I'd gone past that, that he'd pushed me away so much I wouldn't love him anymore. But no. Seeing him again, it all came flooding back." I let out a long sigh, willing myself not to cry again. "Idiot!"

"That was a big sigh, love. You sure you're up to talking more, or do you want to have a kip and we'll talk about all this tomorrow, or not at all? No need to ever mention it again if you don't want to. Like I said, one call is all it'll take." She rapped her nails on the phone. "You thought he'd crossed the line, now you've realised he hasn't, he's still his side of the line and in here." She patted my chest. "Fair enough, we've all done it."

"The line?"

"The thing he would do that you knew would make you leave him. That one thing."

"Not coming home with me from that horrible squat party. After a whole series of *just another hour, just another pill, just another...* That?"

"That's the one. For your dad, it's cheating. I told him if I ever found out he'd cheated on me, that was the end of it. And violence, but then again, can you imagine him being violent?"

"I can't imagine him cheating, but anyway. Maybe that wasn't the line. So what is the line? Where is this line, eh?"

"Cheating, violence?"

"He said he'd never cheat on me. Said no matter how long he disappeared for, he'd always come back to me in our bed."

"And you believed him?" She tapped the ash off her cigarette into the Ibiza-shaped glass ashtray on the table.

"Why not?"

"I'm just asking. Gotta make sure someone's looking out for you. Daft romantic."

"He's had plenty of opportunities, but he hasn't. I know someone would have told me—one of our partying friends would have let me know. But, nothing. Besides, we were the gay DJing couple of Ibiza. Everyone knew we were together. If he'd been shagging around, it would have got back to me somehow, don't you reckon?"

"Fair point, love, fair point. Just checking."

"And he'd never hit me. He might hit himself, for doing something stupid, but never anyone else."

"That's it, then. He's not crossed the line when you thought he had, and now you've seen him again, bang, you're back where you was before. You'd better be careful, love, cos if you don't watch yourself, you'll be back in that afterparty, six o'clock in the morning, surrounded by strangers, asking him to come home as soon as you can say heroin overdose."

"That's what I'm worried about."

"Better help him get through this programme they have at this Friary place, then, hadn't you?"

"Better had, hadn't I?" *Damn. Bollocks. Shit.*

"How many visits, did he say in his letter?"

"Up to six, depending. Barbara explained in her introduction at the first session."

"Do you want me to drive you next time?"

"Do you think there should be a next time?"

"Up to you, my love, but if you're in love with him, I'd say better being in love with an ex-addict than being in love with an addict. Do you know what I mean? I'm no expert, but that's how it looks from where I'm standing." She pulled her bra strap up so it showed above her hot-pink vest top.

***

The next time I visited Paul, Mum drove me.

Of course I went back. Obviously, I couldn't have just left him hanging there, part way through the rehab. Even if we were just friends, and honestly, that's all we were now, I would have helped *just a friend*. So a friend who was also my ex-boyfriend, he was obviously going to get my help.

Mum kissed me while we were inside the car, wished me good luck.

"Come in, you can't wait in here the whole time. They've got magazines and books in reception. You'll have to smoke outside, but I can introduce you to the receptionist, she's nice. She'll look after you."

"That's exactly what I'm afraid of. No fear, I'm staying here, smoking in me own car, thank you very much. This place is freaking me out, even sitting this far away. It's like some big mouth people disappear into and never leave."

"Dramatic much?" I was standing next to the car now, leaning down to meet her eyes.

"Now you know where you get it from. Door, I'll be fine. Go on."

Not long afterwards, after checking the paperwork, I took my seat opposite Paul. Barbara was in hers, this time wearing an aquamarine dress with floaty sleeves that looked like a nightie from the seventies, over stonewashed grey flared jeans, and again with the matching aquamarine chunky jewellery.

She introduced us to the room for the new patients sat round the edge. "Who would like to go first?"

Feeling a bit buoyed up from last time, and having spoken to Mum, I decided to take the awkward dead-auntie's-inheritance bull by the horns. "You said when I left, it all fell apart for you. But it's not my job to look after you. I'm not your mum."

Barbara put her palm near my face to signal I stop speaking. "Feeling words, please. Using words about how you feel, please."

"I feel upset when you say you fell apart after I left. It wasn't just my idea to go to Ibiza, but it was helped by Luella's inheritance.

It wasn't me who was spending all the money on partying. That was you."

"Feeling words, please." She turned to Paul. "How does that make you feel, Paul?"

"Fair enough," Paul said. "I thought she'd want us to enjoy the money. We enjoyed it, didn't we, when we first moved out there?"

"Paul, how do you feel?" Barbara asked.

"I feel we enjoyed ourselves when we first got there. I feel we decided together how to spend the money. I feel my partying got out of hand on my own. I don't blame you, your inheritance, or anything. It was all me. I was the one who took all the drugs, not you."

I said, "What if everything we had wasn't real? What if all the love we had for each other was just based on chemicals, on drugs, not a real relationship? Have you thought about that, eh?"

Barbara started to mention feeling words, but Paul interrupted. "It can't have been. We weren't off our faces the whole time."

Someone laughed from the seats behind me.

Barbara turned, glared at the laugher, returned to focus on us and said, "Paul, say more about what you mean. How often were you off your faces?"

"Sometimes."

"Can you be more specific?"

"Two, maybe three times a week, in peak season, obviously." Paul shrugged.

Obviously. I bit my lip, willing the truth not to escape, but very soon it was too late. I blurted, "More like four or five times a week." The silence filled the room as I stared at Paul. "Ask him about when his parents visited." *This is meant to be hard, so why hold back?* I was going great guns now, a little bit of me was enjoying it slightly.

Barbara turned to Paul, her hands folded in her lap. "Would you like to comment on that, Paul?"

Paul crossed his arms across his chest and turned his back to me.

This time, the silence didn't just fill the room; it crashed in like a wave a surfer would be pleased to ride, filling the room with nothingness. We sat like that for five minutes. I don't know if you've ever sat in complete silence in a room full of people for five minutes. It's a bizarre experience, and I was constantly expecting someone to break it, to dive in and make a joke, but they didn't. I didn't want to speak because I wanted Paul to describe what had happened rather than me harping on like some old fishwife ex. I was particularly keen for him to talk about is since we'd not spoken about it at the time. Even after his parents had gone home, Paul had dismissed it as nothing, saying he was tired, and he needed to see a man about a dog.

The longest five minutes in history passed at a glacial rate. I was beginning to contemplate jumping out the window for some entertainment but noticed the bars on the window and reflected on us being on the ground floor.

Paul said, quietly, slowly, almost inaudibly, "That was a bad time."

"What was that, Paul?" Barbara asked, writing something on her clipboard with three confident strokes, her tongue sticking out between her lips like a piece of ham.

Paul repeated himself, slightly louder this time.

"Can you tell us how that was a bad time, Paul? What made it a bad time for you?" She leant forward, again with the scribbles on the clipboard.

"I was hanging around with some people who were doing a lot of heavy-duty partying. I was in with the wrong crowd."

"Now, Paul, what did we learn about personal responsibility?"

He sighed the sigh of a long-suffering man. "I was influenced by these people. I went to talk about some promo work and ended up getting on it with them. It seemed like a good idea at the time." He looked round the room, trying to catch the eyes of the others sitting by the walls. "Doesn't it always, eh?"

I looked at Paul and said, "Your parents flew over to see you. And you buggered off for most of the time, seeing a man about a dog, or whatever you said. No apology, no explanation, nothing. And who was left holding the fort, entertaining them? Muggins here."

Barbara mentioned feeling words. Again.

I wanted to throttle her but suppressed the urge, pushed it deep, deep down to the bottom of my soul and instead said, "I did it because I loved you. Because that's what you do when you love someone. I listened to you talking about your promotion ideas. When you weren't sure you could do the party planning, I was there, persuading you you could do it. I could have just seen a spoilt rich kid when I first met you, but I knew you were a worker, a grafter, someone who'd work hard for what he wanted. Just like I did.

"But that was the old you, the you I first met. You turned into this whole other person towards the end. Not caring who you upset, what you did—nothing mattered to you except the next party, the next pill, the next sniff of cocaine. Why did you disappear when your parents were visiting, eh? What was so good you had to drop us for hours on end? Which drug is better than seeing your parents and your boyfriend?"

"It all made me feel suffocated. Being tied to a time, an event, people." He briefly looked at me before staring back at the floor. He swallowed. "My name is Paul Stockton and I am a drug addict."

The room filled with applause.

I wanted to jump up from my chair and rip Paul's tongue out of his throat. *All that shitty behaviour and he gets a round of applause? Will they give him a round of applause for being a commitment-phobic selfish prick too?*

Even though I wasn't perfect, I knew I was far from useless, and deserved a fuck's sight better than that.

Above the clapping, I said, "I loved you. I would have done anything for you. In fact, that's why I'm still here. Stupid twat. And all you have to say is you were an addict. Pills and coke were better company than me, is that what you're saying?"

"You were hardly pushing them away if I remember rightly. You're not exactly Mother Theresa when it comes to narcotics."

Barbara put her hand up to stop Paul. "We're here to talk about your addiction, Paul, not Tom's."

"Fucking good job, or we'd be here all day." He glared at me.

What a fucking low blow. Maybe I make men treat me like this. I am useless. I didn't know my left from my right, my wrong from my right anymore. "Did you love me, or was it all a chemical lie? When you used to shout in my ear when we were on the dance floor how much you loved me, what you wanted to do with me when we got home, when you held me so tight I could hardly breathe, did that mean anything, or was it all nothing?"

"I think so. I mean, what's love really?" Paul was staring at his lap. "Yes, I said stuff when I was pilled up, who doesn't? Think of all the things we did straight, all the times I told you I loved you when we were living in London working in shops, before it all got out of hand. All the date nights. All the times I came round to your parents' house for dinner. Nights in on the sofa watching TV. That was all real. Those were real feelings.

"But I can't have a relationship now. I'm not ready for one. It's one of the rules they give us when we come out. We have to get a houseplant and if it's still alive in twelve months, then buy a goldfish. If they're both alive in another year, then we can get a little pet, a hamster, something like that. And only when they're all alive four years after we leave here are we ready for a relationship. That's right, isn't it? It was in the relationship workshop last week."

Barbara nodded. "Well remembered."

"I'm so done with this. Fuck this." I turned to Barbara. "Fuck you and your feelings." I turned to Paul. "Fuck you and not answering my questions. All I wanna know is if you really loved me or if I was wasting my time. All I want is a yes or no. Did you really love me?"

"Dunno. I started loving partying with you."

I stood. "That's all I wanted to know." I left the room, slamming the door behind me, storming past the receptionist shouting for me to sign out, running to Mum's car and telling her to start the car straight away before I exploded.

Mum started the engine. "Good, was it?"

"Drive, please. I must have FUCKING MUG written across my forehead. What the hell was I thinking, agreeing to do this? Four more times. Four more fucking times. I swear to God, if I hear one more person telling me to talk about my feelings, or Paul blaming everything on his addiction, I'm going to kill someone."

Mum offered me a cigarette.

I lit it and inhaled deeply, wishing the day to disappear with the smoke as it blew out the window, wondering why on earth I was putting myself through this, remembering the words he'd said, right before I'd reached the end of my touchy-feely-ness psychobabble tether and left. As I felt the tingling in my hands subside, my shoulders lowered from where they'd been up by my ears and I blew out, watching the smoke fill the car then leave through the window.

"No one said it was gonna be easy, love." Mum squeezed my knee.

"I'm gonna call them and tell 'em to stick it, say Paul can get some other gullible twat to come and play his game." I sucked so hard on the cigarette I thought I might give myself haemorrhoids.

"All right, love. We'll sort it all out when we're home."

An hour of travelling in silence later, as we approached home, I had calmed down, and we decided me doing it all was a bit much.

"Way I see it, love, is Paul's parents should be pulling their weight too. Going to some sessions as well. Take the pressure off you a bit."

"They are paying for it all," I said. "The Friary."

"Throwing money at a problem is the easiest solution, especially if you've got lots of it. Means they're not getting their hands dirty. Think on that, love."

CHAPTER 20

THE NEXT DAY—AFTER trying to write a letter to Paul explaining I wouldn't be coming back to The Friary and ending up with just 'Dear Paul' and three lines of scribbled-out sentences about it being too much for me, about me being very sorry, and how it had been harder than I'd thought—I reluctantly realised I needed Marilyn and Roger's help.

They'll be fine, I told myself on my way to their house. *We've bonded over calamari and Spanish wine. We're practically old friends by now. It's just a little favour I'm asking them, not much really. Just a visit to see their son. Simple.*

I passed Marilyn's bright-red Mercedes cabriolet sports car with matching red wheels, rang the Big Ben–like doorbell and leant against the wall, composing myself, bracing myself for the onslaught.

A Filipino maid in a black and white uniform opened the door and asked who I was and who I wanted to see. Ignoring the maid, I pushed open the door, said I was the ex-son-in-law and wanted to see the lord and lady of the house. The maid ran after me waving her hands.

"Where is Marilyn?" I shouted, opening doors off the entrance hall.

"She said not to be disturbed. Unless it is an emergency."

"Where is she? This is an emergency." I strode into the dining room where, on the table, lay Marilyn, on a white towel, face down, naked except some white material over her bottom, while a large, blond, muscled man massaged her body. Two Filipino women tended to her nails at the same time as another man, this time smaller, thinner and pretty camp, was fiddling about with her hair.

Marilyn removed the cucumbers from her eyes. "Yes, who is this, please?"

I introduced myself, said I wanted to talk about Paul and no, it wouldn't wait.

She sighed. "Must you? I've a ball this evening to prepare for. Roger is entertaining some sheiks and it's all to be on Middle-Eastern time—they don't like to suffer from jet lag, evidently. Their menu choices are very strict. I have a chef working on it as we speak."

"I'm not leaving until we have this conversation. I can have this conversation with these people here, or I can wait until they leave us alone. The choice, Marilyn, is yours." *Fuck me, I'm on fire. But I suppose that's what two sessions in The Friary with Paul has done to me.*

She barked some orders for someone to tell Chef something, and said she'd call them when she was ready. "Any of you leaving without my say-so will not be invited back."

They left her with combs and curlers in her hair, pieces of foam between her toes and half her nails buffed, polished and painted.

Marilyn snapped her fingers. "Robe, please, unless you want to see my Brazilian bikini wax?"

I quickly threw a bathrobe at her, turning away while she slipped it on.

She rang a bell.

The housemaid arrived, took her order for champagne.

Turning her head up towards me, Marilyn asked, "What do you want? Fizzy water or something equally puritanical, I suspect."

"Nothing for me." I smiled at the maid, who then left.

I told Marilyn about the two sessions at The Friary, explained it was too much for me alone and I wasn't sure I could go back. *Because your son has the emotional maturity of a seven-year-old, no thanks to you!*

I knew telling her that wouldn't get what I wanted so instead narrowed my eyes at her, revelling in the silence and waiting for her to jump in with a response. *Thanks, Barbara, for that technique!*

"Can't we pay them for someone to take your place? They must have people who can do this for a fee, surely. Roger can pay whatever it costs."

"I'm afraid this is something you can't just thrown money at. He needs friends and family who've been affected by his behaviour. And apart from lots of random people who may or may not still be in Ibiza, it's us three. I'm doing my bit, but I can't do it on my own."

"We. Are. Paying." She regarded her painted nails then checked out her face in a hand mirror, putting it back on the table with a shudder.

"It could more than double his recovery time if he doesn't have any significant other coming in for his sessions."

She frowned. "It would what?"

"All those extra weeks staying in The Friary, it'll surely add up, won't it." I noticed her diamond earrings and realised I was on the wrong tack. "What have you told the neighbours about where he is? Still in Ibiza, I suppose."

"He's doing very well out there."

"Long time for him to be out there in the off-season, isn't it? These neighbours, do they have children, maybe our age? Wonder if one of them may want to visit Paul in Ibiza? Now it's quiet, they'd get more chance to see him. Be a shame to disappoint them, wouldn't it?"

"How long would he be out if he gets this significant-other therapy?"

"Up to six sessions. One a week. I've done two. I'll do one more, but I wondered if you and Roger could do the other three. Take the strain off me a bit. You know."

She stared straight through me.

I swear I felt the heat of her eyes boring into my chest.

"How long's he been in so far?"

"Long enough that we could do without more than another six weeks."

"Yes."

"Can I ask something please, Marilyn?"

"Haven't you asked enough? Disturbing my morning." She sighed. "Oh, go on, then."

How someone as kind and loving as Paul could have arisen from the union of this woman and Roger was completely beyond me. "Didn't you expect to visit him, even just normal visiting, never mind the significant-other sessions?"

"He was in a terrible state when we collected him. Of course, you didn't see that. You'd abandoned him."

"He's still your son. He still needs support, affection—love even. It's the least you could do."

"And there was me thinking the least we could do was pay for it all, but I must be terribly naïve. Are we done here? If you don't mind, I've a party to prepare for. Maybe he'll help with that again when he's out. Back to his usual self."

"What makes you think he'll ever get back to his old self?"

She frowned. "Might he not?"

"No guarantees. Every bit of support we offer will give him a better chance." I'd had enough and wasn't being walked over by anyone any longer. I wasn't useless or nothing.

Another long sigh as she studied her nails. "I'll talk to Roger."

"Is that a *yes*? It's such a relief."

"It's a *probably yes*."

I kissed her on the cheek. "Always a pleasure." Confidence bubbled up within my stomach, and I felt as if I were floating; a happy, positive, natural floating.

She air-kissed me, pulled back and shouted for the beauty therapists to join her again.

I left her as the hordes of people swarmed closer until they were each latched onto some part of her body they were attending, a bit like a mother cat with its kittens suckling on her teats. Only Marilyn was sucking up the energy and attention from the others.

***

A few days later, I received a short call from Marilyn: "It's done. Myself and Roger will attend some of Paul's significant-other sessions and a few informal normal visiting sessions. We discussed the issue at length with Paul's consultant, who thought it would help his recovery. Also it's clear you're finding it too much of a strain."

Although I wasn't happy with her phrasing, I was happy with the outcome, so I said, "Thank you. Maybe I'll bump into you both at The Friary."

She laughed.

The phone line went dead.

Charming.

I felt guilty for my Machiavellian almost-blackmail, but I'd done it with Paul's interests at heart, knowing there was no way I could have coped with another four visits like the previous two, and wanting him to recover as quickly as possible.

***

Still feeling slightly guilty, I decided to combine my third and final group-therapy session with an informal visit so arrived an hour earlier than necessary and sat in the grounds, under a tree with Paul, a tray of fruit juice between us.

"Sorry about the last session," I said. "I got a bit carried away. Bit emotional."

He passed my juice to me. "Nothing. Don't worry. It shows you give a shit. You turned up and had the row with me. Plenty of other friends and family just ignore the letter asking them to come. When it's their turn, Barbara starts with an empty chair, asking the resident to tell the family member how sorry they are, and she goes ahead like that. It's not as good as when they turn up, have a proper argument, really get the issues out."

"Has your mother been in touch?"

"My consultant said the group therapy was being split between my friend—" he did the air-quotation marks "—and my parents. It's just as hard for you, and you're not in here having all the lessons and the other group therapy. You just turn up, get loads of shit thrown at you, and then go."

I said nothing, instead playing with the plastic cup of juice between my hands.

"Like I said, giving a shit means a lot in this place. And you, and Mother and Father, all give a shit, in some way, and for that I'm grateful. Not sure how I'd have reacted if it was the other way round." He sipped his orange squash.

"What do you mean?" I sipped mine, wishing we were right back at the start in the bar where we went on our first date. Wishing I could turn back time and undo all the stuff we'd been through together.

"If you'd lost the plot, lost yourself, on me, I don't know if I'd have coped. In fact, I know I wouldn't. When you left, I turned to shit. I realised all the stuff you used to do to keep our life ticking over without telling me, and suddenly it was all too much for me. You'd have coped."

"It's just what I do. It's nothing."

"It's not nothing. I realise now it's exactly what we needed, to be together. To be balanced."

I thought back to the months after I'd left him in Ibiza how fucking deeply, terribly, awfully miserable I'd been, how I'd managed to lose a job, a home, and a boyfriend all in one swoop, and how just the thought of trying to go out with someone else had terrified me so I hadn't tried.

He brushed my cheek with his hand. "Penny for 'em?"

"Nothing. I didn't think we'd ever split up. I thought when I met you that would be it, you know, until—" I turned away. "Stupid eh?"

"Neither of us knew what would happen when we moved to Ibiza. That's why it was so exciting. I don't regret going, do you?"

"Not the actual going. I think we had a pretty good life out there. At first, before it all got too much. Before it sort of overtook our lives."

"Before I lost myself and fucked everything up, you mean," Paul said.

"I think we both lost ourselves a bit really, don't you?" I shrugged, noticing the juice glasses were empty. For want of anything else to say, I offered to get some more.

"Don't worry about it. Let's just sit here." He reached past the plastic glasses and held my hand, squeezing it tightly. "You know that time before sunrise when you've been up partying all night, talking philosophy, sharing amazing thoughts with complete strangers, and the warm rush of ecstasy wraps around you like a warm sleeping bag?"

I nodded. I knew it very well. It was such fun, every time we'd done it.

"I wanted to live my life in that space, at that time, always chasing that moment when you feel at peace with the world and the daily worries of life are a thousand miles away. That's why I was always wanting the party to carry on, to never admit defeat when it had keeled over and died."

"That's what I thought."

He stared at me. "I didn't mean for any of the shitty stuff to happen—me disappearing, ending up in that derelict building, your wallet being stolen. None of it was intentional. It was just all me chasing that special, magical time. I suppose I didn't just get addicted to drugs, I got addicted to that time. I was also running too. Away. From structure, organisation, needing to be there for other people other things. Make sense?"

I nodded. "But you can't live in that space, at that time. You've got to live. You've got to be there for people…"

"Otherwise no one's there for you?" Paul smiled weakly.

I nodded. "The practicalities of life—bills, work, food shopping—have to happen or…" I struggled for the phrase, trying to be tactful.

"…or you end up living like some of the party people's squats?"
I nodded at his fair summary.

"Yeah. It's like wanting to live your life like you're on holiday.
You can't. Even out in Ibiza, there's still the everyday stuff to do,
to deal with. The stuff I'm not so good at, I worked out when
you'd left." He smiled weakly.

"The reason that time's so special," I said. "So magical,
like a holiday, is because you're away from the everyday. Away
from reality."

We sat in companionable silence for a few moments, then
I said, "Maybe I did lose myself a bit. But *I* always came back."

Paul shook his head, still holding on to my hand tightly.
"Whereas I moved farther and farther away until…" He swallowed
hard. "I am so, so sorry. It was an illness. And me behaving like
a child. But we didn't know it at the time." He blinked quickly to
stop the tears rolling down his cheeks.

"Come on, this is meant to be the easy bit, when we talk about
the weather, what's been on TV. We should be saving all this good
emotional stuff for Barbara and her clipboard. She'd love this.
Imagine her ticking stuff off, writing things down in her big,
twirly handwriting, licking her lips and crossing her legs."

He looked up at me through teary eyes. "You're amazing, you
know that? Just being here, taking the time to do all this for me.
Even though we're not together. I accept that." He looked away. "I
loved you very much."

Past tense—loved. I swallowed hard, pursed my lips. "I knew
it wasn't all fake. I knew our love was real."

"We'd best get in. If you're late, Barbara can be a bit of a cow
when it comes to punishments."

Each carrying our empty glass, we walked across the sloping
lawn back to The Friary.

My stomach flipped its usual somersault as we walked into the
group-therapy room and took our places in the chairs either side
of Barbara and her kaftan and chunky jewellery.

***

After our much more serious than intended chat under the tree with the orange squash, I was relieved the proper counselling session went smoothly. It was my final session with him; he had some more due with his parents, who it seemed were taking to them like ducks with parenting issues to psychotherapy water.

I say it went well, and it really did. But it put me further into this dilemma I'd been having for some time about whether I wanted to get back together with Paul, whether, after all that had happened, all that had been said, all the desertions—on both sides, to be fair—the excesses and all those had entailed, I could ever get back to the normal, everyday Tom and Paul we'd had at the beginning.

And this was made much worse when, in the final session, he went and did something I really wasn't expecting.

Reader, he said he still loved me.

In front of the room of other residents, and Barbara in another kaftan—beige this time—jeans and matching chunky golden jewellery.

We'd gone over trust and how we thought we were in a different place from where we'd been during the dark days in Ibiza at the height of his partying addiction.

He stared at me. "I'm so grateful for you coming here to help me. It's more than I could ever have expected, especially after what I did."

I tried to argue it wasn't all one-sided, but Barbara told me to let him finish. Damn her and her techniques.

He continued, still staring at me with those bright-blue twinkly eyes. "Being without you made me realise how much I missed you. How you weren't the fun police, as I sometimes thought you were. How together, we balanced each other out. My fun-loving, let's see how things turn out, and your reasoned planning."

Again, I stared to reply, but again with the hand and chunky necklace from Barbara.

"I know I'm not meant to think about relationships, which I'm not—not until I've bought the plant and the goldfish and the hamster anyway."

A few people around the edges of the room laughed.

"I love you, Tom and even if we're never together again, I will always love you. And even if we're just friends, that's something better to take from this mess I made of us, better than losing you from my life completely. I want to be with you, to make plans with you, to create a future together. And I realise that's all you ever wanted for us too. But I spent so much of our time together running away from schedules, plans, from having to be there for other people. Stupid. That's all I wanted to say." He stared at the floor, his hands fidgeting on his lap.

Barbara asked if I had anything to add, anything to say.

And, of course, that was when all my thoughts and questions had chosen to desert me, so instead, I shook my head and said, "That's lovely." I didn't know what else to say. It was a crappy response, but his declaration had come out of nowhere, so I smiled at him and repeated it.

After the session, he told me when he was due to leave The Friary and told me to take care. We did one of those awkward *used to be lovers, but now we're friends* hug and kisses, and then I walked, head hung low, crunching gravel under my feet, back to Mum's car as she sat smoking herself to death. When she asked how it had gone, all I could manage was, "He said he still loves me."

Mum started the car and, looking sideways at me, said, "Love, you are in so much trouble."

CHAPTER 21

THE WEEKS PASSED. Paul's treatment finished, I got a job at a supermarket at the end of Chiswick High Road. The video shop wasn't hiring so, realising I needed to do something other than sit around moping about all I'd lost and feeling sorry for myself, I left my video shop and, on the off-chance, checked if the supermarket had any vacancies. I filled in an application on the spot. It was the wrong side of London for where I was living, but I needed something to occupy my time so when they offered it to me, I accepted. They had a video and CD section, and between stacking shelves, I would hover in that aisle, checking out the latest films and music, occasionally treating myself to one with my staff discount.

One evening, I returned home and Mum handed me a letter with familiar, sloping, twirly handwriting on the envelope.

Paul wanted to meet for a drink, *just as friends*, so we could catch up, *just as friends,* he wrote again, and he wondered, if I didn't mind, could I help him think about what he was going to do with his life now, *just as friends.*

Just. As. Friends.

I told Mum he'd written it three times in one small letter.

Mum asked what I was going to do, "Just as friends?"

I rolled my eyes. "What am I meant to do? I want him in my life. He wants me in his. But don't you think it'll be harder, just as friends, than a clean break?"

"Love, you and him are the only ones who can answer that. Ask how his houseplant's getting on, is it still alive?"

"Funny. What should I wear for this non-date?"

"I'm serious. See how he's getting on now he's outside." She looked at the clock on the wall. "You seen your dad? He was due back anytime now."

"You gonna ask him what I should wear on the non-date?"

"Behave. No, I wanted him to fix those tiles in the bathroom. You might as well ask him to make a time machine from our new Ford Sierra. Flux capacitor or something, isn't it?"

"I can't go too smart or he'll think I made too much effort, but I don't wanna turn up in some old sack, showing him no respect."

"Love, just turn up, be yourself and see how it goes. He's gonna be a bit sore and battered from being inside for so long. Be gentle with him."

"He's not been in prison."

"Didn't look that different from where I was sitting."

***

I arrived early to the café in Chiswick he'd suggested. I'd automatically assumed it would be a pub, but he explained when we spoke on the phone to arrange it: "I've gotta watch out for other gateway substances, and alcohol is my gateway substance. Could lead to drugs cos I've got an addictive personality."

Sitting in the café, I ordered a pot of tea and made myself comfortable by the window, wondering if caffeine and cigarettes counted as gateway drugs too, or were they so low in the addiction pecking order they didn't count? And what about food? I was sure he'd mentioned it could have been anything; if things had turned out differently, he may have been up to thirty boxes of teacakes a day like the overeating man he met when he arrived at The Friary.

I had been so keen to give off a *nonchalant, not taken any effort to get ready* look, it had taken me all afternoon to achieve it. Obviously.

It's like most extremes; rather than being on a long line with one at either end, they're actually a circle, with the two extremes being right next to one another. Looking like an idiot fashion-wise and being very painfully trendy are definitely a good example of this. So is very left wing and very right wing. And camp and butch. Some men's interpretation of super-butch—harnesses, leather, handlebar moustaches and chaps, as in the leather leg-wear, not men—was a gnat's breath away from being very camp.

After discarding piles and piles of clothes, running up and down the stairs showing Mum each outfit option, I had eventually—after she'd shouted at me to make my fucking mind up, she was getting old there and would be drawing her pension soon if I didn't hurry the fuck up—I settled on light-brown chinos, white polo shirt with Union Flag on the front—I, too, had succumbed to the Ginger Spice at the Brit Awards effect, in an ironic way, of course—and a blue hoodie to cover up the Union Flag if I thought it was too dressy.

Now, at the table in the café, I kept the hoodie zipped, feeling, despite my original intention, I'd most definitely overdressed for the non-date.

He arrived at my table, and he shook my hand. I knew Mum was right when I felt his hand in mine and my stomach did a somersault.

"How's things? What you been doing?" he started with once our drinks arrived.

I told him about the supermarket and being back at my parents' place, just generally taking things slower this time. "What about you? How's things on the outside?" I laughed to myself, then regretted it as taking the piss out of him. "Sorry. I wasn't laughing at you. No, it's just… Anyway, how's things?"

"Big change."

"Like what? The music and fashion? You weren't away that long." I laughed quietly, then mentally slapped myself.

"Three months."

"Long time." I stared at my pot of tea. "You going to pour yours, or wait a bit longer? I never know how long to wait. I heard there's an optimum time, but I can never remember if it's three or five minutes."

"Could be four."

"Yeah. Could be." I checked how much the tea had brewed. "I'm going in. I'm pouring it." After pouring mine, I commented that I assumed caffeine was still OK, and not off-limits.

"And cigarettes." He poured his tea. "I think The Friary would burst into flames if they banned cigarettes. They're everything in that place. Currency, friendship, escape. Something else."

Silence descended on the table as we both sipped our tea. *Fuck me, this is hard work. Never used to be like this with Paul. Maybe all the fun, all the ease, all the everything was just the drugs.* I pursed my lips, checked the time. Less than ten minutes we'd been here, and already it felt like an afternoon.

I blurted out something that had been on my mind for some time: "I've not been with anyone since you. I tried, but it didn't feel right. Whatever you've done since we split up doesn't matter. I'm just telling you about me. I felt too broken. Sorry, that must sound really selfish, you've just come out of rehab. We were both broken, I think."

Truth was, it had been a terrible, awful, unrepeatable experience where I'd decided to get out there, to grab myself a piece of the action, and no matter who I looked at, all I could do was compare each man to Paul. Not as cute smile, not as nice eyes, not as strong arms to hold me with. And when I'd actually spoken to one or two, all they wanted was sex, straight away, no getting to know me, no small talk, laughs, clicking, chemistry— nothing. It was always straight to the *what do you like to do in bed* conversation. Even though Paul and I had had some sex problems, all caused by, as ever, the drugs, we always had the spark, the chat, the chemistry. If it was just sex, using someone else's body as a scratching post to release something, I realised I was happier to do that on my own. Of course, I didn't tell Paul any of that.

"I've got the plant they told me to buy. It's on my bedroom windowsill. Still green, still alive. Mind you, it's only been three weeks since I left." He shrugged.

Paul explained how it was living with his parents again. "Mother's treating me like a cross between the prodigal son who's returned from a round-the-world trip and a delicate china vase. They're always asking me how I feel about everything. It's all very consultative when we decide anything, even down to what we eat. It's like a board meeting when we talk about dinner. Sometimes I just wish they'd get the fuck on with it and let me be. But no, it's knocking on my door, checking if everything's all right, do I need anything, would I like to do something with them as a family. I mean, I've not done anything with them as a family since they shipped me off to boarding school. Their visit to Ibiza was so alien, I think that's partly why I fucked off. I couldn't remember when I'd been with them to just be, without having some agenda, some issue, some problem I'd caused to discuss. Weird, eh?"

"Bless Barbara."

"Fuck Barbara. I want my parents back. I want their arm's-length parenting back. I can't cope with this closeness. Just when I think I've got used to the idea of one sort of closeness—a relationship—now I'm having to get used to my parents' closeness. Too much. The other day, I heard Mother asking the maid about her children, and did they want to come round to use the pool. Poor woman nearly fainted. After being treated like an appliance for so many years, she didn't know what the hell to do."

"Warmth from parents is good. I wouldn't change mine if I could. Your mother could do with a few lessons from my mum."

"The hugs. Don't get me started on the hugs. It's hugs in the morning over breakfast, hugs at lunchtime when we sit and eat together. Father's scaled back his work commitments, so he's staying at home more than he's away for the first time ever. Hugs at dinner time. It's like all the hugs I didn't get when I was a child."

"Sweet. They're realising what they would have missed if they'd lost you. They won't get this time again with you, and neither will you. They'll be old soon. They must have been our age when they had us, younger even. And look at how we behave, like we're still teenagers." I laughed, brazenly pouring myself another tea from the pot.

"How's being back at your parents'?"

I explained it wasn't much different. Mum was still very laissez-faire, letting me get on with stuff, not much to want to move away from really. "She even offered for you to move in if you wanted. I explained we weren't together anymore. So there's no spare room for you." *Whoops.* That hadn't come out as I had wanted. I tried to distract myself by putting another two sugars in my tea. I took a sip. "Fuck me, that's sweet." I knew I had to say what I was about to say but had been waiting for the right time in the conversational flow to slip it in. "What you said at the last therapy session—actually, I meant to ask. How were your parents in group therapy? Did she behave like it was her therapy not yours?"

"A little bit." He indicated how little between his thumb and index finger and smiled.

Inside, I felt myself melt. This was really going to be harder than I'd thought, especially since we were face-to-face. Him with his eyes twinkling. Him with his bastard gorgeous smile spreading across his face and now, him holding my hand on the table.

He recounted a story of one of the sessions when Marilyn brought everything back to herself and responded to the questions on her behalf rather than related to Paul. Barbara, it seemed, had met her match and almost called a halt to the session until one of the other residents stepped in with some relevant experience which eventually steered things back to Paul. "Whatever, it worked out in the end. I'm going to NA meetings too."

"NA?"

"Narcotics Anonymous, like Alcoholics Anonymous, but for people who're addicted to drugs."

"What's that like?"

"Keeps me upright. Keeps me together. From being tempted."

"How often do you go?"

"Every day. Mother and Father have been great about it."

"Every day?"

"Every. Day." Paul nodded. "I asked at The Friary how often I should go. They give you a talk before you're discharged, make sure you're ready for the reality of the outside world again. They asked how often I was getting off my face. I said almost every day, so they said I should go to NA almost every day, or every day, just to be safe. I go to them all over West London—Acton, Chiswick, Ealing, Hounslow, Isleworth—during the day, in the evening…"

"Seen any celebrities?"

He tapped the side of his nose. "Confidential. It's like the masons but with shitloads of orange squash, tea, coffee and rich tea biscuits."

I checked my watch. *Has it really been an hour?* The teapots were empty. "I'm so proud of you. You're doing so well. I always knew you could do it. I'll pay, I'm working. Actually, are you working again, or what?"

"Or what." He smiled. "Busy going to all the NA meetings."

"'Course."

I paid at the counter and was about to leave when Paul's waving caught my eye. I returned to our table.

"What I said at the last session?" He stared up at me.

"What about it?" I rested one hand on the table, the other casually in my hoodie pocket.

"You started to talk about it then got distracted talking about Mother."

I was almost out the door. *I could leave this till later. Or never. Never would be good to have this conversation.* I swallowed a lump in my throat.

"I like the Union Flag. Let's have a look." He unzipped my hoodie, revealing the flag in all its red, white and blue overdressed unsuitable glory. "It suits you. Sexy." He held on to the hem of my hoodie.

My stomach clenched. I had to tell him. I had to kick the puppy down the stairs. I had to put him out of his misery because after what he'd said, I'd just let it hang there.

"What you said at the session. It was lovely. It was sweet. No, not sweet. It was kind, it was moving. I didn't expect it. And I wanted you to know I forgive you. For everything you did. I know it wasn't you. I understand why you did it. I was hurt and upset, but I get it now. But this—" I grabbed his hand which was still holding my clothing "—this." I removed his hand and placed it on the table. "This can't happen. This won't happen. I want to be your friend. I can't imagine being without you in my life, but we've moved on now. We've both moved on. Now's the time we work out how to be friends. But that's all. I'm sorry. I can't go through losing you again. I can't do that to my heart."

He blinked quickly, putting his hands in his lap under the table. "'Course. Very sensible. My houseplant's still alive, so maybe when I get the goldfish—no, it's the hamster. Yeah. When I get the hamster, we can."

"No." I shook my head.

He looked up at me, and his smile disappeared instantly, replaced with the face of a man who'd just been given some very bad news.

"Good luck with the meetings!" I said weakly, wanting to punch myself in the stomach. I shook his hand then left in silence. All I could think about was the little puppy I'd just kicked down the stairs.

***

The weeks passed. Despite what we'd said at the non-date, I didn't hear from Paul and neither did I contact him. It felt like we'd split up all over again.

As I finished at work, thinking about the things that had happened—a few short amusing little anecdotes that had punctuated my day—I imagined myself telling Paul about them, and us laughing, and then him telling me about how his day had gone. Even if he'd spent all of it in his bedroom fighting off hugs from his mother, and having a three-quarters-of-an-hour discussion about which meat to have for dinner, I knew it was how I wanted to start my evening.

Yes, I had friends; of course I had friends. I was making some decent ones at work, as I knew I would. Slinky Simon and the others from that part of my life had fallen away. I got the odd call asking if I wanted to DJ at the weekend, but after explaining I wasn't doing that again, I was resting, the calls soon dried up. I realised many of the friends from that period of my life were really just mates, people to go out with, people to have a laugh with, and the only person from then I wanted to still see was Paul.

Only I couldn't see him either because I didn't want to only be friends. Because it felt so wrong, so much like we were holding such a lot of ourselves back from the relationship we were meant to have together.

And then, in the instant when I was about to turn one way to make my way back home, I found myself walking in the other direction.

***

I rang the Big Ben doorbell.

Paul answered the door, smiling weakly. "All right? What you doing here?" He held out his hand for me to shake.

"I'm not, as it goes."

"What's wrong?"

"You know how they always say you don't know what you've got till it's gone?"

"Bit of a cliché, isn't it?" He shrugged, putting his hand by his side, kicking the floor.

"Yeah, but it's a fucking true cliché."

"What you lost now? Can't be as bad as me losing my whole self." He laughed one small breath of laughter, then stared at the gravel on the ground.

I told him about leaving work and the anecdotes, and the way we used to share our days with each other after work. "I want that everyday us back again. With you. Fuck your houseplant and fuck your hamster and seeing if they're alive in three years' time." I took a deep breath. "I don't want to shake your hand."

"Don't blame you. I wouldn't want to shake my hand after what I've done." He stuck his hands in his pockets.

"I'm sorry I haven't been in touch since our non-date."

"That's what I told Mother and Father it was." He looked up at me, his blue eyes crinkling at the edges.

"I've not been in touch…because I don't know how to be with you if I'm not with you, with you."

"With me, with me?"

"No more shaking each other's hands. Boyfriends. Together, together. Do you want me to draw you a diagram? So what I'm saying is, you know that offer in the café, and what you said in The Friary? I don't suppose that offer's still available is it?"

"Yeah."

"Fuck friends, I love you. I want to be with you again, like we were before."

"I thought you'd never ask." He hugged me, holding me tightly as I inhaled his distinctive musky, sweet scent. His strong arms wrapped around me. I felt myself responding inside my trousers as his warmth and hardness pressed against me.

And then he kissed me.

And I kissed him. I opened my mouth to his familiar taste, his soft tongue licking my lips, and as my eyes closed, there was nothing else in the world but his lips, his face, his body. And mine. Entwined. Linked. Together.

Pulling back before I got carried away, I said, "Your parents in?"

Nodding, he said, "Poised like two mother hen sentinels either side of my bedroom door."

I grabbed his hand, and we ran to a secluded spot between some trees on Turnham Green. It wasn't romantic, but it was what we needed. As soon as we were sure no one could see us, we couldn't get at each other's bodies quick enough. I hadn't had sex with anyone since my last time with Paul, and I knew Paul was the same. Frantically unzipping flies, we grabbed at our cocks, face-to-face, breathing in each other's hot breath.

We lasted three minutes. It was the best sex I'd had in such a long time with him. It was *hopeful, enjoying life, grabbing life by the balls* sex. Afterwards, we held each other, leaning against a tree.

"I love you," Paul said.

"I've always loved you," I replied.

"I'm sorry for everything I did."

I pressed my index finger on his lips. "You've apologised enough. Clean slate now." I nodded and he copied me.

We made our way back to my parents' house, holding hands the whole way on the Tube, ignoring some people's disapproving stares.

Bursting through the door, I shouted, "Mum, Paul's here."

Arriving from the kitchen with a cigarette in one hand and a metal spoon in the other, she hugged me, then Paul, and said, "I wondered how long that would take." She took a step back to look him up and down for a moment. "Just as gorgeous as ever. Them blue eyes... Forgive you anything, I would! And that smile." She looked at me as I beamed in happiness. "I've missed seeing that one too, love." Turning to Paul, she said, "Wanna move in? Just while you get yourselves back on your feet."

I looked at Paul, and he nodded at me. Looking back at Mum, I said, "If that's all right."

"'Course it's bloody well all right. You're both my sons, always have been. Welcome back to the family, Paul love."

EPILOGUE

I T WAS A year since my first visit to The Friary.

We lay on the soft, sandy beach, the red sun slowly rising over the sea, gradually filling the air with warmth. We were in that perfect time before anyone had woken for the day, when the beach was covered in clubbers winding down after a night of munching disco biscuits, drinking water and dancing their tits off.

I was at the floaty stage of waves flowing through my body but not so strong as to make me feel nauseous.

Paul's head rested on my chest, his hand slowly stroking my stomach. "What a night, eh? Hope the guy following us wasn't too pissed off when we nicked twenty minutes from his set."

"We were only giving the party people what they wanted. That's all Slinky Simon says you have to do."

"Is he over at the moment?"

"He said he'll drop in on us. I told him your answer would be the same as mine if he asked us to take on more DJing nights. Still, God loves a trier, I suppose."

"And Slinky Simon's definitely trying." Paul sniggered.

"Had a good night?" I asked hesitantly. Despite us being back in the scene for a few months, I still worried he may return to the bad old days.

"You saw me. You were with me for most of it."

"I worry."

"That's sweet of you, but I don't need anyone worrying or feeling sorry for me."

"Being surrounded by people who are off their heads must get boring."

"I've still got the music, the dancing, the people, the mad middle-of-the-night conversations. It's a lot of things, but it's not boring."

"Sure?"

"How you feeling at the moment? Nicely floaty? Want me to give you a hand massage?"

He massaged my hands, pressing firmly so the waves of pleasure radiated from my hand up my arms into my chest, first on one hand then the other. After a while, he said, "What we got today?"

I held his hand. "Nothing. All day, nothing. And we've got such a lot of it to do." After much fanfare of our return to the island, with some help from Slinky Simon and Paul's charm, we'd secured a Friday and Saturday night DJing slot at Ibiza's biggest super club, playing to about fifteen thousand each night.

"When we next working?"

"Friday."

He looked up at me. "And today is Sunday, right?"

"All day long."

"I never thought I'd look forward to a week full of nothing as much as I do now. Eating, walking, sunbathing, seeing friends, isn't nothing, though, I suppose."

"Busy doing nothing."

"Depends on your definition of nothing." After a pause, during which he used his finger to trace a trail from my belly button to inside the top of my shorts, he said, "Your mum's coming over tomorrow…or is it next week?"

In an instant, I felt unsexy again. I laughed. "Oh, shit, forgot that. Yes, tomorrow, but you know what she's like—bit of wine, bit of paella, one of her little romance paperbacks on the beach and she's sorted. She told me she'll amuse herself when she's here."

"What about Dad?"

"Dad's pulled his back resurfacing a car park in Hounslow town centre. He's on bed rest, doctor's orders. Mum said to tell you he says hello."

"Do you think he'll ever meet my father?"

I shrugged. "Probably. No rush though, eh? We've got the rest of our lives to make plans together."

We lay in companionable silence for a while, the sea lapping on the sand, a gentle breeze blowing from the water, the warmth of the sun growing as the morning light filled the sky ready for another day on the island.

Paul linked his hand with mine, our fingers alternating. "I don't think I could love you more than I do now."

I leant forward to kiss him. We kissed for a few moments, then I said, pulling back, staring at his twinkly blue eyes and his broad smile. "Me neither."

The End

ABOUT THE AUTHOR

Liam Livings lives where East London ends and becomes Essex. He shares his house with his boyfriend and cat. He enjoys baking, cooking, classic cars and socialising with friends. He has a sweet tooth for food and entertainment: loving to escape from real life with a romantic book; enjoying a good cry at a sad, funny and camp film; and listening to musical cheesy pop from the eighties to now. He tirelessly watches an awful lot of *Gilmore Girls* in the name of writing 'research'.

Published since 2013 by a number of British and American presses, his gay romance and gay fiction focuses on friendships, British humour and romance with plenty of sparkle. He's a member of the Romantic Novelists' Association, and the Chartered Institute of Marketing. With a Master's in creative writing from Kingston University, he teaches writing workshops with his partner in sarcasm and humour, Virginia Heath, as www.realpeoplewritebooks.com and has also ghostwritten a client's five-star reviewed autobiography.

Social Media

Facebook: http://www.facebook.com/liam.livings
Twitter: https://twitter.com/LiamLivings
Blog: http://www.liamlivings.com/blog

For Liam's other stories check out his website:
www.liamlivings.com

BEATEN TRACK PUBLISHING

For more titles from Beaten Track Publishing,
please visit our website:

https://www.beatentrackpublishing.com

Thanks for reading!